ites of pa

RITES
OF
PASSAGE

Stories About Growing Up
by Black Writers from Around the World

Edited by Tonya Bolden

With a Foreword by Charles Johnson

Hyperion Books for Children
New York

For
My nephew, Bobby Lee Brunson, Jr., aka "BJ," who taught
me everything I know about video games, but more important, who keeps me in touch with all that I might otherwise forget about the woes and wonders of growing up.
&
My molders and main role models, my bridges over adoles-
cent and adult troubled waters: Willie J. Bolden and Georgia
C. Bolden (1937–89). Daddy, I love you mighty much. And,
Mommy, I sure do miss you.

First Edition
1 3 5 7 9 10 8 6 4 2

Library of Congress Cataloging-in-Publication Data
Rites of passage: stories about growing up by black writers from
around the world/edited by Tonya Bolden; with a foreword by Charles Johnson.
p. cm.
Includes bibliographical references.
Summary: Seventeen stories about the experiences of young people
of African descent around the world, by such authors as Toni Cade
Bambara, John Henrik Clarke, Njabulo Ndebele, and Barbara Burford.
ISBN 1-56282-688-3 (trade)
1. Children's stories, American—Afro-American authors.
2. Children's stories—Black authors. 3. Afro-Americans—Juvenile fiction.
4. Blacks—Juvenile fiction. [1. Afro-Americans—Fiction. 2. Blacks—Fiction.
3. Short stories—Afro-American authors.
4. Short stories—Black authors.] I. Bolden, Tonya, ed.
PZ5.R53 1994 [Fic]—dc20 93-31304 CIP AC

Contents

Acknowledgments *Page v*

Foreword by Charles Johnson *Page vii*

Introduction *Page xii*

Raymond's Run by Toni Cade Bambara *Page 1*

The Scar by Cecil Foster *Page 11*

The Day the World Almost Came to an End
by Pearl Crayton *Page 25*

The Late Bud by Ama Ata Aidoo *Page 33*

The Mountain by Martin J. Hamer *Page 45*

Bright Thursdays by Olive Senior *Page 50*

The Boy Who Painted Christ Black
by John Henrik Clarke *Page 71*

BigWater by Charlotte Watson Sherman *Page 79*

Swan Song by Quince Duncan *Page 89*

Getting the Facts of Life by Paulette Childress White *Page 91*

The Test by Njabulo Ndebele *Page 103*

How, Why to Get Rich by J. California Cooper *Page 130*

Johnny Blue by Archie Weller *Page 143*

Marigolds by Eugenia Collier *Page 151*

My Lucy by Howard Gordon *Page 163*

Dreaming the Sky Down by Barbara Burford *Page 177*

My Mother and Mitch by Clarence Major *Page 191*

About the Contributors *Page 203*

Acknowledgments

The joy of it notwithstanding, compiling this anthology proved more arduous than I'd ever imagined. And it might well have been an utterly mind-bending experience had it not been for the help of a lot of good folks and friends. To you all, I give a hug and a heartfelt THANK-YOU, THANK-YOU!

To my agent, Marie Dutton Brown, for your faith in this book, and for being a rock and a refuge during *every* rite of passage of my writing life.

To my editor at Hyperion, Andrea Cascardi, and her assistant, Kristen Behrens, for your enthusiasm, most constructive criticism, and grace.

To Claudette Green Pessin, veteran English teacher and teacher consultant with the New York City Writing Project, for reading SO MANY of my preliminary as well as my final picks and providing such substantive feedback at every turn.

To Jewelle Gomez and Lisa Monroe for being right on time with your story recommendations. And to Marlin L. Adams, Harold Augenbraum, Naadu I. Blankson, James Corry, Susan Curry, Miriam DeCosta-Willis, Constance M. Green, Beverly Guy-Sheftall, Miriam de Himenez, Marvin A. Lewis, Mona Rigaud, Ian I. Smart, and Karim B. Yorose—for your various and sundry helps.

To Sharon M. Howard, curator of General Research and Reference at the Schomburg Center for Research in Black Culture, for being such a ready, willing, and able flow of information, advice, and encouragement. And to her colleagues, Genette McLaurin, Betty Odabashian, and Koreen Duncan, who made researching at the Schomburg an ease and a pleasure.

To my very dear friends and mentors, Elza Dinwiddie-

Boyd and Herb Boyd, for allowing me—as you always so graciously do—continual access to your awesome knowledge bank and fine sensibilities.

To my best-best friend on earth, my sister, Nelta D. Brunson, for being a sounding board and counsel on every leg of my journey with this book.

Special thanks to all the black writers and griots down through the ages and around the world who've had the love, wisdom, passion, and courage to tell our stories and who've given me so much wonderment to read and remember.

Lastly (but first!), I offer praise and thanksgiving to the ultimate source of strength and inspiration for any bit of good I ever do in my personal and professional life: the Blessed Trinity.

Foreword

One of the rules in our Seattle home is that my family never throws away books. Magazines and newspapers (after I've clipped the articles that interest me) will wind up in the wastebasket—but never books, because parting with them seems too much like losing an old friend or casting aside an experience we might someday want to enter again.

From the time I was able to hold one in my hands—picture books or comic books, with the covers winged open upon my knees—books always struck me as being one of this world's special experiences. Today we have video games, VCRs, and more than fifty channels to choose from on television. But coming as I did from a pious Illinois church family, I imagine that back in the 1950s some of the respect that my elders had for the Bible (*the* book) rubbed off on any volume that fell into my hands. No, it didn't matter what the book was about. For me, holding its heftiness in my hands, underlining certain parts, and arguing with the author in the margins (yes, I still do that) meant that I possessed the key to knowledge, to realms of the imagination I could find nowhere else. And remember: during slavery days some states in America made it illegal for black boys and girls to read. With that in mind, the pages beneath my fingers felt like power or contraband. The very act of reading itself was subversive and liberating. Whatever the book's subject, I always knew that as I turned the pages I had that rarest of human privileges: a front-row seat as the best thinkers and storytellers of all ages and cultures presented me—me!—with their most carefully crafted thoughts and feelings.

Of course, *not* throwing away books can lead to problems. Like, where do we put them? Four rooms in our house, just remodeled to hold even more books, have ceiling-to-floor bookshelves with titles covering every topic from aardvarks to Emiliano Zapata in editions published in 1897 and yesterday. There are novels, story collections, science books, philosophy texts, and encyclopedias—over twenty-eight hundred books, and that doesn't count my eighteen-year-old son's collection of Raymond Chandler detective, Ian Fleming spy, and Sax Rohmer adventure novels or my twelve-year-old daughter's young adult books by C. S. Lewis, Roald Dahl, and Betsy Byars.

Or the secret stash we keep in the attic: boxes and boxes of comic books, some rare and preserved in plastic, from the 1940s through the 1960s, which I read as a kid and saved, thinking someday my own children might enjoy seeing E.C. Comics' 1952 adaptations of Ray Bradbury's short stories or original issues of *Tales from the Crypt* and *Challengers of the Unknown.* It doesn't matter where you begin, with classics or comic books, as long as the love of storytelling starts somewhere. Pulitzer Prize–winning short story writer James Alan McPherson says that as a boy his comic book collection numbered over five hundred, but listen: I had him beat because I wanted more than anything in the world to be a cartoonist, so my D.C. and Marvel library easily topped one thousand. But the point remains the same: a lifelong love of reading imaginative stories is the first step toward becoming an accomplished writer.

But in my household things were not always this way. There was a time, I remember, when a steady story diet was harder to come by.

My mother, who'd always wanted to be a schoolteacher but never realized her goal, belonged to a few book clubs when I was a kid. My father, busy working two and sometimes three jobs, had no time for reading, so my mother turned to me to discuss books with her and filled our bookcases with titles that reflected her eclectic taste. On her shelves I found volumes on religion, the Studs Lonigan trilogy (never before had I read stories set so close to me, in the Chicago area), *The Swiss Family Robinson*, and Richard Wright's classic *Black Boy*. (Before I pulled this one down, I never dreamed that black people wrote books about their lives; my schoolteachers didn't present me with even one writer of color.) Yet some of mother's books didn't come from book clubs or rummage sales. Quite a few arrived at our house as orphans from Northwestern University.

No one in my family had gone to college before 1966. However, in the early 1960s my grandmother worked as a cook at the Gamma Phi Beta sorority house when I was in middle school, and sometimes Mother worked there, too, over the holidays as a cleaning woman in order to make a little extra money. According to her, the sorority's chapter said emphatically and in no uncertain terms that black people could never join. Not ever. During the times my mother worked there over school breaks, I remember deeply resenting the bigoted policy of these sorority girls. Along with the clothing they casually threw away after their classes ended, they also tossed out their books. Mother, bless her, brought them home—boxes and boxes of them. Some nights I'd flip them open, lying half on my bed and half off, my toes barely touching the floor. In those boxes I first encountered Shakespeare's *Romeo and Juliet* and *Hamlet*, Mary Shelley's *Frankenstein*, and other college-syllabus classics that I devoured with the pleasure, the delight, the wicked knowledge that the uppity girls of Gamma Phi Beta would never be able to say they knew something their cleaning woman's son didn't know.

And how does this story end? Thirty years later the English Department at Northwestern University offered me a lucrative job, with a distinguished professorship thrown into the bargain, which I turned down, being quite happy where I am in Seattle, thank you. But I like to think that my late mother, who loved books enough to carry home the

castoffs of Northwestern coeds, would find poetic justice in
the way things turned out.

Which brings me to *Rites of Passage*. Like the books I
knew as a boy, this is a collection you will want to keep for
yourself, *your* children, and *their* children. Writer Tonya
Bolden has, through careful selection and editing, created
what every wonderful book for young readers should be—a
magic carpet that carries them to every corner of the world.
Everywhere this book of stories about black children briefly
sets us down, whether in America or South Africa,
Australia or Barbados, we find the wonder and enchantment provided by a rousing good tale that educates at the
same time it entertains. Toni Cade Bambara, a seasoned
veteran of the short story, convincingly portrays in
"Raymond's Run" the possible friendships that await us on
the other side of competition. Eugenia Collier writes mov-
ingly of the real meaning of lost innocence in "Marigolds,"
Howard Gordon writes comically in "My Lucy" of the distance between one's dream girl and the real thing, and J.
California Cooper deftly charts the changes in our world
and in our understanding of others after a first exposure to
the workplace in "How, Why to Get Rich."

Consider yourself fortunate, reader. On these pages
Bolden and company extend to you the equivalent of an
unlimited airline ticket or one of those transporters on the
starship *Enterprise*. You will find yourself immersed in the
rich, poetic language of Australia as Archie Weller conjures
in "Johnny Blue" a universal story of friendship and sacrifice. Then you'll be relocated to a stifling welfare office
with Paulette Childress White's twelve-year-old narrator,
Minerva, who is about to discover fearlessness and the facts
of life in a lovely mother-daughter story. For a superb
mother-son fiction, read Clarence Major's "My Mother and
Mitch," which is as delicately rendered and original an
account of awakening into the world of grown-ups as I've

seen in years. And for sheer heartbreak, the traveler in Tonya Bolden's collection must pause, then linger over Olive Senior's vivid, haunting "Bright Thursdays." The people in this story, as well as the plight of Laura, who is caught between classes and cultures, will drift through your memory for days, like the figures who speak to us in dreams.

Other pleasures, other places, other lives that enrich and expand our own beckon here. These stories will take you everywhere, but their terminus, their final stop, is the one country where all journeys begin and end: the mysterious terrain of the human heart. As with all memorable adventures in the magic theater of the Book, you will want to give *Rites of Passage* a permanent place in your library. And of course, in years to come, revisit these fictional worlds again and again.

—Charles Johnson

INTRODUCTION

During my growing-up years in Harlem and the Bronx, when I wasn't handballing it up or hanging around with my friends talking nonsense and talking dreams, I was oftentimes somewhere reading. For of all the kick-back-and-relax pastimes, reading was my passion. And to paraphrase my childhood enchanter, Dr. Seuss, "Oh! The places I did go!" Anton Chekhov's Russia . . . Dickens's England . . . the America of Mark Twain, Ernest Hemingway, William Faulkner, Flannery O'Connor. I was intrigued and instructed by the life stories of the grown-ups I met in these books. And how I savored those occasions when the hero or heroine was a peer. That was especially nice, especially engaging. My only regret is that I had so few encounters with kids like me. Kids black.

Did many such stories exist? As I now know, yes. But they were not easily available to me, and I didn't have the consciousness to seek them out. And so, I missed out. (Example: Arnold Adoff's anthology, *Brothers and Sisters*—which featured twenty stories about young black Americans—came out in 1970, but, shucks! and alas! nobody told me.)

Thus, this collection of stories is a bit of a selfish act. A gift to the once-young me. It's the kind of anthology I wish I'd had in my 'tween- and teenage years: one that would have given me a chance to "conversate" and commiserate—to say "Amen!" and "You, too?" and "Say *what*?!" and "Hmmm"— with young African Americans and our sisters and brothers in other lands.

But enough about my woulda-shoulda-coulda-been memory lane.

Rites of Passage is a gathering together of black young folks from different places around the world: Africa, Australia, Europe, the Caribbean, Central America—and right here in the United States. It's a collection of seventeen stories about turning points and forks in the road, about pressures from without and sudden dawnings from within, revolving around issues such as family relations, school life, the world of work, oppression, bigotry, identity, love, friendship, betrayal. In short, these stories are about happenings in the lives of girls and boys that journey them one step closer to being women and men.

Is this collection about growing up black?

Well, sort of . . . kind of. Yes and no.

To be sure, each story offers insights into the black experience. Each one spotlights a dilemma or discovery from a uniquely black perspective. And together the stories shed light on the ties that bind all young people of African descent no matter the era, geography, or cultural context. At the same time, the things the characters go through are by and large quite universal and as such reveal the common ground on which all young folks stand—black and nonblack alike. And so, regardless of who you are and whence you come, you'll find a lot here to grow (up) on.

Quite naturally, how you relate to the stories will depend upon who and where you are in the cycle of life. Whereas one story may allow you to relive a precious memory—the making of a friend or the finding of a joy—another may provide a little comfort on a pain you're presently enduring—a broken heart, a parent problem, the shattering of an illusion—and yet another will give you a preview—and much good food for thought!—of something you might be dealing with one soon-coming day. In the mix, you'll discover a thing or two about your peers of the opposite gender and about the lifescapes of those from other times and horizons. You'll find that you share experiences even though the sights and sounds of their surroundings, games played, and characteristic ways with words—non-American spellings, vocabulary, and yes, a little slang, too—may be quite different.

I could stretch out on these points by giving you tidbit summaries of the stories. But uh-uh . . . I'd much rather you just get to the reading and see for yourself.

—Tonya Bolden

RAYMOND'S RUN

❧

(United States)

by *Toni Cade Bambara*

Winning isn't *everything.*

I don't have much work to do around the house like some girls. My mother does that. And I don't have to earn my pocket money by hustling; George runs errands for the big boys and sells Christmas cards. And anything else that's got to get done, my father does. All I have to do in life is mind my brother Raymond, which is enough.

Sometimes I slip and say my little brother Raymond. But as any fool can see he's much bigger and he's older too. But a lot of people call him my little brother cause he needs looking after cause he's not quite right. And a lot of smart mouths got lots to say about that too, especially when George is minding him. But now, if anybody has anything to say to Raymond, anything to say about his big head, they have to come by me. And I don't play the dozens or believe in standing around with somebody in my face doing a lot of talking. I much rather just knock you down and take my chances even if I am a little girl with skinny arms and a squeaky voice, which is how I got the name Squeaky. And if things get too rough, I run. And as anybody can tell you, I'm the fastest thing on two feet.

There is no track meet that I don't win the first place medal. I used to win the twenty-yard dash when I was a little kid in kindergarten. Nowadays, it's the fifty-yard dash. And tomorrow I'm subject to run the quarter-meter relay all by myself and come in first, second, and third. The big kids call me Mercury cause I'm the swiftest thing in the neighborhood. Everybody knows that—except two people who know better, my father and me. He can beat me to Amsterdam Avenue with me having a two fire-hydrant headstart and him running with his hands in his pockets and whistling. But that's private information. Cause can you imagine some thirty-five-year-old man stuffing himself into PAL[1] shorts to race little kids? So as far as everyone's concerned, I'm the fastest and that goes for Gretchen, too, who has put out the tale that she is going to win the first-place medal this year. Ridiculous. In the second place, she's got short legs. In the third place, she's got freckles. In the first place, no one can beat me and that's all there is to it.

I'm standing on the corner admiring the weather and about to take a stroll down Broadway so I can practice my breathing exercises, and I've got Raymond walking on the inside close to the buildings, cause he's subject to fits of fantasy and starts thinking he's a circus performer and that the curb is a tightrope strung high in the air. And sometimes after a rain he likes to step down off his tightrope right into the gutter and slosh around getting his shoes and cuffs wet. Then I get hit when I get home. Or sometimes if you don't watch him he'll dash across traffic to the island in the middle of Broadway and give the pigeons a fit. Then I have to go behind him apologizing to all the old people sitting around trying to get some sun and getting all upset with the pigeons fluttering around them, scattering their newspapers and upsetting the waxpaper lunches in their laps. So I keep Raymond on the inside of me, and he plays like he's driving a stage coach which is O.K. by me so long as he doesn't run me over or interrupt my breathing exercises, which I have to do on account of I'm serious about my running, and I don't care who knows it.

Now some people like to act like things come easy to them, won't let on that they practice. Not me. I'll high-

[1] Police Athletic League.

prance down 34th Street like a rodeo pony to keep my knees strong even if it does get my mother uptight so that she walks ahead like she's not with me, don't know me, is all by herself on a shopping trip, and I am somebody else's crazy child. Now you take Cynthia Procter for instance. She's just the opposite. If there's a test tomorrow, she'll say something like, "Oh, I guess I'll play handball this afternoon and watch television tonight," just to let you know she ain't thinking about the test. Or like last week when she won the spelling bee for the millionth time, "A good thing you got 'receive,' Squeaky, cause I would have got it wrong. I completely forgot about the spelling bee." And she'll clutch the lace on her blouse like it was a narrow escape. Oh, brother. But of course when I pass her house on my early morning trots around the block, she is practicing the scales on the piano over and over and over and over. Then in music class she always lets herself get bumped around so she falls accidently on purpose onto the piano stool and is so surprised to find herself sitting there that she decides just for fun to try out the ole keys. And what do you know—Chopin's waltzes just spring out of her fingertips and she's the most surprised thing in the world. A regular prodigy. I could kill people like that. I stay up all night studying the words for the spelling bee. And you can see me any time of day practicing running. I never walk if I can trot, and shame on Raymond if he can't keep up. But of course he does, cause if he hangs back someone's liable to walk up to him and get smart, or take his allowance from him, or ask him where he got that great big pumpkin head. People are so stupid sometimes.

So I'm strolling down Broadway breathing out and breathing in on counts of seven, which is my lucky number, and here comes Gretchen and her sidekicks: Mary Louise, who used to be a friend of mine when she first moved to Harlem from Baltimore and got beat up by every-

body till I took up for her on account of her mother and my
mother used to sing in the same choir when they were
young girls, but people ain't grateful, so now she hangs out
with the new girl Gretchen and talks about me like a dog;
and Rosie, who is as fat as I am skinny and has a big mouth
where Raymond is concerned and is too stupid to know
that there is not a big deal of difference between herself and
Raymond and that she can't afford to throw stones. So they
are steady coming up Broadway and I see right away that
it's going to be one of those Dodge City scenes cause the
street ain't that big and they're close to the buildings just as
we are. First I think I'll step into the candy store and look
over the new comics and let them pass. But that's chicken
and I've got a reputation to consider. So then I think I'll
just walk straight on through them or even over them if
necessary. But as they get to me, they slow down. I'm
ready to fight, cause like I said I don't feature a whole lot of
chitchat, I much prefer to just knock you down right from
the jump and save everybody a lotta precious time.

"You signing up for the May Day races?" smiles Mary
Louise, only it's not a smile at all. A dumb question like
that doesn't deserve an answer. Besides, there's just me and
Gretchen standing there really, so no use wasting my breath
talking to shadows.

"I don't think you're going to win this time," says Rosie,
trying to signify with her hands on her hips all salty, completely forgetting that I have whupped her behind many
times for less salt than that.

"I always win cause I'm the best," I say straight at
Gretchen who is, as far as I'm concerned, the only one talking in this ventriloquist-dummy routine. Gretchen smiles,
but it's not a smile, and I'm thinking that girls never really
smile at each other because they don't know how and don't
want to know how and there's probably no one to teach us
how, cause grown-up girls don't know either. Then they all
look at Raymond who has just brought his mule team to a

standstill. And they're about to see what trouble they can get into through him.

"What grade you in now, Raymond?"

"You got anything to say to my brother, you say it to me, Mary Louise Williams of Raggedy Town, Baltimore."

"What are you, his mother?" sasses Rosie.

"That's right, Fatso. And the next word out of anybody and I'll be *their* mother too." So they just stand there and Gretchen shifts from one leg to the other and so do they. Then Gretchen puts her hands on her hips and is about to say something with her freckle-face self but doesn't. Then she walks around me looking me up and down but keeps walking up Broadway, and her sidekicks follow her. So me and Raymond smile at each other and he says, "Gidyap" to his team and I continue with my breathing exercises, strolling down Broadway toward the iceman on 145th with not a care in the world cause I am Miss Quicksilver herself.

I take my time getting to the park on May Day because the track meet is the last thing on the program. The biggest thing on the program is the Maypole dancing, which I can do without, thank you, even if my mother thinks it's a shame I don't take part and act like a girl for a change. You'd think my mother'd be grateful not to have to make me a white organdy dress with a big satin sash and buy me new white baby-doll shoes that can't be taken out of the box till the big day. You'd think she'd be glad her daughter ain't out there prancing around a Maypole getting the new clothes all dirty and sweaty and trying to act like a fairy or a flower or whatever you're supposed to be when you should be trying to be yourself, whatever that is, which is, as far as I am concerned, a poor black girl who really can't afford to buy shoes and a new dress you only wear once a lifetime cause it won't fit next year.

I was once a strawberry in a Hansel and Gretel pageant when I was in nursery school and didn't have no better sense than to dance on tiptoe with my arms in a circle over my head doing umbrella steps and being a perfect fool just so my mother and father could come dressed up and clap. You'd think they'd know better than to encourage that kind of nonsense. I am not a strawberry. I do not dance on my toes. I run. That is what I am all about. So I always come late to the May Day program, just in time to get my number pinned on and lay in the grass till they announce the fifty-yard dash.

I put Raymond in the little swings, which is a tight squeeze this year and will be impossible next year. Then I look around for Mr. Pearson, who pins the numbers on. I'm really looking for Gretchen if you want to know the truth, but she's not around. The park is jam-packed. Parents in hats and corsages and breast-pocket handkerchiefs peeking up. Kids in white dresses and light-blue suits. The parkees unfolding chairs and chasing the rowdy kids from Lenox as if they had no right to be there. The big guys with their caps on backwards, leaning against the fence swirling the basketballs on the tips of their fingers, waiting for all these crazy people to clear out the park so they can play. Most of the kids in my class are carrying bass drums and glockenspiels and flutes. You'd think they'd put in a few bongos or something for real like that.

Then here comes Mr. Pearson with his clipboard and his cards and pencils and whistles and safety pins and fifty million other things he's always dropping all over the place with his clumsy self. He sticks out in a crowd because he's on stilts. We used to call him Jack and the Beanstalk to get him mad. But I'm the only one that can outrun him and get away, and I'm too grown for that silliness now.

"Well, Squeaky," he says, checking my name off the list and handing me number seven and two pins. And I'm thinking he's got no right to call me Squeaky, if I can't call him Beanstalk.

"Hazel Elizabeth Deborah Parker," I correct him and tell him to write it down on his board.

"Well, Hazel Elizabeth Deborah Parker, going to give

someone else a break this year?" I squint at him real hard
to see if he is seriously thinking I should lose the race on
purpose just to give someone else a break. "Only six girls
running this time," he continues, shaking his head sadly
like it's my fault all of New York didn't turn out in sneak-
ers. "That new girl should give you a run for your money."
He looks around the park for Gretchen like a periscope in a
submarine movie. "Wouldn't it be a nice gesture if you
were . . . to ahhh . . ."

I give him such a look he couldn't finish putting that idea
into words. Grown-ups got a lot of nerve sometimes. I pin
number seven to myself and stomp away, I'm so burnt.
And I go straight for the track and stretch out on the grass
while the band winds up with "Oh, the Monkey Wrapped
His Tail Around the Flag Pole," which my teacher calls by
some other name. The man on the loudspeaker is calling
everyone over to the track and I'm on my back looking at
the sky, trying to pretend I'm in the country, but I can't,
because even grass in the city feels hard as sidewalk, and
there's just no pretending you are anywhere but in a "concrete jungle" as my grandfather says.

The twenty-yard dash takes all of two minutes cause
most of the little kids don't know no better than to run off
the track or run the wrong way or run smack into the fence
and fall down and cry. One little kid, though, has got the
good sense to run straight for the white ribbon up ahead so
he wins. Then the second-graders line up for the thirty-
yard dash and I don't even bother to turn my head to watch
cause Raphael Perez always wins. He wins before he even
begins by psyching the runners, telling them they're going
to trip on their shoelaces and fall on their faces or lose their
shorts or something, which he doesn't really have to do
since he is very fast, almost as fast as I am. After that is the
forty-yard dash which I use to run when I was in first grade.
Raymond is hollering from the swings cause he knows I'm
about to do my thing cause the man on the loudspeaker has

just announced the fifty-yard dash, although he might just as well be giving a recipe for angel food cake cause you can hardly make out what he's sayin' for the static. I get up and slip off my sweatpants and then I see Gretchen standing at the starting line, kicking her legs out like a pro. Then as I get into place I see that ole Raymond is on line on the other side of the fence, bending down with his fingers on the ground just like he knew what he was doing. I was going to yell at him but then I didn't. It burns up your energy to holler.

Every time, just before I take off in a race, I always feel like I'm in a dream, the kind of dream you have when you're sick with fever and feel all hot and weightless. I dream I'm flying over a sandy beach in the early morning sun, kissing the leaves of the trees as I fly by. And there's always the smell of apples, just like in the country when I was little and used to think I was a choo-choo train, running through the fields of corn chugging up the hill to the orchard. And all the time I'm dreaming this, I get lighter and lighter until I'm flying over the beach again, getting blown through the sky like a feather that weighs nothing at all. But once I spread my fingers in the dirt and crouch over the Get on Your Mark, the dream goes and I am solid again and am telling myself, Squeaky you must win, you must win, you are the fastest thing in the world, you can even beat your father up Amsterdam if you really try. And then I feel my weight coming back just behind my knees then down to my feet then into the earth and the pistol shot explodes in my blood and I am off and weightless again, flying past the other runners, my arms pumping up and down and the whole world is quiet except for the crunch as I zoom over the gravel in the track. I glance to my left and there is no one. To the right, a blurred Gretchen, who's got her chin jutting out as if it would win the race all by itself. And on the other side of the fence is

Raymond with his arms down to his side and the palms tucked up behind him, running in his very own style, and it's the first time I ever saw that and I almost stop to watch my brother Raymond on his first run. But the white ribbon is bouncing toward me and I tear past it, racing into the distance till my feet with a mind of their own start digging up footfuls of dirt and brake me short. Then all the kids standing on the side pile on me, banging me on the back and slapping my head with their May Day programs, for I have won again and everybody on 151st Street can walk tall for another year.

"In first place . . ." the man on the loudspeaker is clear as a bell now. But then he pauses and the loudspeaker starts to whine. Then static. And I lean down to catch my breath and here comes Gretchen walking back, for she's overshot the finish line too, huffing and puffing with her hands on her hips taking it slow, breathing in steady time like a real pro and I sort of like her a little for the first time. "In first place . . ." and then three or four voices get all mixed up on the loudspeaker and I dig my sneaker into the grass and stare at Gretchen who's staring back, we both wondering just who did win. I can hear old Beanstalk arguing with the man on the loudspeaker and then a few others running their mouths about what the stopwatches say. Then I hear Raymond yanking at the fence to call me and I wave to shush him, but he keeps rattling the fence like a gorilla in a cage like in them gorilla movies, but then like a dancer or something he starts climbing up nice and easy but very fast. And it occurs to me, watching how smoothly he climbs hand over hand and remembering how he looked running with his arms down to his side and with the wind pulling his mouth back and his teeth showing and all, it occurred to me that Raymond would make a very fine runner. Doesn't he always keep up with me on my trots? And he surely knows how to breathe in counts of seven cause he's always doing it at the dinner table, which drives my brother George up the wall. And I'm smiling to beat the band cause if I've lost this race, or if me and Gretchen tied, or even if I've won, I can always retire as a runner and begin a whole new career as a coach with Raymond as my champion. After all, with a little more study I can beat Cynthia and her phony self at the spelling bee. And if I bugged my mother, I could get piano lessons and become a star. And I have a big rep as the baddest thing around. And I've got a roomful of ribbons and medals and awards. But what has Raymond got to call his own?

So I stand there with my new plans, laughing out loud by this time as Raymond jumps down from the fence and runs over with his teeth showing and his arms down to the side, which no one before him has quite mastered as a running style. And by the time he comes over I'm jumping up and down so glad to see him—my brother Raymond, a great runner in the family tradition. But of course everyone thinks I'm jumping up and down because the men on the loudspeaker have finally gotten themselves together and compared notes and are announcing "In first place—Miss Hazel Elizabeth Deborah Parker." (Dig that.) "In second place— Miss Gretchen P. Lewis." And I look over at Gretchen wondering what the "P" stands for. And I smile. Cause she's good, no doubt about it. Maybe she'd like to help me coach Raymond; she obviously is serious about running, as any fool can see. And she nods to congratulate me and then she smiles. And I smile. We stand there with this big smile of respect between us. It's about as real a smile as girls can do for each other, considering we don't practice real smiling every day, you know, cause maybe we too busy being flowers or fairies or strawberries instead of something honest and worthy of respect . . . you know . . . like being people.

THE SCAR

(Barbados)

by Cecil Foster

There's a thin line between compromising oneself
and stooping to conquer—or merely survive.

*T*he weight was breaking my neck. I did not feel I could take another step without toppling over. The large crocus bag of potatoes was just too heavy. I was too weak and hungry. And I was mad enough to throw the bag off my head and abandon it beside the road.

"Hold on," Grandmother said. Her voice was soothing but firm. "Hold on! We're soon home. Now ain't the time to give up."

"But look how far we've walked," I said, wiping the sweat from my eyes. "All the way from right up there by Buckley's plantation."

"No. No. You shouldn't look back. Remember what happened to Lot's wife. She turned into a pillar of salt. Why? Because she looked back. But me and you ain't looking back. We pressing on 'til victory is ours in Christ name."

From early morning we had gone sprouting. Grandmother had located the two long iron stakes from the backyard, had wrapped them in two pieces of old cloth and put the grapplers in the big crocus bags. As the soft sun was rising, we left the village behind us and walked along the grass track on our way to the sweet-potato and yam field.

The early morning dew, still fresh on the grass and forming large bubbles in places like multicoloured raindrops, slicked my feet, making them wet and cold. The dew quickly soaked the bottom of Grandma's frock, making it cling to her calves. The wetness caused her canvas shoes to make sloshing sounds with every step.

We had gone on such a trip several times, mostly with others from the village. But for some reason Grandmother had decided we should travel alone that morning. This was welcome news to me as I always looked forward to the two of us doing just about anything together. Walks like this gave me the chance to question her about so many things and for she to teach me even more. Over the years, there were so many times when Grandmother purposely took me aside, when we went walking and exploring, maybe to visit some important person in the area or even to stroll along craggy sections of the beach, where Grandmother said I was never to bathe.

Only a few days earlier, she had consented to allowing me to bathe in the sea unaccompanied by an adult. Several of us had decided on the spur of the moment to have a dip in the ocean and I had run home to ask permission. Grandmother thought long and asked which beach we wanted to visit. I told her. Finally, she said: "I guess it's okay. You are getting to be a big boy now. You got to do some things on your own." I went to the beach, but shortly afterwards Grandmother found a reason for us to have another walk.

That morning was one of those occasions, I had thought. Maybe there was something new she wanted to show me. I eagerly looked forward to hearing and seeing whatever it was. And to hear the story behind what made whatever thing so important. Like the report of the boy who got washed out to sea on the same shoals she had warned me against, and how it was only through the Grace of God that a man was fishing from the top of the rocks and threw out his net to him. In his struggle, the boy broke the net, making it useless for catching the sprats swimming around in large schools. But at least the boy was saved, even if the fisherman made no money that day. Some other boy, especially the hard-luck sort, might not be so fortunate, she had warned.

More than that, being alone with Grandmother gave me the chance to have her undivided attention and for she to tell me how proud she was that I was maturing into a strong African man, that she only had to teach me a few more things before I was fully ready. I knew she told me those things when she wanted me to do deeds that were more of a challenge than usual, or when she was flattering me. Still, I liked these moments because they made me feel important.

The morning of our walk promised to be extra special. As we sauntered along, we dodged the long sugar cane leaves, and occasionally even a stalk of cane itself, bent across the cart road from the weight of the dew. The canes were no more than what was to be expected, so symbolic of the obstacles that could block the path, she had said.

As she spoke, she carefully pushed the leaves and canes aside, clearing the path for us. Nothing was to prevent me from achieving whatever I wanted, Grandmother said, although, once in a while, the sacrifice might be greater than expected. Becoming an adult meant passing the tests of realizing when to compromise, and when to realize that the concession was worth more than what was achieved from it. As happened on some occasions, I did not understand what she was getting at. Grandmother did not bother to explain fully.

But there was something different about this walk. Several times, I noticed Grandmother looking in the distance behind us. Every now and then, she pointed out "good" weeds and grasses that could be used for medicines or food and the "bad" ones that were poisonous. This was a continuation of my education. But her heart didn't seem to be in the teaching. And she was walking faster than usual, even speeding up her steps where, in the past, I might have got her to slow down so I could catch my breath. Her mind seemed to be focused solely on getting the matter at hand over with as soon as possible, before anyone joined us.

This trip was a chance to get free sweet potatoes and yams. By leaving so early, and with only me, I assumed Grandmother wanted us to get first crack before others arrived and joined us in a mad scramble. Grandmother called the potatoes and yams we were to reap pickings, or sprouts. They were the second crop after the plantation workers had harvested the rows of giant sweet potatoes and yams. The best of the crop was usually sent overseas, with the remainder sold in the fancy supermarkets in the city or to the hotels along the white sand coasts. Few poor people like us on the island could afford the exorbitant prices. So we waited our turn, which was usually a week or so after the first harvest, when some tubers left behind in the ground started to sprout new vines, making it easier for us to find them.

As a rule, what was left in the ground could be claimed by anyone coming after the first harvest. This was the only time we could enter onto the plantation property without having to be on the lookout for the watchman. In a sense, we were doing the plantation owner a favour, Grandmother had explained. We were removing the vines that grew wild and choked the newly transplanted sugar cane plants. Grandmother had told me the plantation had to rest the land every seven years from growing sugar cane. This was why yams and potatoes were planted. The rotation made the land fertile again, she said. However, the ratooning[1] potato vines and weeds might be so embedded into the ground, or so scattered from the first harvest, they strangled the young canes. By removing them, we saved the plantation the cost of paying gangs of young boys to crawl on their hands and knees under the scorching sun to clear the fields of the unwanted growth.

"Then they should be paying us, shouldn't they?" I asked.

"You would think so," Grandmother said. "But that's

[1] Sprouting.

not the case. There was a time, way back, when they even tried to charge the people for the pickings. The people said: let them stay and rot in the ground. But the sprouts grew back so fast and strong, the owners soon realized it was better to let the people have the few potatoes and save themselves a whole heap of trouble. When the people went back the potatoes were no good; when you ate them they felt like sponge, with no taste. Too old. They were good only for feeding the pigs. The owners examined a few pickings, saw the worms growing in them because the plantation had stopped spraying the fields, and agreed that they were only fit for hogs. That is why, even now, we always say that we are picking the sprouts for the pigs. That way the plantation owners can pretend we ain't getting the few half-dead pickings for nothing."

"Why do we have to pretend anyway?" I asked.

She thought for a while. Then she spoke slowly. "Once in a while in this life, as you'll learn, there are times to pretend, to swallow your pride, just to get by. As the Good Book says, 'To every thing there is a season, and a time to every purpose under heaven . . . a time to plant, and a time to pluck up that which is planted.' A time when you have to pretend and, I believe, a time when you won't have to." Until we reached the field, Grandmother was unusually quiet. The silence convinced me even more that something was wrong.

Grandmother normally chose a row and I the one beside her. Walking side by side, we looked for the new growth and rooted out the pickings with the iron stakes. On a good day, by the time we reached the head row on the other side, we would be dragging the stuffed bags behind us. Occasionally luck smiled on us when we found a tuber as large as any from the first crop, and in as good condition.

This had been a very good day and for several unexpected reasons. Somehow, Grandmother had got word before the field was fully harvested and we had turned up on a morn-

ing when the men were working elsewhere on the plantation. With nobody around, she had stealthily abandoned
the pickings and had dug up several of the large tubers in
the still unharvested part of the field and had crammed
them into her bag. Grandmother further surprised me
when she quickly raided the pigeon pea trees along the
head row, stuffing the pods into a cloth bag tied around her
waist.

"Come Sunday," she had said, returning to where I was
standing, "we'll eat these peas too-sweet[2] in the rice and
peas I'll be cooking." She must have felt a need to comment on her action. It was so uncharacteristic of her to
take such chances. Maybe she felt uncomfortable from the
way I was staring at how she was shelling some of the very
young pods and nervously throwing the small green peas
into her mouth. She never told me why she took the potatoes and peas. Most certainly we would have landed before
a magistrate if the watchman, or any busybody for that
matter, had happened by at that time and caught us stray-
ing beyond the boundary.

The next challenge was to hoist the bumpy bags on our
heads and carry them home. Grandmother had made two
pads by wrapping cloth rags around her hand in a flat circu-
lar pattern. She placed one on my cap and then helped me
to lift the heavy bag onto my head, balancing it on the pad.
Instantly, my neck felt forced into my shoulders. I steadied
my load with both hands. In the past, Grandmother never
made my bag so heavy.

Grandmother placed the second pad on her straw hat,
bent and picked up the bag, her head held straight all this
time to prevent the pad from shifting. She brought the bag
to rest on a bent knee. Like the men training as body-
builders in the Public Works yard, she lifted the bag over
her head while praising God for the victory and the

---

[2] Delicious.

strength. Grandmother's bag was two or three times bigger than mine.

"But I can't go any farther, Grandma," I protested. We had been walking for what seemed to me like hours. "My head's really hurting me. It looks like you put too many potatoes in my bag and—"

"No, man," she jumped in before I had finished. "You're a strong boy. You can carry your load. Just hold on a bit longer. The harder you sweat, the more satisfaction you should get, for you are labouring for your daily bread, not begging."

"I was thinking I can leave it in the grass and we can come back for it later," I said.

"What! And let somebody come along and thief it?"

"We can cover it with grass. Hide it good-good, so nobody can find it."

"How you don't know somebody ain't watching us right now? How you're to know somebody might just be waiting for a little boy like you to bring a big bag of potatoes this far and then, just before you get home, to leave them so this big able man can thief them and take them home and feed his family food that you work so hard to get this far? But that won't happen. Not today. You'll hold on as I tell yuh. Yes, man, hold on just a little bit more. Won't be too long now. Look, we can already see the houses. There is the top of Violet Jones's house coming into sight. Hold on, son. In this life, you can't give up when things get too hard. I keep telling yuh: We African people, especially the men, like what you're going to be, got to be tough and strong."

"No, Grandma. I don't feel strong anymore and, besides, I'm too hungry."

"I know that," she responded, now walking beside me instead of letting me lead the way. "Hungry? All o' we're hungry. That's why when I get home the first thing I'm going to do is put a pot on the fire and stew a handful of these potatoes, the same ones in your bag. Then we can wash it down with some swank that I'll make from the bottle of the crack-liquor Livingstone Hunte brought for we from the sugar factory."[3]

"But you've done told me how you don't want anybody to use the syrup," I said. "Remember: It was for a special occasion."

"That's right. Special like now. When we get home, I'll mix a big jug of syrup water. I'll even squeeze a lime or two into it, just like how you like it. Like on Sundays. Now, wouldn't that be nice? So hang on. This will help you, and the swank will too, to be a strong and a tough man when you grow up. Just hold on a bit longer. Don't let a small thing like this defeat yuh. What the Bible says: the race isn't for the swift nor the battle for the strong, but he that endureth to the end."

We walked in silence until Grandmother added what must have been an afterthought. "Even so, we'd already rest a while back there, so it ain't make no sense stopping and then having to walk in the hot midday sun. This constant stopping to cool down only to sweat some more again ain't too good for the body." It was almost as if she had continued the conversation in her head.

The sun had long dried the dew. My shirt was stuck to my back and I felt the perspiration running down my face, back and chest. Grandmother had undone the top button of the loose-fitting cotton dress. The grass and black soil were already beginning to look parched and it was only about 11 o'clock. In another hour, the sun would be blazing down on us out of a cloudless sky. The bag of potatoes would hardly provide any shade.

We had stopped briefly some time back, but that wasn't so much for a rest, as Grandmother now claimed, but to allow me to "break" some cane. Grandmother had stayed

[3] Usually, swank is made of sugar and water; but here, it'll be made with the very thick molasseslike substance—the crack-liquor—extracted from the sugar cane in the first refining process.

outside the field, supposedly on the lookout for the despised watchman, Livingstone Hunte. Although he lived in the village with us, the watchman took very seriously his duty to protect the plantation owner's property. Not only could we not pick the first crops of potatoes, yams or peas, but Mr. Hunte was also sure to chase us if he caught us breaking the canes. He always carried a shiny guava-wood stick, which he consistently threatened to use on any thief. The women in the village never hesitated to cuss the watchman, often describing him as a "wo'thless-no-use-whatsoever."

Grandmother had claimed he was the perfect example of what I should strive not to become as a man. "You can always count on one thing: that people like Livingstone Hunte will always sell out to some white master," Grandmother had said. "That's a fact of life. It's no different from when all o' we were slaves on the plantation and the massa used to pick one o' we to keep everybody in check. And they always choose a light skin curly hair fellow like Livingstone Hunte."

With Grandmother watching, I went into the cane field, walking with my elbow in front of my face as protection from the sharp edges of the cane blades. I had been lucky this morning. A short distance into the field was an imposing stand of soft canes, the tall, long-jointed canes with the yellowish peel that we so easily tore away with our teeth to get at the soft inside. Most of the cane in this area were hard enough to break out the teeth of anyone "sucking" them, or to cut the corner of the mouth when stripping away the rind with the teeth.

It was a rare stroke of luck that Grandmother chose this spot. I smashed down several of the plants and broke them into smaller pieces on my knee. I could not wait to get home to suck them. Even then, I imagined sitting in the cool evening breeze, chewing on the cane and feeling the sweet sticky juice running down my throat and making me belch. I might not even need supper. But first I had to get home.

"Come now," Grandmother's voice was calling. "What's keeping you so long? You're going to wait until some of the wo'thless people living around here come along and see you breaking the few canes? That would only give them something more to talk 'bout, to wash their mouths with on poor Livingstone Hunte, as if I care what they say."

I emerged from the field and stuffed the canes into the bags. It was only when helping to lift the bag onto my head that I realized I had damaged my hands. Several of the young prickly hairs from the cane tops were caught in my hands, making them sore.

"Just to show you that, as in life, nothing comes easy," Grandmother said, as she re-headed her bag, now much heavier with the pieces of sugar canes. We walked quickly away from the scene of our crime. "Nothing comes easy in life. Not one little thing. There's always a price, but hopefully, it is something you can live with. When we get home, you can take a bath and treat the hands."

"But not as soon as I get home. I would have to cool down first," I said. "The grass licking at my foot and the prickles from the canes will itch me real bad if I bathe when I'm so sweaty." Unless it was at the beach, I still hated bathing, especially when I didn't have to go to school or church. "Even so, you're always telling me that nobody should bathe when the body is hot from too much sun."

"You like you're learning," Grandmother said approvingly. "I tell yuh: you're learning, yes."

Grandmother's words were more fortuitous than even she might have thought. That very evening, I was forced to confront things I never expected and to learn certain facts of life Grandmother had never told me. Perhaps she felt these were some of the things that I should discover for myself, the same way I had found out that people in the village were talking about us more than usual.

"Like Livingstone Hunte feeding all o' you now, eh," the

woman passing the street had said to me. "Look how you're sitting down there fulling up yuh guts with the plantation cane and everybody done know that if it was someone else Livingstone Hunte will be creating one big fuss. But he's right. He knows what he's getting. He's only feeding the lambie to get to the mammie."

I had ignored her, claiming as Grandmother would have that this woman was simply dropping remarks or had a bad mind. But she had struck a chord. Earlier in the evening I was standing near the rum shop when I heard Livingstone Hunte and some men talking over a bottle of white rum in a darkened corner. Grandmother's name had been mentioned and the men had laughed loudly, the way I had learned to recognize when they said something dirty.

"So I see, Livingstone, boy, that you find your arse in real good grazings these days and nights," one of the men had said. "That Doris Payne still look fine despite her age. Like she still got a couple more drinks in she bottle."

"Yes, man," Livingstone said. "I can swear to that, man. And they're good drinks too."

"So that's why she and she grandson got the run of the plantation?" the man continued.

"I ain't no fool," Livingstone boasted. "It ain't costing me nothing out of my pocket. And how much potatoes or yams can any one woman carry on her head? I don't care how strong she is or how many she crammed into the bag, she can only carry so many. It ain't like she's fulling up a donkey cart or anything so. Only a few kiss-me-arse potatoes and yams. And maybe a few canes and a couple handfuls o' peas. Ain't costing me nothing; can't bankrupt the plantation."

"The price for you controlling the house, eh?" someone said. The light from the big kerosene lamps spilled out the shop and I left before I was discovered.

The conversation lingered in my mind. Of late, the watchman had taken to arriving at our house strange hours of the night, before leaving for his tour of the plantation. Often when he left, I was asleep.

Just as I was finishing the last of the cane, I heard footsteps behind me and looked around to see Livingstone Hunte tottering on uncertain legs, but leaning on his stick, trying to relieve himself in the tall grass at the side of the street.

"Little boy," he said, his words were slurred from too much rum. "Why don't you run along and tell yuh grandmerher I coming soon. Tell she to warm up the little food she said she'd cooked for me."

"What food you're talking 'bout?" I shouted back at him. The overheard conversation was still fresh in my mind. I had grown used to his coming and sharing a meal with us, but naively I thought this was only if he happened to drop in when we were eating. Now, with the rum in his head, he had either turned foolish or too drunk because he was expecting Grandmother to set aside a share of food for him.

"How yuh mean wha' food?" he shouted back. "I'm talking about the damn green peas and rice she's supposed to be cooking. Why you think I'd let she pick all o' Buckley's plantation peas for, if I ain't getting none of it? I's the watchman 'round here, yuh know."

Grandmother had not cooked peas and rice. Perhaps, because of the energy sapped by the sun, she had cooked "stew food." She had boiled the yams and the potatoes and had added a few green bananas in their skins, a ripe plantain, some eddoes and several cornmeal dumplings to the pot. This she served with a yellowish and tasty sauce of Palm Tree butter and flaked salted codfish. It was a quick and delicious meal. But Livingstone Hunte was in no mood for it.

"Didn't I tell you to cook me rice and peas?" he bellowed in the kitchen. "Rice and peas! Why the hell you think I let you pick the masser's damn peas for?"

"But I tell you, they're for Sunday food."

"Sunday is a long time off, man," he shouted. "What I'm

going to do with all that rough food you cook there? I can't eat that food cold and I don't like stew food warmed over. I want rice and peas."

"Sunday, man. You know Sunday is always special." Grandma Doris was speaking softly.

"You can go back and pick some more for Sunday if that was what you want. You could have asked me again; I represent the masser 'round here," Livingstone said.

"I ain't able to walk all the way up there and back," Grandmother protested. "The walk too long, especially in the hot sun. And what if people see me? They'd have something more to talk 'bout."

"Don't you know I have five minds to call the police and lock you up for stealing the damn plantation peas and potatoes," he looked at me, standing in the doorway, "and cane. What the hell I want stew food for!"

He smashed the bowl containing the food with his watchman's stick and knocked everything else off the table, including the red clay pitcher with the swank. It crashed to the floor and broke, spilling the sticky molasses drink on the floor. Livingstone turned away from the table, and, with the stick poised above his head, appeared ready to strike Grandmother.

Instinctively, I jumped on him, but his strength was too much. He flung me against the side of the house and, while I was bent over, brought the stick crashing down on my head. When I came to, Grandma Doris was stooping over me with a towel in one hand and a small bottle of smelling salts in the other. The basin next to me was covered with blood. She had ripped off her long floral dress and put me to rest on it. She looked too scared to talk. Livingstone Hunte had left.

"You'll overcome this," she said some time after I was conscious. As she spoke, she pulled back my lids to look into my eyes. "Lord, how that beast for a man could do a thing like this to a mere child. Only because he thinks he got power; because he's in charge at Buckley's plantation and can give me a potato or two. I don't ever want to set my eyes on the vagabond again. And I got five minds to carry you 'long to hospital even if it means I have to swear out a statement against him and get his arse lock-up in prison. Then we will see who is powerful around here."

But we didn't go to hospital. Even while she consoled me, I knew she was going to do nothing, for her body was tense, and her hands trembled, betraying the fear of what would happen to her if she made too much of this matter. To make me feel better she spoke bravely and threatened, but all the time her body was telling a different story, once again conceding that powerful people like Livingstone Hunte were always unchallengeable. In my wish for revenge, I could not accept her resignation so easily.

That night, Grandmother allowed me to sleep in her bed. Several times, she awoke me to ask if I was alright and if my head was still hurting, and to tell me to use the topsy underneath the bed instead of going outside to pee. For years, I had been used to sleeping in Grandma's bed, but just about the time people started dropping remarks about Livingstone Hunte, I was told to stay in my bed at night.

The wound to my forehead healed eventually, but left a big scar because it had not been stitched. I never forgave Livingstone Hunte for spoiling my features. The next day he had come by the house, sober and remorseful, and with a big bag of peas already shelled. He had offered me a dollar, but I didn't take it. Grandmother did and avoided us the embarrassment.

Livingstone Hunte continued to come around until he got tired and found another woman to spend the night with and to share the fruits of the plantation. Grandmother never talked about him again, as if she was hoping this would expunge her frailty and mistakes.

Soon afterwards, we stopped taking the long walks. Maybe Grandmother felt she had taught me enough. Or that I had become the strong African man she wanted, even with a noticeable scar.

THE DAY THE WORLD ALMOST CAME TO AN END

❧

(United States)

by *Pearl Crayton*

The world is full of Chicken Littles. The sooner you learn to ignore them, the better off you'll be — and better able to get on with the business of living.

*I*f you haven't had the world coming to an end on you when you're twelve years old and a sinner, you don't know how lucky you are! When it happened to me it scared the living daylights and some of the joy of sinning out of me and, in a lot of other ways, messed up my life altogether. But if I am to believe Ralph Waldo Emerson's "Compensation,"[1] I guess I got some good out of it too.

The calamity befell me back in 1936. We were living on a plantation in Louisiana at the time, close to the earth and God, and all wrapped up in religion. The church was the axis around which plantation life revolved, the Mother to whom the folks took their problems, the Teacher who taught them how the Lord wanted them to live, the Chastiser who threatened the sinful with Hell.

In spite of the fact that my parents were churchgoing Christians, I was still holding on to being a sinner. Not that I had anything against religion, it was just a matter of integrity. There was an old plantation custom that in order to be baptized into the church a sinner had to "get religion," a mystical experience in which the soul of the sinner was converted into Christian. A Christian had to live up-

---

[1] Ralph Waldo Emerson (1803–82): writer, philosopher, and Unitarian minister; one of his most well known sayings is Hitch your wagon to a star.

right, and I knew I just couldn't come up to that on account of there were too many delicious sins around to get into. But a world coming to an end can be pretty hard on a sinner.

The trouble began when my cousin Rena came upon me playing in the watermelon patch, running like the devil was behind her. I was making a whole quarter of mud cabins by packing dirt over my foot in the shape of a cabin, putting a chimney on top, then pulling my foot out. The space left by my foot formed the room of the cabin. I'd broken some twigs off chinaberry and sycamore trees which I planted in the ground around the cabins to make "trees." Some blooming wild flowers that I had picked made up a flower yard in front of each cabin. It was as pretty a sight as you ever want to see before she came stepping all over everything. I let her know I didn't like it real loud, but she didn't pay what I said any attention, she just blurted out, "The end of the world is coming Saturday; you'd better go get you some religion in a hurry!"

That was on a Friday afternoon, getting late.

A picture of Hell flashed across my mind but I pushed it back into the subconscious. "The world's NOT coming to an end!" The confidence I tried to put in my voice failed; it quaked a little. "Who told you the world is coming to an end?"

"I heard Mama and Miss Daya talking about it just now. There's going to be an eclipse Sunday. You know what an eclipse is, don't you?"

I didn't know but I nodded anyhow.

"That's when the sun has a fight with the moon. If the sun whips, the world goes on; if the moon whips, then the world comes to an end. Well, they say that Sunday the moon is going to whip the sun!"

I wasn't going to be scared into giving up my sinning that easily. "How do they know the moon is going to whip?" I asked.

"They read it in the almanac. And it's in the Bible too,

in Revelation. It says in Revelation that the world is supposed to end this year. Miss Daya is a missionary sister and she knows all about things like that."

"Nobody knows anything about Revelation, my daddy says so," I rebutted. "Ain't never been nobody born smart enough to figure out Revelation since that Mister John wrote it. He's just going to have to come back and explain it himself."

She acted like she didn't hear that. "And Reverend Davis said in church last Sunday that time is winding up," she said.

"He's been saying that for years now, and time hasn't wound up yet."

"That's what I know, he's been saying it for years, and all the while he's been saying it time's been winding right along, and now it's just about all wound up!"

That made sense to me and I began to consider that maybe she could be right. Then that Miss Daya happened by.

"Lord bless you down there on your knees, baby! Pray to the Lord 'cause it's praying time!"

I hadn't gotten up from where I'd been making mud cabins, but I jumped up quick to let her know I wasn't praying.

"Both of you girls got religion?" she asked, and without waiting for an answer, "That's good. You're both big girls, big enough to go to Hell. You all be glad you all got religion 'cause the Lord is coming soon! He said he was coming and he's coming SOON!" And she went on towards our cabin before I could ask her about the world ending Sunday.

Rena just stood there and looked at me awhile, shaking her head in an "I told you so," and advised me again to get some religion in a hurry. Then she ran off to warn someone else.

Although I was a sinner, I was a regular churchgoing sinner and at our church we had a hellfire-preaching pastor. He could paint pictures of Hell and the Devil in his sermons horrible enough to give a sinner a whole week of nightmares. Nobody with a dime's worth of sense wanted to go to a hot, burning Hell where a red, horned Devil tormented folks with a pitchfork, but I'd been taking a chance on enjoying life another thirty years or so before getting some religion—getting just enough to keep me out of Hell. I hadn't figured on time running out on me so soon, and I still wasn't taking anybody's word before asking my daddy about it first. But it was plowing time and Daddy was way back in the cornfield where I'd already run across a rattlesnake, so I figured even the world coming to an end could wait until suppertime.

I went around the rest of that day with my mind loaded down. Now I didn't exactly believe that the world was coming to an end, but I didn't exactly believe it wasn't either. About two years before, I'd went and read the worst part of Revelation and it had taken my daddy two weeks to convince me that I didn't understand what I had read, which still didn't keep me from having bad dreams about the moon dripping away in blood and a lot of other distressing visions aroused from misunderstood words.

Those dreams were only a vague and frightening memory the Friday I'm talking about, and Revelation an accepted mystery. Yet things like that have a way of sneaking back on you when you need it the least. I got to "supposing" the world did come to an end with earthquakes and hail and fire raining down from the sky and stars falling, exactly like it read in Revelation, and "supposing" the Devil got after me and took me to Hell like folks on the plantation said he would, and "supposing" Hell really and truly was as horrible as the preacher said it was. The way the preacher told it, in Hell a person got burned and burned up and never died, he just kept burning, burning, burning. With "supposing" like that going through it, my mind was really loaded down! I figured there was no use talking to Mama about what was bothering me because Miss Daya had stayed at our cabin for over an hour, and I was sure she had convinced Mama that the moon was going to whip the sun.

It seemed to me like it took Daddy longer than ever to come home. It was the Friday of Council Meeting at the church, and Daddy, a deacon, had to be there. I knew he wouldn't have much time to talk to me before he'd have to leave out for the church, so I started walking up the turn-row through the fields to meet him. When I finally saw him riding towards home on his slide I ran to meet him.

Daddy always hitched a plank under his plow to keep the plow blades from cutting up the turnrow when he came home from plowing the fields. The plank, which he called a slide, was long enough behind the plow for him to stand on and ride home, pulled by his plow horse. Whenever I ran to meet him he'd let me ride home with him on the slide.

"Daddy," I said as soon as he'd put me on the slide in front of him and "gee'd" the horse to go on, "is the world going to come to an end Sunday?"

"I don't know, honey," he replied. "Why do you want to know?"

I told him about Rena's prophecy. That really tickled him! He laughed and laughed like that was the funniest thing he'd ever heard! I laughed a little too, though I didn't get the joke in it.

"There's always somebody coming around prophesying that the world's coming to an end," he said after he'd laughed himself out. "Folks been doing that ever since I was a boy, they were doing it when my daddy was a boy, aw, they've been doing that for hundreds of years and the world is still here. Don't you ever pay any attention to anybody that comes around telling you the world is going to end, baby."

"But ain't the world *ever* going to end?" I wanted to know.

"Yeah, but don't anybody know when. Only the Lord knows that. Why, the world might not end for another thousand years, then again it might end tonight, we just don't know. . . ."

"TONIGHT! You mean the world might end TONIGHT!"

"Sure. I'm not saying it will but it could. A person never can tell about a thing like that. But if you let that bother you, why you'll be scared to death every day of your life looking for the world to end. You're not going to be that silly, are you?"

"Aw, shucks no," I lied. I was that silly. Right then and there I got to looking for the world to end, right there on the *spot!*

Like anybody expecting a calamity, I decided to sit up all night that night but Mama made me go to bed. My room was full of the plantation, the darkest of darkness. Before Daddy returned from church Mama put out the coal oil lamp and went to bed.

The lazy old moon was on its vacation again; there was no light anywhere, not a speck. Although my eyes couldn't see anything in that awful dark, my mind had always been very good at seeing things in the dark that weren't there. I got to "seeing" how it was going to be when the world ended, the whole drama of it paraded right before my mind. Then my imagination marched me up before the judgment seat to give account for my past sins and I tried to figure out how much burning I'd get for each offense. Counting up all the ripe plums and peaches I'd saved from going to waste on the neighbors' trees, neglecting to get the owners' permission, the fights I'd had with that sassy little Catherine who lived across the river, the domino games I'd played for penny stakes with my sinner-cousin, Sam, the times I'd handled the truth careless enough to save myself from a whipping, and other not so holy acts, I figured I'd be in for some real hot burning.

While I lay there in that pitch-black darkness worrying

myself sick about burning in Hell, a distant rumbling disturbed the stillness of the night, so faint that at first I wasn't sure I'd heard it. I sat up in bed, straining my ears listening. Sure enough there was a rumbling, far away. The rumbling wasn't thunder, I was sure of that because thunder rumbled, then died away, but this rumbling grew louder and louder and LOUDER. A slow-moving, terrible, loud rumbling that was to my scared mind the earth quaking, the sky caving in, the world ending!

I got out of there, I got out of there *fast!* I didn't even think about being dressed only in my nightgown or the awful dark outside being full of ghosts and bogeymen and other horrors, I just ran!

"The world is ending! The world is ending! Run! Run for your life!" I shouted a warning to Mama, and I just kept on hollering as I ran down the road past the other plantation cabins. "The world is ending! The world is ending! Run! Run for your life!"

Doors opened and folks came out on the cabin porches, some holding coal oil lamps in their hands. They'd look at me in my white nightgown running down the road as fast as a scared rabbit, then look up at the sky, rumbling like it was caving in, and a few of them hollered something at me as I passed by, but I couldn't make out what any of them said.

I might have run myself plumb to the ocean or death if Daddy and some other deacons hadn't been coming up the road on their way from church. Daddy caught me. He had a hard time holding me though. The fear of the Devil and Hell was stronger in me than reason. I was dead set on escaping them.

Daddy had heard my hollering about the world ending as I ran down the road towards them, so he kept telling me, "That's just an old airplane, honey, the world's not ending. That's just an old airplane making all that racket!"

When his words got through the fear that fogged my

mind I calmed down a bit. "Airplane?" I'd only heard about airplanes, never had I seen one or heard one passing by.

Daddy laughed. "You were just about outrunning that old airplane and keeping up almost as much racket!" He pointed toward the sky. "Look up there, you see, it's gone now. See that light moving towards town? That's it. Those old airplanes sure have scared a lot of folks with all that racket they make."

I looked up. Sure enough there was a light that looked like a star moving across the sky. The rumbling was way off in the distance, going away slowly like it had come. And the sky was whole, not a piece of it had caved in! I broke down and cried because I was so relieved that the world wasn't coming to an end, because I'd been so scared for so long, because I'd made such a fool of myself, and just because.

Daddy pulled off his suit coat and wrapped it around me to hide the shame of my nightgown from the deacons. After I'd had a real good cry we walked home.

As we walked up the ribbon of road bordering the plantation on our way home I felt a new kind of happiness inside me. The yellow squares of light shining from the black shapes of the plantation cabins outline against the night made a picture that looked beautiful to me for the first time. Even the chirping of the crickets sounded beautiful, like a new song I'd never heard before. Even the darkness was beautiful, everything was beautiful. And I was alive, I felt the life within me warming me from the inside, a happy feeling I'd never had before. And the world was here all around me, I was aware of all of it, full of beauty, full of happy things to do. Right then and there I was overwhelmed with a desire to *live*, really *live* in the world and enjoy as much of it as I could before it came to an end. And I've been doing so ever since.

THE LATE BUD

❧

(Ghana)

by Ama Ata Aidoo

Pride goes before destruction, and a haughty spirit before a fall.
—Proverbs 16:18

"*T*he good child who willingly goes on errands eats the food of peace." This was a favourite saying in the house. Maami, Aunt Efua, Aunt Araba . . . oh, they all said it, especially when they had prepared something delicious like cocoyam porridge and seasoned beef. You know how it is.

First, as they stirred it with the ladle, its scent rose from the pot and became a little cloud hanging over the hearth. Gradually, it spread through the courtyard and entered the inner and outer rooms of the women's apartments. This was the first scent that greeted the afternoon sleeper. She stretched herself luxuriously, inhaled a large quantity of the sweet scent, cried "Mm" and either fell back again to sleep or got up to be about her business. The aroma did not stay. It rolled into the next house and the next, until it filled the whole neighbourhood. And Yaaba would sniff it.

As usual, she would be playing with her friends by the Big Trunk. She would suddenly throw down her pebbles even if it was her turn, jump up, shake her cloth free of sand and announce, "I am going home."

"Why?"

"Yaaba, why?"

But the questions of her amazed companions would reach her faintly like whispers. She was flying home. Having crossed the threshold, she then slunk by the wall. But there would be none for her.

Yaaba never stayed at home to go on an errand. Even when she was around, she never would fetch water to save a dying soul. How could she then eat the food of peace? Oh, if it was a formal meal, like in the morning or evening, that was a different matter. Of that, even Yaaba got her lawful share. . . . But not this sweet-sweet porridge. "Nsia, Antobam, Naabanyin, Adwoa, come for some porridge." And the other children trooped in with their little plates and bowls. But not the figure by the wall. They chattered as they came and the mother teased as she dished out their titbits.

"Is yours alright, Adwoa? . . . and yours, Tawia? . . . yours is certainly sufficient, Antobam. . . . But my child, this is only a titbit for us, the deserving. Other people," and she would squint at Yaaba, "who have not worked will not get the tiniest bit." She then started eating hers. If Yaaba felt that the joke was being carried too far, she coughed. "Oh," the mother would cry out, "people should be careful about their throats. Even if they coughed until they spat blood none of this porridge would touch their mouths."

But it was not things and incidents like these which worried Yaaba. For inevitably, a mother's womb cried out for a lonely figure by a wall and she would be given some porridge. Even when her mother could be bile-bellied enough to look at her and dish out all the porridge, Yaaba could run into the doorway and ambush some child and rob him of the greater part of his share. No, it was not such things that worried her. Every mother might call her a bad girl. She enjoyed playing by the Big Trunk, for instance. Since to be a good girl, one had to stay by the hearth and not by the Big Trunk throwing pebbles, but with one's hands folded quietly on one's lap, waiting to be sent everywhere by all the mothers, Yaaba let people like Adwoa who wanted to be called "good" be good. Thank you, she was not interested.

But there was something which disturbed Yaaba. No one knew it did, but it did. She used to wonder why, every time Maami called Adwoa, she called her "My child Adwoa," while she was always merely called "Yaaba."

"My child Adwoa, pick me the drinking can. . . . My child you have done well. . . ."

Oh, it is so always. Am I not my mother's child?

"Yaaba, come for your food." She always wished in her heart that she could ask somebody about it. . . . Paapa . . . Maami . . . Nana, am I not Maami's daughter? Who was my mother?

But you see, one does not go round asking elders such questions. Take the day Antobam asked her grandmother where her own mother was. The grandmother also asked Antobam whether she was not being looked after well, and then started weeping and saying things. Other mothers joined in the weeping. Then some more women came over from the neighbourhood and her aunts and uncles came too and there was more weeping and there was also drinking and libation-pouring. At the end of it all, they gave Antobam a stiff talking-to.

No, one does not go round asking one's elders such questions.

But Adwoa, my child, bring me the knife. . . . Yaaba . . . Yaaba, your cloth is dirty. Yaaba, Yaaba . . .

It was the afternoon of the Saturday before Christmas Sunday. Yaaba had just come from the playgrounds to gobble down her afternoon meal. It was kenkey[1] and a little fish stewed in palm oil. She had eaten in such a hurry that a bone had got stuck in her throat. She had drunk a lot of water but still the bone was sticking there. She did not want to tell Maami about it. She knew she would get a scolding or even a knock on the head. It was while she was

---

[1] A Ghanaian staple, cooked from corn dough.

in the outer room looking for a bit of kenkey to push down the troublesome bone that she heard Maami talking in the inner room.

"Ah, and what shall I do now? But I thought there was a whole big lump left. . . . O . . . O! Things like this irritate me so. How can I spend Christmas without varnishing my floor?"

Yaaba discovered a piece of kenkey which was left from the week before, hidden in its huge wrappings. She pounced upon it and without breaking away the mildew, swallowed it. She choked, stretched her neck and the bone was gone. She drank some water and with her cloth, wiped away the tears which had started gathering in her eyes. She was about to bounce away to the playgrounds when she remembered that she had heard Maami speaking to herself.

Although one must not stand by to listen to elders if they are not addressing one, yet one can hide and listen. And anyway, it would be interesting to hear the sort of things our elders say to themselves. "And how can I celebrate Christmas on a hardened, whitened floor?" Maami's voice went on. "If I could only get a piece of red earth. But I cannot go round my friends begging, 'Give me a piece of red earth.' No. O . . . O! And it is growing dark already. If only my child Adwoa was here. I am sure she could have run to the red-earth pit and fetched me just a hoeful. Then I could varnish the floor before the church bells ring tomorrow." Yaaba was thinking she had heard enough.

After all, our elders do not say anything interesting to themselves. It is their usual complaints about how difficult life is. If it is not the price of cloth or fish, then it is the scarcity of water. It is all very uninteresting. I will always play with my children when they grow up. I will not grumble about anything. . . .

It was quite dark. The children could hardly see their own hands as they threw up the pebbles. But Yaaba insisted that they go on. There were only three left of the eight girls who were playing *soso-mba*. From time to time mothers, fathers or elder sisters had come and called to the others to go home. The two still with Yaaba were Panyin and Kakra. Their mother had travelled and that was why they were still there. No one came any longer to call Yaaba. Up till the year before, Maami always came to yell for her when it was sundown. When she could not come, she sent Adwoa. But of course, Yaaba never listened to them.

What is the point in breaking a game to go home? She stayed out and played even by herself until it was dark and she was satisfied. And now, at the age of ten, no one came to call her.

The pebble hit Kakra on the head.

"*Ajii.*"

"What is it?"

"The pebble has hit me."

"I am sorry. It was not intentional." Panyin said, "But it is dark Kakra, let us go home." So they stood up.

"Panyin, will you go to church tomorrow?"

"No."

"Why? You have no new cloths?"

"We have new cloths but we will not get gold chains or earrings. Our mother is not at home. She has gone to some place and will only return in the afternoon. Kakra, remember we will get up very early tomorrow morning."

"Why?"

"Have you forgotten what mother told us before she went away? Did she not tell us to go and get some red earth from the pit? Yaaba, we are going away."

"*Yoo.*"

And the twins turned towards home.

Red earth! The pit! Probably, Maami will be the only woman in the village who will not have red earth to varnish her floor. *Oo!*

"Panyin! Kakra! Panyin!"

"Who is calling us?"

"It is me, Yaaba. Wait for me."

She ran in the darkness and almost collided with someone who was carrying food to her husband's house.

"Panyin, do you say you will go to the pit tomorrow morning?"

"Yes, what is it?"

"I want to go with you."

"Why?"

"Because I want to get some red earth for my mother."

"But tomorrow you will go to church."

"Yes, but I will try to get it done in time to go to church as well."

"See, you cannot. Do you not know the pit? It is very far away. Everyone will already be at church by the time we get back home."

Yaaba stood quietly digging her right toe into the hard ground beneath her. "It doesn't matter, I will go."

"Do you not want to wear your gold things? Kakra and I are very sorry that we cannot wear ours because our mother is not here."

"It does not matter. Come and wake me up."

"Where do you sleep?"

"Under my mother's window. I will wake up if you hit the window with a small pebble."

"*Yoo*. . . . We will come to call you."

"Do not forget your *apampa*² and your hoe."

"*Yoo*."

When Yaaba arrived home, they had already finished eating the evening meal. Adwoa had arrived from an errand it seemed. In fact she had gone on several others. Yaaba was slinking like a cat to take her food which she knew would be under the wooden bowl, when Maami saw her. "Yes, go and take it. You are hungry, are you not? And very soon

---

² A wide, flat wooden tray used for carrying farm produce.

you will be swallowing all that huge lump of fufu as quickly as a hen would swallow corn." Yaaba stood still.

"*Aa*. My Father God, who inflicted on me such a child? Look here, Yaaba. You are growing, so be careful how you live your life. When you are ten years old you are not a child any more. And a woman that lives on the playground is not a woman. If you were a boy, it would be bad enough, but for a girl, it is a curse. The house cannot hold you. *Tchia*."

Yaaba crept into the outer room. She saw the wooden bowl. She turned it over and as she had known all the time, her food was there. She swallowed it more quickly than a hen would have swallowed corn. When she finished eating, she went into the inner room, she picked her mat, spread it on the floor, threw herself down and was soon asleep. Long afterwards, Maami came in from the conversation with the other mothers. When she saw the figure of Yaaba, her heart did a somersault. Pooh, went her fists on the figure in the corner. Pooh, "You lazy lazy thing." Pooh, pooh! "You good-for-nothing, empty corn husk of a daughter . . ." She pulled her ears, and Yaaba screamed. Still sleepy-eyed, she sat up on the mat.

"If you like, you scream, and watch what I will do to you. If I do not pull your mouth until it is as long as a pestle, then my name is not Benyiwa."

But Yaaba was now wide awake and tearless. Who said she was screaming, anyway? She stared at Maami with shining tearless eyes. Maami was angry at this too.

"I spit in your eyes, witch! Stare at me and tell me if I am going to die tomorrow. At your age . . ." and the blows came pooh, pooh, pooh. "You do not know that you wash yourself before your skin touches the mat. And after a long day in the sand, the dust and filth by the Big Trunk. *Hoo! Pooh!* You moth-bitten grain. *Pooh!*"

The clock in the chief's house struck twelve o'clock midnight. Yaaba never cried. She only tried, without success, to ward off the blows. Perhaps Maami was tired herself, perhaps she was satisfied. Or perhaps she was afraid she was putting herself in the position of Kweku Ananse[3] tempting the spirits to carry their kindness as far as to come and help her beat her daughter. Of course, this would kill Yaaba. Anyway, she stopped beating her and lay down by Kofi, Kwame and Adwoa. Yaaba saw the figure of Adwoa lying peacefully there. It was then her eyes misted. The tears flowed from her eyes. Every time, she wiped them with her cloth but more came. They did not make any noise for Maami to hear. Soon the cloth was wet. When the clock struck one, she heard Maami snoring. She herself could not sleep even when she lay down.

Is this woman my mother?

Perhaps I should not go and fetch her some red earth. But the twins will come. . . .

Yaaba rose and went into the outer room. There was no door between the inner and outer rooms to creak and wake anybody. She wanted the *apampa* and a hoe. At ten years of age, she should have had her own of both, but of course, she had not. Adwoa's hoe, she knew, was in the corner left of the door. She groped and found it. She also knew Adwoa's *apampa* was on the bamboo shelf. It was when she turned and was groping towards the bamboo shelf that she stumbled over the large water-bowl. Her chest hit the edge of the tray. The tray tilted and the water poured on the floor. She could not rise up. When Maami heard the noise her fall made, she screamed "Thief! Thief! Thief! Everybody, come, there is a thief in my room."

She gave the thief a chance to run away since he might attack her before the men of the village came. But no thief rushed through the door and there were no running footsteps in the courtyard. In fact, all was too quiet.

She picked up the lantern, pushed the wick up to blazing

[3] A Ghanaian name for the ever clever and cunning Trickster Spider of West African folklore. His "cousins" are Annancy the Spider in the Caribbean and Br'er Rabbit in the United States.

point and went gingerly to the outer room. There was Yaaba, sprawled like a freshly-killed overgrown cock on the tray. She screamed again.

"Ah Yaaba, why do you frighten me like this? What were you looking for? That is why I always say you are a witch. What do you want at this time of the night that you should fall on a water-bowl? And look at the floor. But of course, you were playing when someone lent me a piece of red earth to polish it, eh?" The figure in the tray just lay there. Maami bent down to help her up and then she saw the hoe. She stood up again.

"A hoe! I swear by all that be that I do not understand this." She lifted her up and was carrying her to the inner room when Yaaba's lips parted as if to say something. She closed the lips again, her eyelids fluttered down and the neck sagged. "My Saviour!" There was nothing strange in the fact that the cry was heard in the north and south of the village. Was it not past midnight?

People had heard Maami's first cry of "Thief" and by the time she cried out again, the first men were coming from all directions. Soon the courtyard was full. Questions and answers went round. Some said Yaaba was trying to catch a thief, others that she was running from her mother's beating. But the first thing was to wake her up.

"Pour anowata[4] into her nose!"—and the mothers ran into their husbands' chambers to bring their giant-sized bottles of the sweetest scents. "Touch her feet with a little fire.". . . "Squeeze a little ginger juice into her nose."

The latter was done and before she could suffer further ordeals, Yaaba's eyelids fluttered up.

"*Aa*. . . . *Oo* . . . we thank God. She is awake, she is awake." Everyone said it. Some were too far away and saw her neither in the faint nor awake. But they said it as they trooped back to piece together their broken sleep. Egya Yaw, the village medicine-man, examined her and told the

[4] Perfume.

now-mad Maami that she should not worry. "The impact was violent but I do not think anything has happened to the breast-bone. I will bind her up in beaten herbs and she should be all right in a few days." "Thank you, Egya," said Maami, Paapa, her grandmother, the other mothers and all her relatives. The medicine-man went to his house and came back. Yaaba's brawniest uncles beat up the herbs. Soon, Yaaba was bound up. The cock had crowed once, when they laid her down. Her relatives then left for their own homes. Only Maami, Paapa and the other mothers were left. "And how is she?" one of the women asked.

"But what really happened?"

"Only Benyiwa can answer you."

"Benyiwa, what happened?"

"But I am surprised myself. After she had eaten her kenkey this afternoon, I heard her movements in the outer room but I did not mind her. Then she went away and came back when it was dark to eat her food. After our talk, I went to sleep. And there she was lying. As usual, she had not had a wash, so I just held her . . ."

"You held her what? Had she met with death you would have been the one that pushed her into it—beating a child in the night!"

"But Yaaba is too troublesome!"

"And so you think every child will be good? But how did she come to fall in the tray?"

"That is what I cannot tell. My eyes were just playing me tricks when I heard some noise in the outer room."

"Is that why you cried 'Thief'?"

"Yes. When I went to see what it was, I saw her lying in the tray, clutching a hoe."

"A hoe?"

"Yes, Adwoa's hoe."

"Perhaps there was a thief after all? She can tell us the truth . . . but . . ."

So they went on through the early morning. Yaaba slept. The second cock-crow came. The church bell soon did its Christmas reveille. In the distance, they heard the songs of the dawn procession. Quite near in the doorway, the regular pat, pat of the twins' footsteps drew nearer towards the elderly group by the hearth. Both parties were surprised at the encounter.

"Children, what do you want at dawn?"

"Where is Yaaba?"

"Yaaba is asleep."

"May we go and wake her, she asked us to."

"Why?"

"She said she will go with us to the red-earth pit."

"O . . . O!" The group around the hearth was amazed but they did not show it before the children.

"*Yoo.* You go today. She may come with you next time."

"*Yoo*, Mother."

"Walk well, my children. When she wakes up, we shall tell her you came."

"We cannot understand it. Yaaba? What affected her head?"

"My sister, the world is a strange place. That is all."

"And my sister, the child that will not do anything is better than a sheep."

"Benyiwa, we will go and lie down a little."

"Good morning."

"Good morning."

"Good morning."

"*Yoo.* I thank you all."

So Maami went into the apartment and closed the door. She knelt by the sleeping Yaaba and put her left hand on her bound chest. "My child, I say thank you. You were getting ready to go and fetch me red earth? Is that why you were holding the hoe? My child, my child, I thank you."

And the tears streamed down her face. Yaaba heard "My

child" from very far away. She opened her eyes. Maami was weeping and still calling her "My child" and saying things which she did not understand.

Is Maami really calling me that? May the twins come. Am I Maami's own child?

"My child Yaaba . . . "

But how will I get red earth?

But why can I not speak . . . ?

"I wish the twins would come . . . "

I want to wear the gold earrings . . .

I want to know whether Maami called me her child. Does it mean I am her child like Adwoa is? But one does not ask our elders such questions. And anyway, there is too much pain. And there are barriers where my chest is.

Probably tomorrow . . . but now Maami called me "My child!" . . .

And she fell asleep again.

THE MOUNTAIN

❧

(United States)

by Martin J. Hamer

*From adolescence to death there is something very per-
sonal about being a Negro in America.*
    —*J. Saunders Redding*
                    (writer, critic, educator, 1906–88)

*I*n the summer of 1943, Charlie was my best friend. We
were in the same class in elementary school and we lived
right next door to each other. He, in the first high stoop
house from the corner, and I in the second. By standing on
our backyard fire escapes and reaching out, we could pass
things to one another. My mother came home late in the
evening and my father never until much later, so when I
came in from school, and my sister wasn't there to tell on
me, I would climb out on the fire escape and call to
Charlie. To do this, we each had a long string with a stone
wrapped in cloth tied to it, hanging from our fire escapes.
Once, when Charlie had been mean to the lady under him,
she cut his string. Anyway, to call to each other, we would
swing the stones so that they tapped the window.

The day of graduation from elementary school, Charlie
was so excited when he came home that he almost broke
my window. When I climbed out on the fire escape, he
was there all dressed up in his blue suit with a tragic look
on his face.

"I thought you were dead," he said. "Why didn't you
come to school?"

"I was sick," I answered.

"You don't look sick now . . . "

"How was it?" I interrupted.

"You didn't get left back, did you?"

"Of course I didn't."

"You know what somebody said?" he continued. "They said your mama couldn't afford to buy you a new suit."

"They were right."

"You mean you missed graduation because you didn't have a new suit?"

"Would you have gone if you didn't have one?"

"Yeah," he answered, "I guess you're right. I probably wouldn't have. . . . It's all that stupid principal's fault. If he hadn't announced that everybody had to wear blue suits and all that, this wouldn't have happened . . . "

Then as an afterthought he added, "Couldn't your mama afford to buy you a new suit?"

"I don't know," I replied. "I guess not."

But really I didn't know. We weren't any poorer than Charlie's family, and from the way Mama had explained it when I had asked her, I had been unable to figure out whether we could afford it or not.

She had said that the Sunday suit I had was good enough for anybody's graduation, and that if any of the other kids were getting new ones, she hoped it was because they needed them. When I tried to explain that it wasn't the other kids I was thinking of, but my teachers, she looked at me real hard and said, "I *know* you don't want a new suit because the white man says so!"

"My principal says we should all . . . "

"Your principal, huh? A hundred boys sitting up there in blue suits may be the most important thing in the world to him, but it's not to me. If how you look is all that counts then maybe you'd better stay home."

"But Mama, I can't stay home," I cried.

"Then go in what you got!"

I stared at her, unable to believe this lack of understanding, then turned and walked away.

I was sitting at the fire escape window indulging in a fantasy of how I would kill myself and she would have to buy the new suit to bury me in, when I felt her come up behind me.

"Look here," she said, "I want to talk to you." I dragged

myself around, and saw her standing there, wiping her hands in her apron.

"Honey," she began softly, "a new suit isn't going to change you as far as the white man is concerned. To him you'll still be a little colored boy . . . "

"That man," she continued, looking off out of the window, "is up there on a mountain, and he'll probably be up there all your life . . . but remember, you're as good as he is, new suit or no new suit."

Tears began to run down my cheeks, but I gave no sign of even noticing them. She didn't understand me, my own mother. Here she was talking about mountains, and all I wanted was a new suit.

"Did you hear what I said?"

The tears came faster, and finally unable to ignore them, I wiped my shirtsleeve across my face, and blurted out, "All I want is a new suit!" Just then, the door opened and Daddy came in. When Mama turned around, I ran off.

I didn't tell Charlie any of this that day on the fire escape, and it wasn't until August that I realized what she meant. In August, Charlie and I decided to visit Columbia University. We planned the trip one day in advance, and the following morning arose very early and set out through Morningside Park, which separated the valley where we lived, from the area where the university lay. The park, a two block wide strip of trees, grass, rocks, and sand, rose steeply from Morningside Heights. Its many planned paths and beaten trails having long since given up their secrets to us, we crossed it rapidly, pausing only twice. Once to cautiously inspect a man who was lying in the bushes; we thought we had accidentally stumbled onto a murder, but it turned out he was a drunk. And the other time to throw stones at two dogs to prevent them from doing what we had been told would be injurious to their health.

At the top, we rested in an oval from where we could look out over the whole of Harlem. It was bunched up it seemed, between Central Park and the Yankee Stadium, its old buildings spilling almost into the East River with cars and people filling the remaining spaces like black lava. We tried to count all the parked cars we could see but, after reaching two hundred, we tired, turned, and headed toward the university.

We found ourselves in another world. The buildings were tall and immaculate, their polished brass fronts opening onto glistening tile floors which beckoned towards cool dark opulent depths. Awnings everywhere. And the streets were large and clean, the white granite faces of the buildings meeting the sidewalks in a line unbroken from corner to corner. After two blocks, we came to a sprawling group of buildings and Charlie said, "This must be it."

We stood, two small dark boys, before the Taj Mahal, before the Parthenon, and the Sphinx of Egypt. We stood, two small dark boys, before the reality of our dreams. There were steps of stone that ran for almost a block, with lions, one at either end, from which a king might speak. And red bricks where girls in veils could dance before a great feast. And a pool. And tennis courts. And flagstone walks, that led through gardens with benches hewed from stone by slaves. We climbed the stairs, stood before the doors, and read the inscription carved there in the stone: "The Lowe Library, Columbia University."

Then we continued westward to the Hudson River and south along Riverside Drive, finding ourselves by four in the afternoon in Columbus Circle. With our last bit of change we paid our subway fare for the ride home. The trains were crowded, and Charlie and I were pressed up against the doors hardly able to breathe as the express left 59th Street. We were grinning at each other, our day having been filled with wonders that only we two shared, when the lady in front of me suddenly looked down, saw that her purse was open, fumbled around inside it for a moment; then turned to me and said, "Little boy, give me back my wallet!" All noises ceased. All except the roar of the fans. "Little boy, *please* give me back my wallet!" All pressures ceased. The surrounding bodies moving away from us. All except the pressure of shame and humiliation that came with her words. I finally replied, "I haven't got your wallet, Miss."

The train rushed on towards 125th Street. A man pushed his way to the front of the crowd. The woman repeated her plea. And Charlie and I stood, our hands locked together, their perspiration forming a bond that was our only salvation.

It takes seven minutes for the express to travel between 59th Street and 125th Street. After five of those minutes, the man offered to search us. The woman, busily searching her purse, either did not hear him or did not care to commit herself. Seconds later, she found her wallet—in her purse.

She apologized. And the man, feeling perhaps even more ashamed, reached into his pocket, brought out a half dollar, and tried to press it into Charlie's hand. Water reached the crotch of Charlie's trousers, chose the left leg, coursed its way down his thigh, across his knee, into his socks, over his shoe, and puddled at its tip. And my shame gave way to anger as it grew in size. I raised my head, looking directly at no one, but into the crowd and said, "No thank you mister. No thank you."

That evening we met on the fire escape. We passed things to each other for a while and then Charlie said, "Some trip today, huh?" I was staring off towards the park and didn't answer. "Yeah," he continued, "that was some trip . . . You know what? I bet if we had been dressed up, I bet that woman wouldn't have thought we robbed her."

"Yes she would have, too," I replied. "It wouldn't have made any difference."

"How do you know it wouldn't have made any difference?" I almost told him what Mama had said, but changed my mind.

"I just do, that's all . . . I just do."

We stood looking at each other; I'm sure he knew what I meant. Then two cats began fighting in the backyard, we turned to watch, and night fell.

BRIGHT THURSDAYS

✣

(Jamaica)

by Olive Senior

*The longing for the love of those who've given us life is a
natural and blessed thing; but love can be neither hurried
nor forced.*

*T*hursday was the worst day. While she had no expecta-
tions of any other day of the week, every Thursday turned
out to be either very good or very bad, and she had no way
of knowing in advance which one it would be. Sometimes
there would be so many bad Thursdays in a row that she
wanted to write home to her mother, "Please please take
me home for I cannot stand the clouds." But then she
would remember her mother saying, "Laura this is a new
life for you. This is opportunity. Now dont let yu mama
down. Chile, swallow yu tongue before yu talk lest yu say
the wrong thing and dont mek yu eye big for everything yu
see. Dont give Miss Christie no cause for complain and
most of all, let them know you have broughtuptcy."

Miss Christie was the lady she now lived with, her
father's mother. She didn't know her father except for a
photograph of him on Miss Christie's bureau where he was
almost lost in a forest of photographs of all her children and
grandchildren all brown skinned with straight hair and confident smiles on their faces. When she saw these photographs she understood why Miss Christie wouldn't put
hers there. Every week as she dusted the bureau, Laura
looked at herself in the mirror and tried to smile with the
confidence of those in the photographs, but all she saw was

a being so strange, so far removed from those in the pictures, that she knew that she could never be like them. To smile so at a camera one had to be born with certain things—a big house with heavy mahogany furniture and many rooms, fixed mealtimes, a mother and father who were married to each other and lived together in the same house, who would chastise and praise, who would send you to school with the proper clothes so you would look like, be like everyone else, fit neatly into the space Life had created for you.

But even though others kept pushing her, and she tried to ease, to work her way into that space too, she sometimes felt that Life had played her tricks, and there was, after all, no space allotted for her. For how else could she explain this discomfort, this pain it caused her in this her father's house to confront even the slightest event. Such as sitting at table and eating a meal.

In her mother's house she simply came in from school or wherever and sat on a stool in a corner of the lean-to kitchen or on the steps while Mama dished up a plate of food which one ate with whatever implement happened to be handy. Mama herself would more often than not stand to eat, sometimes out of the pot, and the boys too would sit wherever their fancy took them. Everything would be black from the soot from the fireside which hung now like grotesque torn ribbons from the roof. After the meal, Laura would wash the plates and pots in an enamel basin outside and sweep out the ashes from the fireside. A meal was something as natural as breathing.

But here in this house of her father's parents a meal was a ritual, something for which you prepared yourself by washing your hands and combing your hair and straightening your dress before approaching the Table. The Table was in the Dining Room and at least twelve could have comfortably sat around it. Now Laura and the grandparents huddled together at one end and in the sombre shadows of the room. Laura sometimes imagined that they so unbalanced the table that it would come toppling over on to them. At other times, when she polished the mahogany she placed each of the children of the household at a place around this table, along with their mother and father and their bewhiskered and beribboned grandparents who looked down from oval picture frames. When they were all seated, they fitted so neatly in their slots that there was now no place left for her. Sometimes she didn't mind.

But now at the real mealtimes, the ghosts were no longer there and she sat with the old people in this empty echoing space. Each time she sat down with dread in her heart, for mealtime was not a time to eat so much as a time for lessons in Table Manners.

First Mirie the cook would tinkle a little silver bell that would summon them to the dining room, and the house would stir with soft footsteps scurrying like mice and the swish of water in the basin. All the inhabitants of the house were washing and combing and straightening themselves in preparation for the Meal. She tried not to be the last one to the table for that was an occasion for chastisement. Then she had to remember to take the stiffly starched white napkin from its silver ring and place it in her lap.

"Now sit up straight, child. Don't slump so," Miss Christie would say as she lifted the covers off tureens. Miss Christie sat at the table uncovering dishes of food, but by the time Laura was served, her throat was already full and she got so confused that she would forget the knife and start to eat with her fork.

"Now dear, please use your knife. And don't cut your meat into little pieces all at once."

At the sulky look which came over Laura's face, Miss Christie would say, "You'll thank me for this one day you know, Laura. If you are going to get anywhere, you must learn how to do things properly. I just can't imagine what your mother has been doing with you all this time. How a child your age can be so ignorant of the most elementary things is beyond me."

The first time Miss Christie had mentioned her mother in this way, Laura had burst into tears and fled from the room. But now, remembering her mother's words, she refused to cry.

Laura's father had never married her mother. The question never came up for, said Myrtle without even a hint of malice in her voice, "Mr Bertram was a young man of high estate. Very high estate." She was fond of telling this to everyone who came to her house and did not know the story of Laura's father. How Mr Bertram had come visiting the Wheelers where Myrtle was a young servant. They had had what she liked to call "a romance" but which was hardly even imprinted on Mr Bertram's mind, and Laura was the result. The fact that Mr Bertram was a man of "high estate" had in itself elevated Miss Myrtle so far in her own eyes that no one else could understand how she could have managed to bear her sons afterwards for two undoubtedly humble fathers.

Laura had come out with dark skin but almost straight hair which Miss Myrtle did her best to improve by rubbing it with coconut oil and brushing it every day, at the same time rubbing cocoa butter into her skin to keep it soft and make it "clear."[1] Miss Myrtle made the child wear a broad straw hat to keep off the sun, assuring her that her skin was "too delicate."

Miss Myrtle had no regrets about her encounter with Mr Bertram even though his only acknowledgement of the birth was a ten dollar note sent to her at the time. But then he had been shipped off to the United States by his angry parents and nothing further had been heard from him.

[1] That is, lighter.

Miss Myrtle was unfortunate in her choice of fathers for her children for none of them gave her any support. She single-handedly raised them in a little house on family land and took in sewing to augment what she got from her cultivation of food for the pot and ginger for the market. She did not worry about the fate of her sons for they were after all, boys, and well able to fend for themselves when the time came. But her daughter was a constant source of concern to her, for a child with such long curly hair, with such a straight nose, with such soft skin (too bad it was so dark) was surely destined for a life of ease and comfort. For years, Miss Myrtle sustained herself with the fantasy that one day Laura's father would miraculously appear and take her off to live up to the station in life to which she was born. In the meantime she groomed her daughter for the role she felt she would play in life, squeezing things here and there in order to have enough to make her pretty clothes so that she was the best-dressed little girl for miles around. For the time being, it was the only gift of her heritage that she could make her.

Then after so many years passed that it was apparent even to Myrtle that Mr Bertram had no intention of helping the child, she screwed up her courage, aided and abetted by the entire village it seemed, and wrote to Mr Bertram's parents. She knew them well, for Mr Bertram's mother was Mrs Wheeler's sister and in fact came from a family that had roots in the area:

> Dear Miss Kristie
> Greetings to you in Jesus Holy Name I trust that this letter will find that you an Mister Dolfy ar enjoin the best of helth. Wel Miss Kristie I write you this letter in fear and trimblin for I am the Little One and you are the Big One but I hope you will not take me too for-

rard but mr. Bertram little girl now nine year old and bright as a button wel my dear Mam wish you could see her a good little girl and lern her lesson wel she would go far in Life if she could have some Help but I am a Poor Woman! With Nothing! To Help I am in the fidls morning til night. I can tel you that in looks she take after her Father but I am not Asking Mr Bertram for anything I know. He have his Life to live for but if you can fine it in YourPower to do Anything for the little girl God Richest Blessing wil come down on You May the Good Lord Bles and Keep you Miss Kristie also Mas Dolfy. And give you a long Life until you find Eternal Rest Safe in the arms of the Savor

Your Humble Servant

Myrtle Johnstone.

The letter caused consternation when it was received by the old people for they had almost forgotten about what the family referred to as "Bertram's Mistake" and they thought that the woman had forgotten about it too. Although Myrtle was only 17 at the time and their son was 28, they had never forgiven what Miss Christie called the uppity black gal for seducing their son. "Dying to raise their colour all of them," Miss Christie had cried, "dying to raise their colour. That's why you can't be too careful with them." Now like a ghost suddenly materialising they could see this old scandal coming back to haunt them.

At first the two old people were angry, then as they talked about the subject for days on end, they soon dismissed their first decision which was to ignore the letter, for the little girl, no matter how common and scheming her mother was, was nevertheless family and something would have to be done about her. Eventually they decided on limited help—enough to salve their consciences but not too much so that Myrtle would get the idea that they were a limitless source of wealth. Miss Christie composed the first of her brief and cool letters to the child's mother.

> Dear Myrtle,
>
> In response to your call for help we are sending a little money for the child, also a parcel which should soon arrive. But please don't think that we can do this all the time as we ourselves are finding it hard to make ends meet. Besides, people who have children should worry about how they are going to support them before they have them.
> Yours Truly,
> Mrs. C. Watson

They made, of course, no reference to the child's father who was now married and living in New Jersey.

Myrtle was overjoyed to get the letter and the parcel for they were the tangible indications that the child's family would indeed rescue her from a life of poverty in the mountains. Now she devoted even more care and attention to the little girl, taking pains to remind her of the fineness of her hair, the straightness of her nose, and the high estate of her father. While she allowed the child to continue to help with the chores around the house, she was no longer sent on errands. When all the other children were busy minding goats, fetching water or firewood, all of these chores in her household now fell on Laura's brothers. Myrtle was busy grooming Laura for a golden future.

Because of her mother's strictures, the child soon felt alienated from others. If she played with other children, her mother warned her not to get her clothes too dirty. Not to get too burnt in the sun. Not to talk so broad.[2] Instead of making her filled with pride as her mother intended, these attentions made the child supremely conscious of being different from the children around her, and she soon became withdrawn and lacking in spontaneity.

Myrtle approved of the child's new quietness as a sign of "quality" in her. She sent a flood of letters to Miss Christie, although the answers she got were meagre and few. She kept her constantly informed of the child's progress in school, of her ability to read so well, and occasionally made the child write a few sentences in the letter to her grandmother to show off her fine handwriting. Finally, one Christmas, to flesh out the image of the child she had been building up over the years, she took most of the rat-cut coffee money[3] and took the child to the nearest big town to have her photograph taken in a professional studio.

It was a posed, stilted photograph in a style that went out of fashion thirty years before. The child was dressed in a frilly white dress trimmed with ribbons, much too long for her age. She wore long white nylon socks and white T-strap shoes. Her hair was done in perfect drop curls, with a part to the side and two front curls caught up with a large white bow. In the photograph she stood quite straight with her feet together and her right hand stiffly bent to touch an artificial rose in a vase on a rattan table beside her. She did not smile.

Her grandparents who were the recipients of a large framed print on matte paper saw a dark-skinned child with long dark hair, a straight nose, and enormous, very serious eyes. Despite the fancy clothes, everything about her had a countrified air except for the penetrating eyes which had none of the softness and shyness of country children. Miss Christie was a little embarrassed by this gift, and hid the picture in her bureau drawer for it had none of the gloss of

[2] Loudly and crudely; coarsely.
[3] In other words, she was scraping the bottom of the barrel.

the photos of her children and grandchildren which stood on her bureau. But she could not put the picture away entirely; something about the child haunted her and she constantly looked at it to see what in this child was of her flesh and blood. The child had her father's weak mouth, it seemed, though the defiant chin and the bold eyes undoubtedly came from her mother. Maybe it was the serious, steady, unchildlike gaze that caused Miss Christie sometimes to look at the picture for minutes at a time as if it mesmerised her. Then she would get hold of herself again and angrily put the picture back into the drawer.

Despite her better judgement, Miss Christie found herself intensely curious about this child whose mother made her into such a little paragon and whose eyes gazed out at the world so directly.

Soon, she broached the subject obliquely to her husband. One evening at dusk as the two of them sat on the verandah, she said, "Well, just look at the two of us. Look how many children and grandchildren we have, and not a one to keep our company."

"Hm. So life stay. Once your children go to town, country too lonely for them after that."

"I suppose so. But it really would be nice to have a young person about the house again." They dropped the subject then, but she kept bringing it up from time to time.

Finally she said, as if thinking about it for the first time, "But Dolphie, why don't we get Myrtle's little girl here?"

"What! And rake up that old thing again? You must be mad."

"But nobody has to know who she is."

"Then you dont know how ol'nayga fas'.[4] They bound to find out."

"Well, they can't prove anything. She doesn't have our name. She bears her mother's name."

They argued about it on and off for weeks, then finally they decided to invite the child to stay for a week or two.

[4] The Jamaican patois expression "how ol'nayga fas' " translates into something like "how black folks get all into your business."

When Laura came, she was overawed by the big house, the patrician old couple who were always so clean and sweet-smelling as if perpetually laundered each day anew by Mirie the cook. She fell even more silent, speaking only when spoken to, and then in a low voice which could hardly be heard.

Miss Christie was gratified that she was so much lighter than the photograph (indeed, Myrtle had quarrelled with the photographer for just this reason) and although she was exactly like a country mouse, she did fill the house with her presence. Already Miss Christie was busy planning the child's future, getting her into decent clothes, correcting her speech, erasing her country accent, teaching her table manners, getting her to take a complete bath every day—a fact which was so novel to the child who came from a place where everyone bathed in a bath pan once a week since the water had to be carried on their heads one mile uphill from the spring.

In the child Miss Christie saw a lump of clay which held every promise of being moulded into something satisfactory. The same energy with which Miss Christie entered into a "good" marriage, successfully raised six children and saw that they made good marriages themselves, that impelled her to organise the Mothers Union and the School Board— that energy was now to be expended on this latest product which relatives in the know referred to as "Bertram's stray shot."

Although her husband fussed and fumed, he too liked the idea of having a child in the house once more though he thought her a funny little thing who hardly made a sound all day, unlike the boisterous family they had reared. And so, as if in a dream, the child found herself permanently transported from her mother's two-room house to this mansion of her father's.

Of course her father was never mentioned and she only knew it was him from the photograph because he had signed it. She gazed often at this photograph, trying to transmute it into a being of flesh and blood from which she had been created, but failed utterly. In fact, she was quite unable to deduce even the smallest facet of his character from the picture. All that she saw was a smiling face that in some indefinable way looked like all the faces in the other photographs. All were bland and sweet. In none of these faces were there lines, or frowns, or blemishes, or marks of ugliness such as a squint eye, or a broken nose, or kinky hair, or big ears, or broken teeth which afflicted all the other people she had known. Faced with such perfection, she ceased to look at herself in the mirror.

She had gone to live there during the summer holidays and Miss Christie took every opportunity to add polish to her protegé whom she introduced everywhere as "my little adopted." As part of the child's education, Miss Christie taught her to polish mahogany furniture and to bake cakes, to polish silver and clean panes of glass, all of which objects had been foreign to the child's former upbringing.

The child liked to remain inside the house which was cool and dark and shaded for outside, with its huge treeless lawn and beyond, the endless pastures, frightened her.

She had grown up in a part of the mountain cockpits where a gravel road was the only thing that broke the monotony of the humpbacked hills and endless hills everywhere. There were so many hills that for half of the day their house and yard were damp and dark and moss grew on the sides of the clay path. It was only at midday when the sun was directly overhead that they received light. The houses were perched precariously up the hillsides with slippery paths leading to them from the road, and if anyone bothered to climb to the tops of the hills, all they would see was more mountains. Because it was so hilly the area seemed constantly to be in a dark blue haze, broken only by the occasional hibiscus or croton and the streams of brightly coloured birds dashing through the foliage. They were hemmed in by the mountains on all sides and Laura liked it, because all her life was spent in space that was enclosed and finite, protecting her from what dangers she did not even know.

And then, from the moment she had journeyed to the railway station some ten miles away and got on to the train and it had begun to travel through the endless canefields, she had begun to feel afraid. For suddenly the skies had opened up so wide all around her; the sun beat down and there was the endless noisy clacking of the train wheels. She felt naked and anxious, as if suddenly exposed, and there was nowhere to hide.

When she got off the train at the other end, there were no canefields there, but the land was still flat and open, for this was all rolling pastureland. Her curiosity about the herds of cattle she saw grazing in the shade of an occasional tree could not diminish the fear she felt at being so exposed.

Her father's parents' house was set on the top of a hill from where they could see for miles in all directions. Whenever she went outside she felt dizzy for the sky was so wide it was like being enclosed within a huge blue bowl. The summer was cloudless. And the hills were so far away they were lost in blue. But then summer came to an end and it was time for her to go to school. The nearest school was three miles away. Her grandmother, deciding that this was too far for her to walk—though walking greater distances had meant nothing in her former life—had arranged for her to travel to and from school on the bus which went by at the right time each day. This single fact impressed her most as showing the power and might of her grandmother.

She was glad of the bus for she did not want to walk

alone to school. Now the clear summer days were ending, the clouds had begun to gather in the sky, fat cumulus clouds that travelled in packs and in this strange and empty country became ugly and menacing. They reminded her of the pictures she used to get in Sunday School showing Jesus coming to earth again, floating down on one of these fat white clouds. And because the Jesus of their church was a man who had come to judge and punish sinners, these pictures only served to remind her that she was a sinner and that God would one day soon appear out of the sky flashing fire and brimstone to judge and condemn her. And until he came, the clouds were there to watch her. For why else did they move, change themselves, assume shapes of creatures awesome and frightful, if not to torment her with her unworthiness? Sometimes when she stood on the barbecue[5] and looked back at the house outlined against the sky, the house itself seemed to move and she would feel a wave of dizziness as if the whole earth was moving away off course and leaving her standing there alone in the emptiness.

She would run quickly inside and find Miss Christie or Mirie or somebody. As long as it was another human being to share the world with.

While all day long she would feel a vague longing for her mother and brothers and all the people she had known since childhood, she never felt lonely, for if her mother had given her nothing else, in taking her out of one life without guaranteeing her placement in the next, she had unwittingly raised her for a life of solitude. Here in this big house she wandered from room to room and said nothing all day, for now her lips were sealed from shyness. To her newly sensitised ears, her words came out flat and unmusical and she would look with guilt at the photographs and silently beg pardon for being there.

There were no other children around the house and she

---

[5] Similar to a patio, only not attached to the house.

was now so physically removed from others that she had no chance to meet anyone. Sometimes she would walk down the driveway to the tall black gate hoping that some child would pass along and talk so that they could be friends, but whenever anyone happened by, her shyness would cause her to hide behind the stone pillar so they would not see her. And although her grandmother said nothing on the subject, she instinctively knew after a while that she would never in this place find anyone good enough to bring into Miss Christie's house.

Although she liked the feeling of importance it gave her to get on and off the bus at the school gate—the only child to do so—most times she watched with envy the other children walking home from school, playing, yelling, and rolling in the road. They wore no shoes and she envied them this freedom, for her feet, once free like theirs except for Sundays, were now encased in socks and patent leather shoes handed down from one or the other of the rightful grandchildren who lived in Kingston or New York.

Most days the bus was on time. Every morning she would wait by the tall black gate for the bus to arrive. The bus would arrive on time every day. Except Thursdays. Sometimes on Thursdays the bus wouldn't arrive until late evening. She would nevertheless every Thursday go to the gates and wait, knowing in her heart that the bus would not come. Miss Christie would sometimes walk out and stand by the gate and look the road up and down.

Sometimes Mass Dolphie passing on his way from one pasture to the next would rein in his horse and would also stand by the gate and look up the road. All three would stand silently. The road swayed white in an empty world. The silence hummed like telegraph wires. Her life hung in the air waiting on a word from Miss Christie. Her chest began to swell like a balloon getting bigger and bigger. "The bus isn't coming. You'll have to walk," Miss Christie pronounced with finality.

"Oh Miss Christie, just a few minutes more," she begged. It was the only thing she begged for. But she knew that the bus wouldn't come, and now, at this terribly late hour, she would have to walk alone the three miles to school in a world that was empty of people. She would walk very fast, the dust of the marl road swirling round her ankles, along this lonely road that curved past the graveyard. Above, following every step of the way, the fat clouds sat smirking and smug in the pale blue sky. She hated them for all they knew about her. Her clumsiness, her awkwardness, the fact that she did not belong in this light and splendid place. They sat there in judgement on her every Thursday. Thursday, the day before market day. The day of her Armageddon.

Thursdays the old bus would sit on the road miles above, packed with higglers and their crocus bags, bankras[6] and chickens. The bus would start right enough: somewhere on the road above the bus would start in the dawn hours, full and happy. And then, a few miles after, the bus would gently shudder and like a torn metal bird would ease to a halt with a cough and sigh and settle down on the road, too tired and worn out to move. It would remain there until evening, the market women sitting in the shade and fanning the flies away with the men importantly gathered around the machine, arguing and cursing until evening when the earth was cool again and the driver would go slowly, everything patched up till next Thursday when the higglers descended with their crocus bags and their bankras, their laughter and their girth and their quarrelling and their ferocious energy which would prove too much for the old bus. Then with a sigh it would again lie still on the road above her. Every Thursday.

Sometimes though if she managed to dawdle long enough Miss Christie would say, "Heavens, it's 10 o'clock.

---

[6] Straw baskets or trays used for carrying produce or other wares atop the head.

You can't go to school again."

"Oh Miss Christie" she would cry silently "thank you, thank you."

Sometimes when she didn't go to school Mass Dolphie would let her dig around in his irish potato patch collecting the tiny potatoes for herself.

Digging potatoes was safe. She could not see the sky. And she never knew when a really big potato would turn up among all the tiny ones.

"Like catching fish, eh?" Mass Dolphie said and she agreed though she didn't know how that was having never seen the sea. But she would laugh too.

II

One day they got a letter from the child's father. He was coming home with his wife on a visit. It wasn't long after their initial joy at hearing the news that the grandparents realised that difficulties were bound to arise with the child. For one thing, they hadn't told their son about her, being a little ashamed that they had not consulted him at all before coming to the decision to take her. Besides, it was a little awkward to write to him about such matters at his home, since from all they had heard of American women they believed that there was a strong possibility that his wife would open his letters.

Their immediate decision was to send the child home, but that too presented certain problems since it was still during the school term and they couldn't quite make up their minds what they would tell her mother to explain a change of heart. They certainly couldn't tell her the truth for even to them the truth seemed absurd: that they wanted to return the little girl because her father was coming. For once, Miss Christie was at a loss. It was Mr Dolphie who took a firm line. "Write and ask him what to do," he instructed his wife, "after all, it's his child. If he doesn't want her here when he comes then he can tell us what we should do with her."

They were surprised but not overly so when their son wrote that they should do nothing about the child as he would be greatly amused to see her.

Mr Dolphie didn't see any cause for amusement in the situation and thought that it was just like his youngest son to take a serious thing and make a joke of it and all in all act in a reckless and irresponsible manner. He had certainly hoped that Bertram had finally settled down to the seriousness of life.

Long before they told the child the news of her father's coming, she knew, for without deliberately listening to their conversations, she seemed to absorb and intuitively understand everything that happened in the house.

Since hearing the news there had been joy in her heart, for her mother had told her so often that one day this mysterious father of hers would come and claim her as his own that she had grown to believe it. She knew that he would come and rescue her from fears as tenuous as clouds and provide her with nothing but bright Thursdays.

But when she searched out the photograph from the ones on the bureau, his face held that unreadable, bland smile and his eyes gave off nothing that would show her just how he intended to present his love for her.

One day Miss Christie said to her, "Laura, our son is coming on a visit. Mr Bertram." She said it as if the child and the man bore no relationship to each other. "He is coming with his wife. We haven't seen him for so many years."

Yes. Since I was born, Laura thought.

"Now Laura, I expect you to be on your best behaviour

when they are here."

"Yes mam."

Laura showed no emotion at all as Miss Christie continued to chat on the subject. How does one behave with a
father? Laura thought. She had no experience of this.
There were so few fathers among all the people she knew.

Miss Christie turned the house upside down in a frenzy
of preparation for her son's visit. Without being told so,
Laura understood that such preparation was not so much
for the son as for his white wife. She was quite right, for as
Miss Christie told Mirie, "these foreign women are really
too fresh, you know. Half of them don't really come from
anywhere but they believe that everybody from Jamaica is a
monkey and live in trees. I am really glad my son is bringing her here so that she can see how we live." Laura silently assented to that, for who in the wide world could
keep up a life that was as spotless and well-ordered as Miss
Christie's?

Laura longed to talk to somebody about her father. To
find out what he was really like. But she did not want to
ask Miss Christie. She thought of writing secretly to her
mother and telling her that Mr Bertram was coming, asking
what he was really like, but she was too timid to do anything behind Miss Christie's back for Miss Christie was so
all-knowing she was bound to find out. Sometimes she
wanted to ask Mirie the cook who had been working with
the family for nearly forty years. But although she got into
the habit of dropping into the roomy kitchen and sitting at
the table there for hours, she never got up the nerve to
address Mirie, and Mirie, a silent and morose woman, never
addressed her at all. She believed, though, that Mirie liked
her, for frequently, without saying a word, she would give
her some tidbit from the pot, or a sample of the cookies, or
bread and guava jelly, though she knew that Miss Christie
did not approve of eating between meals. But apart from

grunting every now and then as she went about her tasks, Mirie said nothing at all on the subject of Mr Bertram or any other being. Laura wished that Mirie would talk to her, for she found the kitchen the most comforting part of the house.

Her father and his wife arrived one day when she was at school. When she got home, she was too shy to go in, and was hanging around trying to hide behind a post when Miss Christie spotted her.

"Oh Laura, come and meet my son," said Miss Christie and swept her into the living room. "Mina," she said to a yellow-haired woman sitting there, "this is Laura, the little adopted I was telling you about." Laura first vaguely made out the woman, then Mass Dolphie, then a strange man in the shadows, but she was too shy to give him more than a covert glance. He did not address her but gave a smile which barely moved his lips. In days to come she would get accustomed to that smile, which was not as bland as in the photograph. To his daughter, he paid no more attention. It was his wife who fussed over the little girl, asking questions and exclaiming over her curls. Laura could hardly understand anything the woman said, but was impressed at how trim and neat she was, at the endless fascination of her clothes, her jewellery, her laughter, her accent, her perfume, her assurance. Looking at her long polished nails, Laura had a picture of her mother's hands, the nails cracked and broken like a man's from her work in the fields; of her mother's dark face, her coarse shrill voice. And she was bitterly ashamed. Knowing the mother she had come from, it was no wonder, she thought, that her father could not acknowledge her.

She was extremely uneasy with the guests in the house. Their presence strained to the fullest the new social graces that Miss Christie had inculcated in her. Now she had a two-fold anxiety: not to let her mother down to Miss

Christie, and not to let Miss Christie down in front of this white woman from the United States of America.

For all the woman's attentions, it was the man that she wanted to attend her, acknowledge her, love her. But he never did. She contrived at all times to be near him, to sit in his line of vision, to "accidentally" appear on the path when he went walking through the pastures. The man did not see her. He loved to talk, his voice going on and on in a low rumble like the waves of the sea she had never seen, the ash on his cigarette getting longer till it fell on his clothes or Miss Christie's highly polished floor. But he never talked to her. This caused her even greater anxiety than Miss Christie's efforts at "polishing" her, for while she felt that Miss Christie was trying, however painful it was, to build her up, she could not help feeling that her father's indifference did nothing so much as to reduce her, nullify her. Laura would have wondered if he knew who she was if she hadn't known that Miss Christie had written to him on the subject. She decided then that all his indifference was merely part of a play, that he wanted to surprise her when he did claim her, and was working up to one magical moment of recognition that would thereafter illuminate both their lives forever and ever. In the daytime that is how she consoled herself but at nights she cried in the little room where she slept alone in the fearful shadow of the breadfruit tree against the window pane.

Then Thursday came round again and in this anxiety she even forgot about her father. As usual the bus was late and Laura hung around the gate hoping that Miss Christie would forget she was there until it was too late to walk to school. The road curved white and lonely in the empty morning, silent save for the humming of bees and the beating of her own heart. Then Miss Christie and Mina appeared on the verandah and obviously saw her. Talking together, they started to walk slowly towards the gate where she stood, trapped by several impulses. Laura's heart beat faster then almost stopped as her father appeared from the orange grove and approached the two women. Now the three of them were walking towards her. They were now near enough for Laura to hear what they were saying but her eyes were only on her father.

"Oh dear, that old bus. Laura is going to be late again," Miss Christie said.

"Oh for chrissake. Why don't you stop fussing so much about the bloody little bastard," her son shouted.

Laura heard no more for after one long moment when her heart somersaulted once there was no time for hearing anything else for her feet of their own volition had set off at a run down the road and by the time she got to the school gates she had made herself an orphan and there were no more clouds.

THE BOY WHO PAINTED
CHRIST BLACK

❧❧❧

(United States)

by John Henrik Clarke

It is one thing to "talk that talk" about pride in your heritage, but another thing altogether to "walk that walk"—head held high. Then you know you're not only growing up but growing strong.

*H*e was the smartest boy in the Muskogee County School—for colored children. Everybody even remotely connected with the school knew this. The teacher always pronounced his name with profound gusto as she pointed him out as the ideal student. Once I heard her say: "If he were white he might, some day, become president." Only Aaron Crawford wasn't white; quite the contrary. His skin was so solid black that it glowed, reflecting an inner virtue that was strange, and beyond my comprehension.

In many ways he looked like something that was awkwardly put together. Both his nose and his lips seemed a trifle too large for his face. To say he was ugly would be unjust and to say he was handsome would be gross exaggeration. Truthfully, I could never make up my mind about him. Sometimes he looked like something out of a book of ancient history . . . looked as if he was left over from that magnificent era before the machine age came and marred the earth's natural beauty.

His great variety of talent often startled the teachers. This caused his classmates to look upon him with a mixed feeling of awe and envy.

Before Thanksgiving, he always drew turkeys and pumpkins on the blackboard. On George Washington's birthday, he drew large American flags surrounded by little hatchets. It was these small masterpieces that made him the most talked-about colored boy in Columbus, Georgia. The Negro principal of the Muskogee County School said he would some day be a great painter, like Henry O. Tanner.[1]

For the teacher's birthday, which fell on a day about a week before commencement, Aaron Crawford painted the picture that caused an uproar, and a turning point, at the Muskogee County School. The moment he entered the room that morning, all eyes fell on him. Besides his torn book holder, he was carrying a large-framed concern wrapped in old newspapers. As he went to his seat, the teacher's eyes followed his every motion, a curious wonderment mirrored in them conflicting with the half-smile that wreathed her face.

Aaron put his books down, then smiling broadly, advanced toward the teacher's desk. His alert eyes were so bright with joy that they were almost frightening. The children were leaning forward in their seats, staring greedily at him; a restless anticipation was rampant within every breast.

Already the teacher sensed that Aaron had a present for her. Still smiling, he placed it on her desk and began to help her unwrap it. As the last piece of paper fell from the large frame, the teacher jerked her hand away from it suddenly, her eyes flickering unbelievingly. Amidst the rigid tension, her heavy breathing was distinct and frightening. Temporarily, there was no other sound in the room.

Aaron stared questioningly at her and she moved her hand back to the present cautiously, as if it were a living thing with vicious characteristics. I am sure it was the one thing she least expected.

---

[1] Henry Ossawa Tanner (1859–1937): the Pittsburgh-born painter who emigrated to Paris, France, in 1891 in large part because, as he once said, he couldn't "fight prejudice and paint at the same time." Tanner was the first black American artist to receive international acclaim. Two of his most well known paintings are *The Banjo Lesson* and *The Thankful Poor*.

With a quick, involuntary movement I rose up from my desk. A series of submerged murmurs spread through the room, rising to a distinct monotone. The teacher turned toward the children, staring reproachfully. They did not move their eyes from the present that Aaron had brought her. . . . It was a large picture of Christ—painted black!

Aaron Crawford went back to his seat, a feeling of triumph reflecting in his every movement.

The teacher faced us. Her curious half-smile had blurred into a mild bewilderment. She searched the bright faces before her and started to smile again, occasionally stealing quick glances at the large picture propped on her desk, as though doing so were forbidden amusement.

"Aaron," she spoke at last, a slight tinge of uncertainty in her tone, "this is a most welcome present. Thanks. I will treasure it." She paused, then went on speaking, a trifle more coherent than before. "Looks like you are going to be quite an artist. . . . Suppose you come forward and tell the class how you came to paint this remarkable picture."

When he rose to speak, to explain about the picture, a hush fell tightly over the room, and the children gave him all of their attention . . . something they rarely did for the teacher. He did not speak at first; he just stood there in front of the room, toying absently with his hands, observing his audience carefully, like a great concert artist.

"It was like this," he said, placing full emphasis on every word. "You see, my uncle who lives in New York City teaches classes in Negro History at the Y.M.C.A. When he visited us last year he was telling me about the many great black folks who have made history. He said black folks were once the most powerful people on earth. When I asked him about Christ, he said no one ever proved whether he was black or white. Somehow a feeling came over me that he was a black man, 'cause he was so kind and forgiving, kinder than I have ever seen white people be. So, when I painted his picture I couldn't help but paint it as I thought it was."

After this, the little artist sat down, smiling broadly, as if he had gained entrance to a great storehouse of knowledge that ordinary people could neither acquire nor comprehend.

The teacher, knowing nothing else to do under prevailing circumstances, invited the children to rise from their seats and come forward so they could get a complete view of Aaron's unique piece of art.

When I came close to the picture, I noticed it was painted with the kind of paint you get in the five-and-ten-cent stores. Its shape was blurred slightly, as if someone had jarred the frame before the paint had time to dry. The eyes of Christ were deep-set and sad, very much like those of Aaron's father, who was a deacon in the local Baptist church. This picture of Christ looked much different from the one I saw hanging on the wall when I was in Sunday School. It looked more like a helpless Negro, pleading silently for mercy.

For the next few days, there was much talk about Aaron's picture.

The school term ended the following week and Aaron's picture, along with the best handwork done by the students that year, was on display in the assembly room. Naturally, Aaron's picture graced the place of honor.

There was no book work to be done on commencement day and joy was rampant among the children. The girls in their brightly colored dresses gave the school the delightful air of Spring awakening.

In the middle of the day all the children were gathered in the small assembly. On this day we were always favored with a visit from a man whom all the teachers spoke of with mixed esteem and fear. Professor Danual, they called him, and they always pronounced his name with reverence. He was supervisor of all the city schools, including those small and poorly equipped ones set aside for colored children.

The great man arrived almost at the end of our commencement exercise. On seeing him enter the hall, the children rose, bowed courteously, and sat down again, their eyes examining him as if he were a circus freak.

He was a tall white man with solid gray hair that made his lean face seem paler than it actually was. His eyes were the clearest blue I have ever seen. They were the only life-like things about him.

As he made his way to the front of the room the Negro principal, George Du Vaul, was walking ahead of him, cautiously preventing anything from getting in his way. As he passed me, I heard the teachers, frightened, sucking in their breath, felt the tension tightening.

A large chair was in the center of the rostrum. It had been daintily polished and the janitor had laboriously recushioned its bottom. The supervisor went straight to it without being guided, knowing that this pretty splendor was reserved for him.

Presently the Negro principal introduced the distinguished guest and he favored us with a short speech. It wasn't a very important speech. Almost at the end of it, I remember him saying something about he wouldn't be surprised if one of us boys grew up to be a great colored man, like Booker T. Washington.[2]

After he sat down, the school chorus sang two spirituals and the girls in the fourth grade did an Indian folk dance. This brought the commencement program to an end.

After this the supervisor came down from the rostrum, his eyes tinged with curiosity, and began to view the array of handwork on display in front of the chapel.

Suddenly his face underwent a strange rejuvenation. His clear blue eyes flickered in astonishment. He was looking at Aaron Crawford's picture of Christ. Mechanically he moved his stooped form closer to the picture and stood gaz-

[2] Booker Taliaferro Washington (1856–1915): founder of Tuskegee Institute (1881) in Alabama and one of the most prominent black leaders of his time who did a great deal for "the uplift of the race" and whose autobiography, *Up from Slavery*, became a national best-seller when it was published in 1901. Washington was far more conservative than his ideological rival, the great activist-intellectual W. E. B. Du Bois. This is to say that there's perhaps more than meets the eye to the school supervisor's comment.

ing fixedly at it, curious and undecided, as though it were
a dangerous animal that would rise any moment and spread
destruction.

We waited tensely for his next movement. The silence
was almost suffocating. At last he twisted himself around
and began to search the grim faces before him. The fiery
glitter of his eyes abated slightly as they rested on the
Negro principal, protestingly.

"Who painted this sacrilegious nonsense?" he demanded
sharply.

"I painted it, sir." These were Aaron's words, spoken
hesitantly. He wetted his lips timidly and looked up at the
supervisor, his eyes voicing a sad plea for understanding.

He spoke again, this time more coherently. "Th' principal said a colored person have jes as much right paintin'
Jesus black as a white person have paintin' him white. And
he says . . ." At this point he halted abruptly, as if to search
for his next words. A strong tinge of bewilderment
dimmed the glow of his solid black face. He stammered
out a few more words, then stopped again.

The supervisor strode a few steps toward him. At last
color had swelled some of the lifelessness out of his lean
face.

"Well, go on!" he said, enragedly, ". . . I'm still listening."

Aaron moved his lips pathetically but no words passed
them. His eyes wandered around the room, resting finally,
with an air of hope, on the face of the Negro principal.
After a moment, he jerked his face in another direction,
regretfully, as if something he had said had betrayed an
understanding between him and the principal.

Presently the principal stepped forward to defend the
school's prize student.

"I encouraged the boy in painting that picture," he said
firmly. "And it was with my permission that he brought

the picture into this school. I don't think the boy is so far wrong in painting Christ black. The artists of all other races have painted whatsoever God they worship to resemble themselves. I see no reason why we should be immune from that privilege. After all, Christ was born in that part of the world that had always been predominantly populated by colored people. There is a strong possibility that he could have been a Negro."

But for the monotonous lull of heavy breathing, I would have sworn that his words had frozen everyone in the hall. I had never heard the little principal speak so boldly to anyone, black or white.

The supervisor swallowed dumfoundedly. His face was aglow in silent rage.

"Have you been teaching these children things like that?" he asked the Negro principal, sternly.

"I have been teaching them that their race has produced great kings and queens as well as slaves and serfs," the principal said. "The time is long overdue when we should let the world know that we erected and enjoyed the benefits of a splendid civilization long before the people of Europe had a written language."

The supervisor coughed. His eyes bulged menacingly as he spoke. "You are not being paid to teach such things in this school, and I am demanding your resignation for overstepping your limit as principal."

George Du Vaul did not speak. A strong quiver swept over his sullen face. He revolved himself slowly and walked out of the room toward his office.

The supervisor's eyes followed him until he was out of focus. Then he murmured under his breath: "There'll be a lot of fuss in this world if you start people thinking that Christ was a nigger."

Some of the teachers followed the principal out of the chapel, leaving the crestfallen children restless and in a quandary about what to do next. Finally we started back to our rooms. The supervisor was behind me. I heard him murmur to himself: "Damn, if niggers ain't getting smarter."

A few days later I heard that the principal had accepted a summer job as art instructor of a small high school somewhere in south Georgia and had gotten permission from Aaron's parents to take him along so he could continue to encourage him in his painting.

I was on my way home when I saw him leaving his office. He was carrying a large briefcase and some books tucked under his arm. He had already said good-bye to all the teachers. And strangely, he did not look brokenhearted. As he headed for the large front door, he readjusted his horn-rimmed glasses, but did not look back. And air of triumph gave more dignity to his soldierly stride. He had the appearance of a man who had done a great thing, something greater than any ordinary man would do.

Aaron Crawford was waiting outside for him. They walked down the street together. He put his arm around Aaron's shoulder affectionately. He was talking sincerely to Aaron about something, and Aaron was listening, deeply earnest.

I watched them until they were so far down the street that their forms had begun to blur. Even from this distance I could see they were still walking in brisk, dignified strides, like two people who had won some sort of victory.

BIGWATER

✿

(United States)

by *Charlotte Watson Sherman*

The onset of menstruation is at once terrifying and excit-ing: a time for both contemplation and celebration.

*I*t was almost time to go there. Keta felt it in her bones. Water coming down and her twelve-year-old frame filling and rounding. Water pushing past her lungs when she laid on her back in her skinny wooden bed, pushing past and up until her soft brown skin formed small rounded hills on her chest.

Keta tried to make herself small, tried to hide the secret of her body's slow unfolding.

"Stop hunching your shoulders, girl."

"Let us get a good look at you."

"Where'd you get those skinny legs?"

Her aunts' smiling litany of questions made Keta blink her eyes and drop her head.

These were the women—the overflowing thighs and hips of Aunt Sarah, the softening belly of Aunt Ruth, Aunt Ethel's branchlike limbs, the proud, wise head of Aunt Josephine. Keta would look at the bodies of these women when they gathered every Wednesday to sit in a circle in the early evening light on straight-backed chairs in her mother's living room.

She would stare at the abundant swells of her mother's warm flesh and then feel the two small lumps on her chest and say, "I'm never going to look like that."

"You have to start somewhere," Aunt Sarah would smile.

"You have plenty of time to grow, girl."

Aunt Ethel would hide her smile behind her hands and say, "Mine never did grow."

"They're not what make you a woman," Aunt Ruth would snort. Then, cigarettes in place, they'd all turn, clicking their heads back into their secret dark circle.

Keta looked at the shapes and sizes of the women as they laughed and fussed over grown-woman things. She stood at the edge of their laughter, a long black wire, wondering, what does it take to make a real woman?

BigWater. Her mother had gone there. And Aunt Ethel. And Aunt Ruth and Sarah. And Aunt Josephine forced to go, physically forced against her protests.

"It's coming."

"It's coming. She's almost there."

"Doesn't make any sense. Taking me out to that water. Doesn't make any sense."

In the end, though, even Aunt Josephine had gone: out past the edge of town, past a hundred miles of whispering trees, deep into the forest where old stones hold secrets, past walls of chiseled granite, over a silver ribbon bridge into mountains rising like indigo breasts, moving up, into air so blue your bones fill with light.

BigWater. Her mother had gone, and her mother's mother, and her mother before her, and all the way back to the very first. And soon, very soon it would be Keta's turn to listen to the old words of the women.

> *In the old before time, before the people's spirits were broken, before the many tongues were lost, before the ceremonies were hidden from those who would not understand, women bled together. The moon called out to the water in their bodies, and they bled. One simultaneous stream of blood that carried*

them from world to world. They were one flesh. One blood. One Mother. The women left the nonbleeding girls, the boys and men, and went into the menstrual huts to wash the moon.

Then one morning, Keta woke to golden light filtering through the curtains, her body slashed with yellow light from her toes to the braids that lay across her head.

It started as a seed of water planted deep within her brain. With the whisper of a roar, it grew into a stream soaring through her body toward her pubis, moving straight to the heart of her womb, where it circled, a liquid burning star, before rushing toward the mouth between her legs. First it paused, then pushed past the brown girlish lips and flowed freely, a soft, strong, shining red river.

BigWater. Keta spent the first hours in bed with thick cotton pads clenched between her legs tight as Aunt Ruth's lips on her menthol cigarettes. She didn't know when the women were coming, but she knew they were all going to come. It was time.

Keta's mother entered a room made new.

"I knew it," her mother said, glancing at Keta's face. "I knew it soon as I smelled that new-woman smell, drifting down the steps like clouds. You feeling alright?" she asked.

Keta nodded. "Feel alright, but kind of funny."

"That's natural. You're changing, baby. Changing from one kind of being into another," her mother said as she rubbed Keta's stomach with lavender oil.

The day after her bleeding stopped, the women brought gifts to Keta's room.

Keta fingered a satin brassiere, a bottle of lavender oil, a photograph of her great-grandmother, a gold robe. She stroked her grandmother's collection of sacred writings.

"Tonight we're going to take you."

"Don't be afraid."

"You're growing up."

"Now, you're one of us."

Aunt Josephine put her hands on Keta's stomach and said, "The blood is the line, Keta. The line passing through all of us. The ceremony marks the line, so you know how special it is. I thought I could be a woman without all that. But I didn't know what being a woman was. I didn't know about the power and the responsibility, until BigWater."

Keta was a bit afraid. Her mother leaned forward, brushing Keta's face with her lips.

"It's important what you are and what you're going to be. I want you to know that I'm proud."

"But I didn't do nothing."

"You're you, aren't you?"

"Yeah, but . . ."

"That's enough for me," her mother said and each woman hugged Keta fiercely.

As Keta lay in bed she felt herself grow big and small, light and dark, up and down. The blood had changed her, but she didn't know how. When would her breasts start to grow, when would her hips widen? Was she really now a woman?

"Here, drink this," her mother said, holding a cup of black liquid to Keta's lips. "You have to sleep until we get there."

Keta frowned as the warmth moved down her throat.

"We'll get you ready," Keta heard the women say as she began to float inside a deep black silence, warm as her mother's embrace.

"BigWater," breathed Aunt Sarah.

"It seems a hundred years since we've been here," Aunt Josephine said.

"Speak for yourself," growled Aunt Ruth.

"Are you ready?" Keta's mother asked.

Keta nodded, shaking herself fully awake. Her mother squeezed her hand.

"It's time," she said, pulling Keta from the car. "Watch out for the robe."

Keta stroked the softness of the golden robe while her mother covered her head with its hood.

"Queen Mother for a day."

"For an evening."

"For the rest of your life, if that's what you choose."

The sun left an orange light in the sky as shadows twisted and stretched across the ground.

"Do we have everything?" Aunt Josephine asked after they walked a short way into the trees.

Each woman stopped until they formed a dark knot in the path.

"Of course I know we have everything," Josephine said as she started the line moving toward the clearing once again.

Soon, they stepped from the darkness of the trees onto rocks shining like a skin holding water. BigWater, spreading before the women now, a sheet of shimmering blue-green glass.

"There it is, there's the one," Aunt Sarah cried as she pointed to the broad granite stone sitting in the center of a nest of white rocks.

"Here's where we walk."

"Careful, it's slick."

And the group moved slowly into the water across small dark rocks. The women led the way and behind dipped Keta, the hem of the robe floating on the water like a soft yellow flower.

"This is it. This is the one," Aunt Sarah whispered as she sat on the smooth-skinned rock. The others sat too, in a tight dark ring around Keta.

Her mother opened the basket and removed five yellow candles, a cup of white ashes, a spoonful of honey, a packet of bitterroot, a bottle of wine, and a large carved wooden cup.

When the moon's white eye began shining through the trees, Aunt Sarah said, "Let's begin."

Josephine started to hum, an old sound each of the others in turn pushed into the circle until it melted into one long hum rolling over water.

Keta's mother began:

"This is the place where we come to be women. This is the place we come to be whole. We are following the line of our mothers and their mothers back to the very first one. When the first blood comes and a mother's house fills with its heavy, warm scent, it is time. Are you ready to follow the path of your mothers?"

Keta nodded, though she didn't know yet what her mother meant.

"Don't be afraid, we're going to show you," Aunt Josephine soothed.

The women removed their shoes and eased their bare feet into the water. Then Keta was surrounded by a ring of heavy laughter that held her in a wild embrace before lifting into the air.

Her mother dipped her fingers into the cup of ashes and lightly brushed Keta's face with the soft white powder.

"The bones of the dead. Now you wear the mask of your ancestors, the women who have gone before you and the women yet to come."

"Open your mouth."

Slowly, Keta complied. Her mother placed a drop of the root's bitter, milky sap on the left side of Keta's tongue and a drop of honey on the right.

"One side for the bitterness, one side for the sweetness of Life. Even your body will allow you goodness and sadness. To be a woman means knowing there are two sides of Life."

This was how Keta had felt when she became blood sisters, with her best friend Johnna. They had slit their fingertips with a paring knife, then mixed their blood. She felt safe now, in this circle of women.

"Be still and learn to listen to your body," her mother advised, as her aunts rose from the circle and laughed as they ran barefoot toward the lake's shore. They quickly returned, their long skirts dragging in the water.

"Eat the clay from their hands," her mother said. Each aunt presented a palm holding red clay to Keta.

"Our First Mother's blood poured from the moon into this clay. Her body is in this clay. We take Her body into our bodies so we will gain Her power, Her wisdom. We come here to eat this clay, to be still, to listen to our bodies' prayers. Smell the clay."

Aunt Sarah held the clay to Keta's nose. It smelled like wet dirt.

"This is the smell of our monthly blood, our blood that comes from the moon. People are made of moon-blood and clay. The spirits of our people flow in our blood. It is the blood of Life."

Keta ate some clay from each of her aunts' hands. The women also ate the clay.

"Take off your robe," Keta's mother instructed. Keta removed her robe and handed it to her mother. The women smeared Keta's body with the red clay.

Her mother's fingers gripped the slim bottle of wine and filled the wooden cup.

"This wine is the red water flowing inside you, the liquid cord winding from the women before us, through me to you, connecting us all to our First Mother, the source of all living things. This bloodwine is Her power, now yours. We will all drink from this cup. My mother told me this cup was carved by her mother's mother when she was a girl. You take the first sip, daughter."

Keta held the cup in both hands and raised it to her lips. She dipped her tongue into the pungent red liquid and smiled. This was her first taste of wine. It filled her head with a swirling watery glow.

"We are going to wash you after your first moon," her mother said. "For the last time, you will be bathed as a child. From now on, you will bathe as a woman and will be responsible for your own body."

Keta placed her bare feet in the water. Naked, she stepped from rock to rock as her aunts sat on the old stone laughing, water lapping at the hems of their skirts.

"Always remember how your body feels tonight. This is what happened to me and my mother and her mother before her," her mother said.

Keta watched her mother pass the candles to her aunts. As if looking through water, she saw her mother strike a match. Then Keta felt herself moving, her bones shifting, the candles' glow a fire inside her. She felt something more ancient than memory move through her blood as she moved among the smooth-skinned rocks.

Aunt Ethel leaned forward into the light of her candle and took Keta's right arm. "We're going to wash you like we wash the sacred stones of our dead. We wash them so we can bring them back again, as you will come back. When you were born, the moon was white and had stood up again. It was your beginning."

Keta moved through the water and gave her left arm to Aunt Josephine, who leaned forward, face dancing in the candle's narrow flame. She rubbed the silken water into Keta's arm. "Now the moon is yellow and turning, twisting and turning like a woman trying to get full of herself, trying to become herself, as you will become. It is another beginning."

Keta moved around the circle to Aunt Ruth and put her foot in Aunt Ruth's lap. Aunt Ruth set her glass of wine on the rock and then moved her face from the darkness into her candle's light. As she bathed Keta's foot she said,

"Soon, the moon will be full and red. After loving, after battling, the moon will sit down like a woman who has arrived, a woman who belongs, like you will belong. That, too, will be a beginning."

Aunt Sarah grabbed Keta's left leg, let the water drip over her foot. She moved her candle close to Keta's face and looked into the girl's eyes until satisfied with what she saw, then she backed away and said, "This long body is life, girl. Nothing but life. And a woman holds all these moons, all these beginnings inside her body. When the moon is black, it is the dying moon."

Aunt Sarah pressed her fingertips to Keta's forehead, streaking her skin with clay.

"But when the moon is dying," Aunt Sarah continued, "the circle is only half-complete. We must die to be reborn, to complete the circle of Life. That is why we are washing you like we wash the stones to bring back our dead. One part of life is dying, another being born."

Keta's mother stepped into the water with Keta. She splashed Keta's body, using her hands as cups to pour water over Keta's head, her shoulders, her breasts and buttocks. Keta smiled as the water cascaded over her skin. The water flowed over her body as it had flowed over her mother's body and her mother's before her.

"This will be the only time I will do this," her mother said, kneeling in front of Keta's gleaming body to wash her pubis.

Finally, Keta's mother held her candle to her daughter's face and said, "After tonight, you will be clothed in the knowledge of all these women. This is what makes you a woman. Every month now you'll be reborn and you'll hear a sound like WHOOSHWHOOSHWHOOSH-WHOOSHWHOOSHWHOOSHWHOOSH flowing through the water in your body. It's the old sound of where we all come from."

BigWater. The women were unashamedly drenched with water and wine, and Keta could see the magnificent outlines of their bodies. They talked into the night, their voices inflating Keta's head with notions she had never known until she felt herself swelling, growing larger than the tall black trees, felt her body opening with the sound of words shifting inside water, the bitterroot and honey on her tongue turning to water, her body brimmed with WHOOSHWHOOSHWHOOSHWHOOSH, growing larger, her body rounding with sound, with the women's laughter, and she grew larger still, grew past old granite walls, over indigo mountains, and into the blue-black air so high her body filled with light and the ancient shimmering of water.

SWAN SONG
(LAS OROPÉNDOLAS)

꙰

(Costa Rica)

by Quince Duncan

Translated by Dellita L. Martin-Ogunsola

Sometimes, only birds of a feather ought to flock together.

*T*hey always fly with divine help. In the mornings they soar through the heavens southward bound; they return at evening time, dragging the setting sun behind their golden tails.

You stare into the water. The orioles' reflection is girded with harmonic crystal from depths more profound than the riverbed to the sky, higher than the leaves of the *pejibaye* tree. And each day of that encounter of a close kind grew more meaningful according to the years that passed over our youthful heads.

Every day we would go to visit them. And on our daily pilgrimage we learned to love them. But we never could explain why it didn't occur to them to change nests, to find a better location in Mr. Frederic's cornfield. They never even thought about it. At least that's what Ronald and I deduced during those years that live forever in the galleries of our memory.

We were twelve years old. At that age, when we had hardly awakened from our childhood lethargy, everything had sentimental value for us. Our devotion to the golden orioles was worth the implacable punishment from adults, who did not understand the great truth: We didn't run away from home because we were bad, like they used to say, but because we were poets. And daily in the shadow of the trees, quiet as life, and like life breathing turbulently, we poured the contradictions of our very beings into a burning love that all of us are capable of at twelve years old.

We never dared to disturb our friends' peace. We would watch them from a distance, feeling like playmates in their games and quarrels, ecstatic, deploring noise from the woods, fearful that it would rob us of such priceless company.

And time slipped silently over our hands and foreheads, revealing to us bit by bit the intimate aspects of nature.

But one day we got the idea of inviting a third party along to our daily rendezvous. Neither Ronald nor I have ever forgiven ourselves for that serious mistake. Because the truth is we should have foreseen that our guest would bring a bow and arrow.

As always, when evening falls, the orioles fly with divine help. They surge through the heavens, displaying their golden tails, dragging behind them the last sighs of each dusk, bound northward. We watch them go by with a sadness that digs and sinks into the most sensitive recesses of our spirits. At the place where we daily met, over in Mr. Frederic's cornfield, they never came back. Perhaps they could not forget that there one sunny morning on the well-lit green plain, the rigid body of a friend who had been ruthlessly betrayed lay dead, caressing the earth.

GETTING THE FACTS OF LIFE

❧

(United States)

by Paulette Childress White

It's a cold, cold world after all. But, hey, you can't let that stand between you and your dignity.

The August morning was ripening into a day that promised to be a burner. By the time we'd walked three blocks, dark patches were showing beneath Momma's arms, and inside tennis shoes thick with white polish, my feet were wet against the cushions. I was beginning to regret how quickly I'd volunteered to go.

"Dog. My feet are getting mushy," I complained.

"You should've wore socks," Momma said, without looking my way or slowing down.

I frowned. In 1961, nobody wore socks with tennis shoes. It was bare legs, Bermuda shorts, and a sleeveless blouse. Period.

Momma was chubby but she could really walk. She walked the same way she washed clothes—up-and-down, up-and-down until she was done. She didn't believe in taking breaks.

This was my first time going to the welfare office with Momma. After breakfast, before we'd had time to scatter, she corralled everyone old enough to consider and announced in her serious-business voice that someone was going to the welfare office with her this morning. Cries went up.

Junior had his papers to do. Stella was going swimming

at the high school. Dennis was already pulling the *Free Press* wagon across town every first Wednesday to get the surplus food—like that.

"You want clothes for school, don't you?" That landed. School opened in two weeks.

"I'll go," I said.

"Who's going to baby-sit if Minerva goes?" Momma asked.

Stella smiled and lifted her small golden nose. "I will," she said. "I'd rather baby-sit than do *that*."

That should have warned me. Anything that would make Stella offer to baby-sit had to be bad.

A small cheer probably went up among my younger brothers in the back rooms where I was not too secretly known as "The Witch" because of the criminal licks I'd learned to give on my rise to power. I was twelve, third oldest under Junior and Stella, but I had long established myself as first in command among the kids. I was chief baby-sitter, biscuit-maker and broom-wielder. Unlike Stella, who'd begun her development at ten, I still had my girl's body and wasn't anxious to have that changed. What would it mean but a loss of power? I liked things just the way they were. My interest in bras was even less than my interest in boys, and that was limited to keeping my brothers—who seemed destined for wildness—from taking over completely.

Even before we left, Stella had Little Stevie Wonder turned up on the radio in the living room, and suspicious jumping-bumping sounds were beginning in the back. They'll tear the house down, I thought, following Momma out the door.

We turned at Salliotte, the street that would take us straight up to Jefferson Avenue where the welfare office was. Momma's face was pinking in the heat, and I was huffing to keep up. From here, it was seven more blocks on the colored side, the railroad tracks, five blocks on the white side and there you were. We'd be cooked.

"Is the welfare office near the Harbor Show?" I asked. I knew the answer, I just wanted some talk.

"Across the street."

"Umm. Glad it's not way down Jefferson somewhere."

Nothing. Momma didn't talk much when she was outside. I knew that the reason she wanted one of us along when she had far to go was not for company but so she wouldn't have to walk by herself. I could understand that. To me, walking alone was like being naked or deformed— everyone seemed to look at you harder and longer. With Momma, the feeling was probably worse because you knew people were wondering if she were white, Indian maybe or really colored. Having one of us along, brown and clearly hers, probably helped define that. Still, it was like being a little parade, with Momma's pale skin and straight brown hair turning heads like the clang of cymbals. Especially on the colored side.

"Well," I said, "here we come to the bad part."

Momma gave a tiny laugh.

Most of Salliotte was a business street, with Old West– looking storefronts and some office places that never seemed to open. Ecorse, hinged onto southwest Detroit like a clothes closet, didn't seem to take itself seriously. There were lots of empty fields, some of which folks down the residential streets turned into vegetable gardens every summer. And there was this block where the Moonflower Hotel raised itself to three stories over the poolroom and Beaman's drugstore. Here, bad boys and drunks made their noise and did an occasional stabbing. Except for the cars that lined both sides of the block, only one side was busy—the other bordered a field of weeds. We walked on the safe side.

If you were a woman or a girl over twelve, walking this block—even on the safe side—could be painful. They usually hollered at you and never mind what they said. Today, because it was hot and early, we made it by with only one weak *Hey baby* from a drunk sitting in the poolroom door.

"Hey baby yourself," I said but not too loudly, pushing my flat chest out and stabbing my eyes in his direction.

"Minerva girl, you better watch your mouth with grown men like that," Momma said, her eyes catching me up in real warning though I could see that she was holding down a smile.

"Well, he can't do nothing to me when I'm with you, can he?" I asked, striving to match the rise and fall of her black pumps.

She said nothing. She just walked on, churning away under a sun that clearly meant to melt us. From here to the tracks it was mostly gardens. It felt like the Dixie Peach I'd used to help water-wave my hair was sliding down with the sweat on my face, and my throat was tight with thirst. Boy, did I want a pop. I looked at the last little store before we crossed the tracks without bothering to ask.

Across the tracks, there were no stores and no gardens. It was shady, and the grass was June green. Perfect-looking houses sat in unfenced spaces far back from the street. We walked these five blocks without a word. We just looked and hurried to get through it. I was beginning to worry about the welfare office in earnest. A fool could see that in this part of Ecorse, things got serious.

We had been on welfare for almost a year. I didn't have any strong feelings about it—my life went on pretty much the same. It just meant watching the mail for a check instead of Daddy getting paid, and occasional visits from a social worker that I'd always managed to miss. For Momma and whoever went with her, it meant this walk to the office and whatever went on there that made everyone hate to go. For Daddy, it seemed to bring the most change. For him, it meant staying away from home more than when he was working and a reason not to answer the phone.

At Jefferson, we turned left and there it was, halfway down the block. The Department of Social Services. I discovered some strong feelings. That fine name meant nothing. This was the welfare. The place for poor people. People who couldn't or wouldn't take care of themselves. Now I was going to face it, and suddenly I thought what I knew the others had thought, *What if I see someone I know?* I wanted to run back all those blocks home.

I looked at Momma for comfort, but her face was closed and her mouth looked locked.

Inside, the place was gray. There were rows of long benches like church pews facing each other across a middle aisle that led to a central desk. Beyond the benches and the desk, four hallways led off to a maze of partitioned offices. In opposite corners, huge fans hung from the ceiling, humming from side to side, blowing the heavy air for a breeze.

Momma walked to the desk, answered some questions, was given a number and told to take a seat. I followed her through, trying not to see the waiting people—as though that would keep them from seeing me.

Gradually, as we waited, I took them all in. There was no one there that I knew, but somehow they all looked familiar. Or maybe I only thought they did, because when your eyes connected with someone's, they didn't quickly look away and they usually smiled. They were mostly women and children, a few low-looking men. Some of them were white, which surprised me. I hadn't expected to see them in there.

Directly in front of the bench where we sat, a little girl with blond curls was trying to handle a bottle of Coke. Now and then, she'd manage to turn herself and the bottle around and watch me with big gray eyes that seemed to know quite well how badly I wanted a pop. I thought of asking Momma for fifteen cents so I could get one from the machine in the back but I was afraid she'd still say no so I just kept planning more and more convincing ways to ask. Besides, there was a water fountain near the door if I could make myself rise and walk to it.

We waited three hours. White ladies dressed like secretaries kept coming out to call numbers, and people on the benches would get up and follow down a hall. Then more people came in to replace them. I drank water from the fountain three times and was ready to put my feet up on the bench before us—the little girl with the Coke and her momma got called—by the time we heard Momma's number.

"You wait here," Momma said as I rose with her.

I sat down with a plop.

The lady with the number looked at me. Her face reminded me of the librarian's at Bunch school. Looked like she never cracked a smile. "Let her come," she said.

"She can wait here," Momma repeated, weakly.

"It's okay. She can come in. Come on," the lady insisted at me.

I hesitated, knowing that Momma's face was telling me to sit.

"Come on," the woman said.

Momma said nothing.

I got up and followed them into the maze. We came to a small room where there was a desk and three chairs. The woman sat behind the desk and we before it.

For a while, no one spoke. The woman studied a folder open before her, brows drawn together. On the wall behind her there was a calendar with one heavy black line drawn slantwise through each day of August, up to the twenty-first. That was today.

"Mrs. Blue, I have a notation here that Mr. Blue has not reported to the department on his efforts to obtain employment since the sixteenth of June. Before that, it was the tenth of April. You understand that department regulations

require that he report monthly to this office, do you not?"
Eyes brown as a wren's belly came up at Momma.

"Yes," Momma answered, sounding as small as I felt.

"Can you explain his failure to do so?"

Pause. "He's been looking. He says he's been looking."

"That may be. However, his failure to report those
efforts here is my only concern."

Silence.

"We cannot continue with your case as it now stands if
Mr. Blue refuses to comply with departmental regulations.
He is still residing with the family, is he not?"

"Yes, he is. I've been reminding him to come in . . . he
said he would."

"Well, he hasn't. Regulations are that any able-bodied
man, head-of-household and receiving assistance who
neglects to report to this office any effort to obtain work for
a period of sixty days or more is to be cut off for a mini-
mum of three months, at which time he may reapply. As of
this date, Mr. Blue is over sixty days delinquent, and offi-
cially, I am obliged to close the case and direct you to other
sources of aid."

"What is that?"

"Aid to Dependent Children would be the only source
available to you. Then, of course, you would not be eligible
unless it was verified that Mr. Blue was no longer residing
with the family."

Another silence. I stared into the gray steel front of the
desk, everything stopped but my heart.

"Well, can you keep the case open until Monday? If he
comes in by Monday?"

"According to my records, Mr. Blue failed to come in
May and such an agreement was made then. In all, we
allowed him a period of seventy days. You must understand that what happens in such cases as this is not wholly
my decision." She sighed and watched Momma with hope-

less eyes, tapping the soft end of her pencil on the papers before her. "Mrs. Blue, I will speak to my superiors on your behalf. I can allow you until Monday next . . . that's the"— she swung around to the calendar—"twenty-sixth of August, to get him in here."

"Thank you. He'll be in," Momma breathed. "Will I be able to get the clothing order today?"

Hands and eyes searched in the folder for an answer before she cleared her throat and tilted her face at Momma. "We'll see what we can do," she said, finally.

My back touched the chair. Without turning my head, I moved my eyes down to Momma's dusty feet and wondered if she could still feel them; my own were numb. I felt bodyless—there was only my face, which wouldn't disappear, and behind it, one word pinging against another in a buzz that made no sense. At home, we'd have the house cleaned by now, and I'd be waiting for the daily appearance of my best friend, Bernadine, so we could comb each other's hair or talk about stuck-up Evelyn and Brenda. Maybe Bernadine was already there, and Stella was teaching her to dance the bop.

Then I heard our names and ages—all eight of them— being called off like items in a grocery list.

"Clifford, Junior, age fourteen." She waited.

"Yes."

"Born? Give me the month and year."

"October 1946," Momma answered, and I could hear in her voice that she'd been through these questions before.

"Stella, age thirteen."

"Yes."

"Born?"

"November 1947."

"Minerva, age twelve." She looked at me. "This is Minerva?"

"Yes."

No. I thought, no, this is not Minerva. You can write it down if you want to, but Minerva is not here.

"Born?"

"December 1948."

The woman went on down the list, sounding more and more like Momma should be sorry or ashamed, and Momma's answers grew fainter and fainter. So this was welfare. I wondered how many times Momma had had to do this. Once before? Three times? Every time?

More questions. How many in school? Six. Who needs shoes? Everybody.

"Everybody needs shoes? The youngest two?"

"Well, they don't go to school . . . but they walk."

My head came up to look a Momma and the woman. The woman's mouth was left open. Momma didn't blink.

The brown eyes went down. "Our allowances are based on the median cost for moderately priced clothing at Sears, Roebuck." She figured on paper as she spoke. "That will mean thirty-four dollars for children over ten . . . thirty dollars for children under ten. It comes to one hundred ninety-eight dollars. I can allow eight dollars for two additional pairs of shoes."

"Thank you."

"You will present your clothing order to a salesperson at the store, who will be happy to assist you in your selections. Please be practical as further clothing requests will not be considered for a period of six months. In cases of necessity, however, requests for winter outerwear will be considered beginning November first."

Momma said nothing.

The woman rose and left the room.

For the first time, I shifted in the chair. Momma was looking into the calendar as though she could see through the pages to November first. Everybody needed a coat.

I'm never coming here again, I thought. If I do, I'll stay

out front. Not coming back in here. Ever again.

She came back and sat behind her desk. "Mrs. Blue, I must make it clear that, regardless of my feelings, I will be forced to close your case if your husband does not report to this office by Monday, the twenty-sixth. Do you understand?"

"Yes. Thank you. He'll come. I'll see to it."

"Very well." She held a paper out to Momma.

We stood. Momma reached over and took the slip of paper. I moved toward the door.

"Excuse me, Mrs. Blue, but are you pregnant?"

"What?"

"I asked if you were expecting another child."

"Oh. No, I'm not," Momma answered, biting down on her lips.

"Well, I'm sure you'll want to be careful about a thing like that in your present situation."

"Yes."

I looked quickly at Momma's loose white blouse. We'd never known when another baby was coming until it was almost there.

"I suppose that eight children are enough for anyone," the woman said, and for the first time her face broke into a smile.

Momma didn't answer that. Somehow, we left the room and found our way out onto the street. We stood for a moment as though lost. My eyes followed Momma's up to where the sun was burning high. It was still there, blazing white against a cloudless blue. Slowly, Momma put the clothing order into her purse and snapped it shut. She looked around as if uncertain which way to go. I led the way to the corner. We turned. We walked the first five blocks.

I was thinking about how stupid I'd been a year ago, when Daddy lost his job. I'd been happy.

"You-all better be thinking about moving to

Indianapolis," he announced one day after work, looking like he didn't think much of it himself. He was a welder with the railroad company. He'd worked there for eleven years. But now, "Company's moving to Indianapolis," he said. "Gonna be gone by November. If I want to keep my job, we've got to move with it."

We didn't. Nobody wanted to move to Indianapolis—not even Daddy. Here, we had uncles, aunts and cousins on both sides. Friends. Everybody and everything we knew. Daddy could get another job. First came unemployment compensation. Then came welfare. Thank goodness for welfare, we said, while we waited and waited for the job that hadn't yet come.

The problem was that Daddy couldn't take it. If something got repossessed or somebody took sick or something was broken or another kid was coming, he'd carry on terribly until things got better—by which time things were always worse. He'd always been that way. So when the railroad left, he began to do everything wrong. Stayed out all hours. Drank and drank some more. When he was home, he was so grouchy we were afraid to squeak. Now when we saw him coming, we got lost. Even our friends ran for cover.

At the railroad tracks, we sped up. The tracks were as far across as a block was long. Silently, I counted the rails by the heat of the steel bars through my thin soles. On the other side, I felt something heavy rise up in my chest and I knew that I wanted to cry. I wanted to cry or run or kiss the dusty ground. The little houses with their sun-scorched lawns and backyard gardens were mansions in my eyes. "Ohh, Ma . . . look at those collards!"

"Umm-humm," she agreed, and I knew that she saw it too.

"Wonder how they grew so big?"

"Cow dung, probably. Big Poppa used to put cow dung

out to fertilize the vegetable plots, and everything just grew like crazy. We used to get tomatoes this big"—she circled with her hands—"and don't talk about squash or melons."

"I bet y'all ate like rich people. Bet y'all had everything you could want."

"We sure did," she said. "We never wanted for anything when it came to food. And when the cash crops were sold, we could get whatever else that was needed. We never wanted for a thing."

"What about the time you and cousin Emma threw out the supper peas?"

"Oh! Did I tell you about that?" she asked. Then she told it all over again. I didn't listen. I watched her face and guarded her smile with a smile of my own.

We walked together, step for step. The sun was still burning, but we forgot to mind it. We talked about an Alabama girlhood in a time and place I'd never know. We talked about the wringer washer and how it could be fixed, because washing every day on a scrub-board was something Alabama could keep. We talked about how to get Daddy to the Department of Social Services.

Then we talked about having babies. She began to tell me things I'd never known, and the idea of womanhood blossomed in my mind like some kind of suffocating rose.

"Momma," I said, "I don't think I can be a woman."

"You can," she laughed, "and if you live, you will be. You gotta be some kind of woman."

"But it's hard," I said, "sometimes it must be hard."

"Umm-humm," she said, "sometimes it is hard."

When we got to the bad block, we crossed to Beaman's drugstore for two orange crushes. Then we walked right through the groups of men standing in the shadows of the poolroom and the Moonflower Hotel. Not one of them said a word to us. I supposed they could see in the way we walked that we weren't afraid. We'd been to the welfare office and back again. And the facts of life, fixed in our minds like the sun in the sky, were no burning mysteries.

THE TEST

❧

(South Africa)

by Njabulo Ndebele

*A little defiance is a needful thing if you're ever to let loose
the apron strings.*

As he felt the first drops of rain on his bare arms, Thoba
wondered if he should run home quickly before there was a
downpour. He shivered briefly, and his teeth chattered for a
moment as a cold breeze blew and then stopped. How cold
it had become, he thought. He watched the other boys who
seemed completely absorbed in the game. They felt no
rain, and no cold. He watched. The boys of Mayaba Street
had divided themselves into two soccer teams. That was
how they spent most days of their school vacation: playing
soccer in the street. No, decided Thoba, he would play on.
Besides, his team was winning. He looked up at the sky
and sniffed, remembering that some grown-ups would say
one can tell if it is going to rain by sniffing at the sky the
way dogs do. He was not sure if he could smell anything
other than the dust raised by the soccer players around him.
He could tell, though, that the sky, having been overcast for
some time, had grown darker.

Should I? he thought. Should I go home? But the ball
decided for him when it came his way accidentally, and he
was suddenly swept into the action as he dribbled his way
past one fellow. But the next fellow took the ball away
from him, and Thoba gave it up without a struggle. It had
been a quick thrill. He had felt no rain, no cold. The trick
is to keep playing and be involved, he thought. But he

stopped, and looked at the swarm of boys chasing after the tennis ball in a swift chaotic movement away from him, like a whirlwind. They were all oblivious of the early warnings of rain. He did not follow them, feeling no inclination to do so. He felt uncertain whether he was tired or whether it was the fear of rain and cold that had taken his interest away from the game. He looked down at his arms. There they were: tiny drops of rain, some sitting on goose pimples, others between them. Fly's spit, he thought.

Soon there was a loud yell. Some boys were jumping into the air, others shaking their fists, others dancing in all sorts of ways. Some, with a determined look on their faces, trotted back to the centre, their small thumbs raised, to wait for the ball to be thrown in again. Someone had scored for Thoba's team. The scorer was raised into the air. It was Vusi. But Vusi's triumph was short-lived for it was just at that moment that the full might of the rain came. Vusi disappeared from the sky like a mole reversing into its hole. The boys of Mayaba Street scattered home, abandoning their match. The goal posts on either side disappeared when the owners of the shoes repossessed them. Thoba began to run home, hesitated, and changed direction to follow a little group of boys towards the shelter of the walled veranda of Simangele's home.

Thoba found only Simangele, Vusi, Mpiyakhe, and Nana on the veranda. He was disappointed. In the rush, it had seemed as if more boys had gone there. Perhaps he really should have run home, he thought. Too late, though. He was there now, at the veranda of Simangele's home, breathing hard like the others from the short impulsive sprint away from the rain. They were all trying to get the rain water off them: kicking it off their legs, or pushing it down their arms with their fingers, the way windscreen wipers do. Simangele wiped so hard that it looked as if he was rubbing the water into his skin. Only Vusi, who had scored the last goal, was not wiping off the water on him. There was an angry scowl on his face as he slowly massaged his buttocks, all the while cursing:

"The bastards," he said. "The bastards! They just dropped me. They let go of me like a bag of potatoes. I'll get them for that. One by one. I'll get them one by one."

"What if you *are* a bag of potatoes?" said Simangele laughing. "What do you think, fellows?" He was jumping up and down like a grown-up soccer player warming up just before the beginning of a game. He shadow-boxed briefly then jumped up and down again.

Simangele got no response from the others. It would have been risky for them to take sides. Thoba rubbed his arms vigorously, making it too obvious that he was shamming a preoccupation with keeping warm in order to avoid answering Simangele's question. But Vusi did not fear Simangele.

"This is no laughing matter," he said.

"Then don't make me laugh," replied Simangele, shadow-boxing with slow easy sweeps of his arms.

Vusi uttered a click of annoyance and looked away from Simangele. He continued to massage his buttocks.

Simangele looked at Vusi for a while, and then turned away to look at Nana.

"Are you warm?" he asked, suddenly looking gentle.

Nana, who was noticeably shivering, sniffed back mucus and nodded.

"Perhaps you should sit there at the corner," said Simangele.

Thoba looked at Nana and felt vaguely jealous that Nana should receive such special attention from Simangele. But then Nana always received special attention. This thought made Thoba yearn for the security of his home. He began to feel anxious and guilty that he had not run home. Not only did he feel he did not matter to Simangele and Vusi, he also feared the possibility of a fight between these two. Quarrels made him uneasy. Always. What would his mother say if he was injured in a fight? Rather, wouldn't she be pleased to hear that he had run home as soon as the rain started? The rain. Yes, the rain. He looked at it, and it seemed ominous with its steady strength, as if it would go on raining for ever, making it impossible for him to get home before his mother. And how cold it was now! Should he? Should he run home? No. There was too much rain out there. Somewhat anxiously, he looked at the others, and tried to control his shivering.

The other three boys were looking at Nana huddling himself at the corner where the house and the veranda walls met. He looked frailer than ever, as if there were a disease eating at him all the time. Thoba wished he had a coat to put over Nana. But Nana seemed warm, for he had embraced his legs and buried his head between his raised knees. The only sound that came from him was a continuous sniff as he drew back watery mucus, occasionally swallowing it. Thoba wondered if Nana's grandmother was home. Or did the rain catch her far in the open fields away from the township, where it was said she dug all over for roots and herbs? She was always away looking for roots to heal people with. And when she was away, Nana was cared for by everyone in Mayaba Street. Thoba looked at Nana and wished that he himself was as lucky.

Just then, Mpiyakhe turned round like a dog wanting to sit, and sat down about a foot from Nana. He began to put his shoes on. Mpiyakhe's shoes had been one of the two pairs that had been used as goal posts. Thoba looked at Mpiyakhe's feet as Mpiyakhe slipped them into socks first, and noticed how smooth those feet were compared to Nana's which were deeply cracked. Then he looked at Vusi's and Simangele's feet. Theirs too were cracked. His were not. They were as smooth as Mpiyakhe's. Thoba remembered that he had three pairs of shoes, and his mother had always told him to count his blessings because most boys had only one pair, if any shoes at all, for both school and special occasions like going to church. Yet Thoba yearned to have cracked feet too. So whenever his mother and father were away from home, he would go out and play without his shoes. But Mpiyakhe never failed to wear his shoes. Perhaps that was why Mpiyakhe's shoes were always being used as goal posts. They were always available.

Soon, Thoba, Mpiyakhe, Vusi, and Simangele stood in a row along the low wall of the veranda, looking at the rain, and talking and laughing. The anxiety over a possible fight had disappeared, and Thoba felt contented as he nestled himself into the company of these daring ones who had not run home when the rain started. And it no longer mattered to him that his mother had always said to him: "Always run home as soon as it begins to rain. I will not nurse a child who has said to illness 'Come on, friend, let's hold hands and dance.' Never!" And Thoba would always wonder how a boy could hold hands with a disease. He must ask his uncle next time he came to visit.

For the moment, Thoba was glad that there was nobody at home. His mother was on day duty at the Dunnotar Hospital, and, although it was the December vacation, his father still went to school saying there was too much preparation to be done.

"You ought to take a rest, Father," Thoba's mother had said on the last Sunday of the school term. The two had been relaxing in the living room, reading the Sunday papers.

"Never!" Thoba's father had replied with offended conviction. "Moulding these little ones requires much energy and self-sacrifice. I will not ever say 'wait a minute' to duty. Don't you know me yet?"

"Oh, you teachers!" Thoba's mother had said with a sigh.

"Thoba!" called his father.

"*Baba!*" responded Thoba who had been in his bedroom memorising Psalm 23. He had to be ready for the scripture oral examination the following morning.

"Show yourself," said his father. Thoba appeared timidly at the door and leaned against it.

"What," his father asked, "is the square root of three hundred and twenty-five?" Thoba looked up at the ceiling. After some silence his father looked up from his newspaper and cast a knowing glance at his wife.

"You see," he said. "It takes time."

Thoba's mother rose from her chair, dropped her paper and walked towards Thoba, her arms stretched out before her in order to embrace him. Thoba allowed himself to be embraced, all the while wishing his mother had not done that. It made him too helpless.

"Only yesterday," his father drove the point home, "we were working on square roots, and he has already forgotten. What kind of exams he is going to write this coming week is anybody's guess. Son, there has got to be a difference between the son of a teacher and other boys. But never mind. Einstein, if you care to know. . . . Do you know him? Do you know Einstein?"

Thoba shook his head, brushing his forehead against his mother's breasts.

"Well, well," his father said, "you will know him in time. But that great mathematics genius was once your age; and then, he did not know his square roots."

That was three weeks ago. And now, as Thoba looked at the other boys with him on the veranda, he felt glad that his father had gone to work, or else the man would certainly have turned the day into a tortuous tutorial. Instead, there was Thoba with Simangele and Vusi and Mpiyakhe, all by themselves, looking at the rain from the shelter of the famed veranda of Mayaba Street.

The veranda of Simangele's home was very popular with the boys of Mayaba Street. Simangele's parents had done all they could to chase the boys away. But then, it was the only veranda in the neighbourhood that was walled round. To most boys, its low front wall came up to their shoulders, so that anyone looking at them from the street would see many little heads just appearing above the wall. The boys loved to climb on that wall, run on it, chasing one another. There had been many broken teeth, broken arms, and slashed tongues. Yet the boys, with the memory of chickens, would be back not long after each accident.

Once, Simangele's parents decided to lock the gate leading into the yard. But the boys of Mayaba Street, led by none other than Simangele himself, simply scaled the fence. Then it became a game to race over it: either from the street into the yard, or from the yard into the street. The fence gave in. By the time it was decided to unlock the gate, it was too late. People either walked in through the gate, or walked over the flattened fence. Simangele's father then tried to surprise the boys by sneaking up on them with a whip. But it did not take long for them to enjoy being surprised and then chased down the street. He gave up.

Thoba, who was never allowed to play too long in the street, always felt honoured to be on that veranda. He was feeling exactly this way when, as he looked at the rain, he gave way to an inner glow of exultation.

"Oh!" he exclaimed, "it's so nice during the holidays. We just play soccer all day." He spoke to no one in particular. And nobody answered him. The others, with the exception of Mpiyakhe, really did not share Thoba's enthusiasm. They were always free, always playing in the street. Just whenever they wanted. Thoba envied these boys. They seemed not to have demanding mothers who issued endless orders, inspected chores given and done, and sent their children on endless errands. Thoba smiled, savouring the thrill of being with them, and the joy of having followed the moment's inclination to join them on the veranda.

"How many goals did we score?" asked Mpiyakhe.

"Seven," replied Vusi.

"Naw!" protested Simangele. "It was six."

"Seven!" insisted Vusi.

"Six!" shouted Simangele.

The two boys glared at each other for the second time. Thoba noticed that Nana had raised his head and was looking fixedly at the brewing conflict.

The rain poured gently now; it registered without much intrusion in the boys' minds as a distant background to the brief but charged silence.

"It doesn't matter, anyway," said Vusi with some finality. "We beat you."

"Naw!" retorted Simangele. "You haven't beaten us yet. The game was stopped by the rain. We are carrying on after the rain."

"Who said we'll want to play after the rain?" asked Vusi.

"That's how you are," said Simangele. "I've long seen what kind you are. You never want to lose."

"Of course! Who likes to lose, anyway," said Vusi triumphantly.

There followed a tense silence, longer this time. All the boys looked at the rain, and as it faded back into their consciousness, the tension seemed to dissolve away into its sound. They crossed their arms over their chests, clutching at their shoulders firmly against the cold. They seemed lost in thought as they listened to the sound of the rain on the corrugated roofs of the township houses. It was loudest on the roof of the A.M.E.[1] church which stood some fifty yards away, at the corner of Mayaba and Thelejane Streets. The sound on this roof was a sustained, heavy patter which reverberated with the emptiness of a building that was

[1] African Methodist Episcopal.

made entirely of corrugated iron. Even when the rain was a light shower, the roar it made on the church roof gave the impression of hail. Occasionally, there would be a great gust of wind, and the noise of the rain on the roofs would increase, and a gust of sound would flow away in ripples from house to house in the direction of the wind, leaving behind the quiet, regular patter.

"If there was a service in there," said Thoba breaking the silence, and pointing towards the church with his head, "would the people hear the sermon?"

"Reverend Mkhabela has a big voice," said Mpiyakhe, demonstrating the size of the voice with his hands and his blown up cheeks.

"No voice can be bigger than thunder," said Vusi matter-of-factly.

"Who talked about thunder?" asked Simangele, and then declared emphatically, "There's no thunder out there. It's only rain out there."

"Well," said Vusi who probably had not meant his observation to be scrutinised, "it seems like thunder."

"Either there is thunder, or there is no thunder," declared Simangele.

"Exactly what do you want from me?" asked Vusi desperately. "I wasn't even talking to you."

"It's everybody's discussion," said Simangele. "So you don't have to be talking to me. But if I talk about what you have said, I will talk to you directly. So, I'm saying it again: either there is thunder there, or there is no thunder out there. And right now there is no thunder out there."

Vusi stepped away from the wall and faced Simangele, who also stepped away from the wall, faced Vusi, and waited. There was only Thoba between them. A fight seemed inevitable, and Thoba trembled, out of fear, and then also from the cold, which he could now feel even more, because it again reasserted both itself and the rain as the reasons he should have gone home in order to avoid a silly fight. He should have gone home. His mother was right. Now, he could be caught in the middle. He felt responsible for the coming danger, because he had said something that had now gone out of control.

Mpiyakhe moved away from the wall and squatted next to Nana, who was also looking at the conflict. But a fight did not occur. Vusi stepped towards the wall, rested his hands on it, and looked out at the rain. Simangele made a click of annoyance and then turned towards the wall. Mpiyakhe sprang to his feet, and everybody looked at the rain once more. Thoba desperately tried to think of something pleasant to say; something harmless.

Then he saw two horses that were nibbling at the grass that loved to grow along the fence that surrounded the church. Horses loved to nibble at that grass, thought Thoba. And when they were not nibbling at the grass, they would be rubbing themselves against the fence. They loved that too. Horses were strange creatures. They just stood in the rain, eating grass as if there was no rain at all.

"Does a horse ever catch cold?" asked Thoba, again to no one in particular. It had been just an articulated thought. But Vusi took it up with some enthusiasm.

"Ho, boy! A horse?" exclaimed Vusi. "A horse? It's got an iron skin. Hard. Tough." He demonstrated with two black bony fists. "They just don't get to coughing like people."

"Now you want to tell us that a horse can cough," said Simangele.

Nobody took that one up. The others looked at the two horses. Thoba considered Vusi's explanation, while at the same time frantically trying to find something to say before Simangele pressed his antagonism any further. An iron skin? thought Thoba, and then spoke again.

"What sound does the rain make when it falls on the

back of a horse?" But Vusi ignored the question and made another contentious statement.

"Me," said Vusi, "I don't just catch cold. Not me!" he declared.

"Now, you are telling us a lie," said Simangele. "And you know that very well."

"Now, don't ever say I tell lies," shouted Vusi.

"There's no person in this world who never gets ill," insisted Simangele.

"I never said 'never,'" Vusi defended himself. "I said, 'don't just.'"

Simangele did not pursue the matter. He had made his point. He was a year or two older than the other boys, and by far the tallest. The wall of the veranda came up to his chest. He had a lean but strong body. It was said he was like that because he was from the farms, and on the farms people are always running around and working hard all day, and they have no chance to get fat. So they become lean and strong. And when they get to the towns they become stubborn and arrogant because they don't understand things, and people laugh at them; and when people laugh at them they start fighting back. Then people say "beware of those from the farms, they will stab with a broad smile on their faces."

Simangele had lived in the township for two years now, but he was still known as the boy from the farms. And he could be deadly. Whenever there were street fights between the boys of Mayaba Street and those of Thipe Street, Simangele would be out there in front, leading the boys of Mayaba Street and throwing stones at the enemy with legendary accuracy. Sometimes Simangele would retreat during a fight, and then watch the boys of Mayaba Street being forced to retreat. Then he would run to the front again, and the enemy would retreat. And everybody would have seen the difference. Few boys ever took any chances with Simangele.

Vusi, on the other hand, was one of those boys who were good at many things. He was very inventive. He made the best bird traps, the best slings, the best wire cars; and four-three, and six-one, and five-two, always came his way in a game of dice. But it was in soccer that he was most famous. He was known to all the boys in the township, and everybody wanted to be on his side. He was nick-named after Sandlane, Charterston Rovers' great dribbling wizard, who had a deformed right hand that was perpetu-ally bent at the wrist, with the fingers stretched out firmly. And Vusi would always bend his wrist whenever the ball was in his possession. And his teammates would cheer "Sandla-a-a-ne-e-e-!" And they would be looking at his deformed hand and its outstretched fingers, dry and dusty on the outside like the foot of a hen when it has raised its leg. And Vusi would go into a frenzy of dribbling, scoring goals with that sudden, unexpected shot.

Vusi was the only boy in Mayaba Street who could stand up to Simangele. The two had never actually fought, but they had been on the brink of fighting many times. The general speculation was that Simangele really did not want to take a chance; for who knew what would happen? Vusi was known to have outbraved many boys, even those acknowledged to be stronger than he. The problem with Vusi was that he fought to the death. All the boys knew he was a dangerous person to fight with, because you would be hitting and hitting him, but Vusi would keep coming and coming at you, and you would begin to lose hope. And then he might defeat you not because he was stronger, but because he kept coming at you, and you lost all hope. That is why it was thought Simangele never wanted to go all the way. In any case, there was really nothing awesome about Simangele's bravery. He had to be brave: he was older. But Vusi? He was a wonder.

It was for this reason that Thoba was busy considering Vusi's claim that he never got ill. It sounded familiar. Vusi was like Thoba's father. He was just that kind of person. Thoba's father was not the sick type; and Thoba's mother had always told visitors that her husband was a very strong man. And since Thoba felt instinctively on Vusi's side, he felt a pressing need to bear witness, if only to establish the truthfulness of Vusi's claim.

"My own father doesn't just get ill," he declared. There was a brief silence after this and then the others began to laugh. And Thoba felt how terrible it was to be young and have no power. Whatever you said was laughed at. It was a deeply indulgent laugh that helped to blow away all the tension that had existed just before. They just laughed. It was always the case when you are not very strong, and you have to say something.

"What is he telling us, this one?" said Mpiyakhe in the middle of a guffaw. "Your family gets knocked down with all kinds of diseases. Everybody knows that. Softies, all of you. You're too higher-up. That's your problem. Instead of eating *papa*[2] and beans, you have too many sandwiches."

"Now, that is a lot of shit you are saying," said Thoba trying to work up anger to counter the laughter.

"Don't ever say that about what I'm saying," threatened Mpiyakhe.

"And what if I say it?" retorted Thoba.

"Take him on, boy, take him on," said Simangele nudging Mpiyakhe in the stomach with an elbow.

Thoba began to feel uneasy. It was strange how the conflict had suddenly shifted down to him and Mpiyakhe who were at the lower end of the pecking order among the boys of Mayaba Street. He had fought Mpiyakhe a few times, and it was never clear who was stronger. Today he would win, tomorrow he would lose. That was how it was among the weak; a constant, unresolved struggle. Why should a

[2] That is, pap, a cornmeal porridge.

simple truth about one's father lead to ridicule and then to a fight? Thoba looked at Mpiyakhe and had the impulse to rush him. Should he? What would be the result of it? But the uncertainty of the outcome made Thoba look away towards the rain. He squeezed his shoulders, and felt deeply ashamed that he could not prove his worth before Vusi and Simangele. He had to find a way to deal with his rival.

Mpiyakhe's father was a prosperous man who ran a flourishing taxi service. His house, a famous landmark, was one of the biggest in the township. If a stranger was looking for some house in that neighbourhood, he was told: "Go right down Mayaba Street until you see a big, green house. That will be Nzima's house. Once there, ask again. . . ."

Screwed on to the front gate of the big, green house was a wooden board on which was painted "Love Your Wife" in white paint. And whenever a man got into Mpiyakhe's father's taxi, he was always asked: "Do you love your wife?" Thus, Mpiyakhe's father was known throughout the township as "Love Your Wife." As a result, Mpiyakhe was always teased about his father by the boys of Mayaba Street. And whenever that happened, he would let out steam on Thoba, trying to transfer the ridicule. After all, both their families were "higher-ups" and if one family was a laughing stock the same should be applied to the other.

Thoba and Mpiyakhe were prevented from fighting by Nana, who suddenly began to cough violently. They all turned towards him. The cough was a long one, and it shook his frail body until he seemed to be having convulsions. Thoba wondered if Nana was going to die. And what would Nana's grandmother do to them if Nana died in their presence? If she healed people, surely she could kill them. Nana continued to cough. And the boys could see his head go up and down. They looked at each other anxiously as if wondering what to do. But the cough finally ceased; and when Nana looked up, there were tears in his eyes and much mucus flowing down in two lines over his lips. He swept his lower arm over his lips and nose and then rubbed it against the side of his shirt.

"You should go home," said Vusi to Nana.

"How can he go home in this rain?" said Simangele, taking advantage of Nana's refusal. Vusi turned away indignantly. Thoba wondered if he should take off his shirt and give it to Nana. But he quickly decided against it. He himself could die. He turned away to look at the rain. He saw that Vusi was looking at the horses eating grass in the rain. He saw the concentration on Vusi's face. He watched as a sudden gleam came to Vusi's eye, and Vusi slowly turned his face away from the rain to fix an ominously excited gaze on Simangele. He looked at the rain again, and then his look took on a determined intensity. He turned to Simangele again.

"Simangele," called Vusi. "How would you like to be a horse in the rain?"

"A horse in the rain?" said Simangele tentatively. He looked at Thoba and Mpiyakhe, and seemed embarrassed, as if there was something he could not understand.

"Yes, a horse in the rain," said Vusi. There was a look of triumph in his face. "Look at the horses. They are in the rain. Yet they have nothing on them. I bet you can never go into the rain without your shirt."

Simangele laughed. "That is foolishness," he said.

"No," said Vusi. "It is not foolishness." And as he spoke, Vusi was slowly pulling out his shirt without loosening the belt that held it tightly round the waist where it was tucked into the trousers. All the while he was looking steadily at Simangele.

Simangele stopped laughing and began to look uneasy. Once more he looked at Vusi and Mpiyakhe. And then he looked at Nana on the floor. Their eyes met, and

Simangele looked away quickly. Meanwhile, his jaws
tightened, Vusi was unbuttoning his shirt from the rum-
pled bottom upwards. Then he took off his shirt slowly,
exposing a thin, shining, black body, taut with strength.
Thoba felt a tremor of iciness through his body as if it was
his body that had been exposed. Vusi had thrust his chest
out and arched his arms back so that his shirt dangled from
his right hand. Soon his body was looking like a plucked
chicken.

"I'm a horse now," said Vusi. "Let's see if you too can be
a horse." He did not wait for an answer. Dropping his shirt
with a flourish, Vusi flung himself into the rain. He braced
his head against the rain and ran up Thelejane Street,
which was directly opposite Simangele's home and formed
a T-junction with Mayaba Street. Thelejane Street went
right up and disappeared in the distance. Vusi ran so fast,
he seemed to have grown shorter. Soon he was a tiny black
speck in the rain; and the far distance of the street seemed
to swallow him up. Not once did he look back.

It had all happened so suddenly, Thoba thought. Just like
the day a formation of military jets had suddenly come
from nowhere and flown low round the township a number
of times, deafening the place with noise. And then they
were gone, leaving behind a petrifying, stunned silence
which totally blocked thinking until many minutes later.

Simangele looked like someone who thought he had
enough time, but when he got to the station found that the
train was already pulling out, and that he had to suffer the
indignity of running after it. He looked at Thoba and
Mpiyakhe. They looked back. Then a wave of anger and
frustration crossed his face.

"What are you doing here on my veranda?" he yelled at
the two boys. They moved towards a corner away from
him. There was silence. Then Simangele looked at Nana.

"I didn't mean you," he said with a faint plea in his

voice. Then he looked at the small figure in the rain. It was so far now that it did not even seem to be moving. He looked at the sky. It was grey, and the rain was grey. He looked at the two boys, again. Thoba cringed, and looked well into Simangele's eyes. And then suddenly Thoba did not feel afraid any more. As he looked into Simangele's eyes, he felt a strange sense of power over Simangele. Simangele did not want to go into the rain, but he would go, because Thoba was looking at him. Mpiyakhe was looking at him with those large eyes. And they had all been there when Simangele was challenged. He would have to go.

Slowly, and seemingly with much pain, Simangele fingered the buttons of his shirt. He unbuttoned only the three upper buttons and pulled the shirt over his head. Just then, a gust of wind swept the rain, making it sound harder on the roofs of houses. Simangele shuddered. He threw his shirt on the floor and then stretched his leg out into the rain and watched his grey, dry skin turn brown and wet. Then he eased himself into the rain. He shivered, and that made him seem to decide he had better run. He was out there now, running in the street, following Vusi. But his strides were much less confident than Vusi's magnanimous strides. Simangele jumped over puddles where his challenger had just waded in and out of them like a galloping horse. Thoba and Mpiyakhe watched him in silence until he vanished into the distance.

Thoba and Mpiyakhe moved out of the corner at the same time, and went to stand before the low wall. They stood there looking at the streets in silence. Thoba became aware that he was stealing glances at Mpiyakhe. Of course he was not afraid of him. Yes, indeed, Mpiyakhe was stealing glances at him too. But now that there were only the two of them, there really seemed no reason to quarrel. There was nobody else to entertain at the expense of each other. Nana? Thoba looked at him. Their eyes met. He looked away. Wouldn't questions be asked later? What did Thoba and Mpiyakhe do after Vusi and Simangele had run into the rain to settle scores? Weren't Thoba and Mpiyakhe known rivals? And then there was Nana to tell the story. There was the rain. There were the empty streets. It was cold out there. But there could be glory out there for a shirtless boy.

Thoba wondered if he should issue a challenge. That was certainly attractive. But less attractive was the ordeal of running in the rain. But there was no thunder. Only water. That's all. No lightning to fear. Only water falling from sky. What was water? Only water. And the cold? Once he was out there he would forget about it, because he would be involved in the running. That's the trick. The horses went on eating wet grass. They were involved. How was the sound of the rain on the back of a horse? What sound would the rain make on a boy's body?

Thoba and Mpiyakhe looked at each other again, only to look away once more. Clearly there was something they could not confront. When Thoba stole a glance at Mpiyakhe through the corner of his eye, he noticed that Mpiyakhe was looking at him. When Mpiyakhe finally spoke, it was slowly and tentatively.

"Do you . . ." he asked, "do you want to go into the rain?"

Thoba pretended he had not heard, and continued to look at the rain. But then he broke into a smile, and turned his face to look at Mpiyakhe. Mpiyakhe had not issued a challenge. He had not. He had merely asked a question. Here was an uneasy boy who was trying to persuade him into an intimate truce. Here was a boy who assumed there were mutual fears; who did not know for sure. Here was a boy asking his way into a compromise. This boy did not deserve an answer.

Slowly and deliberately, and with a gleam in his eye, Thoba unbuttoned his shirt, and as he pulled it over his head, he felt the warmth of his breath on his chest. And that gave him a momentary impression of dreaming, for he had a clear image of Vusi taking off his shirt. But the image did not last; it was shattered by the re-emergence of his head into the cold. He shivered as goose pimples literally sprang out on his skin before his eyes. But he would have to be reckless. That was bravery. Bravery meant forgetting about one's mother.

Thoba threw his shirt on to the floor where it joined Vusi's and Simangele's. And the last thing he did before he burst into the rain was look at Nana, as if pleading for approval. Their eyes met. Those were the eyes he would carry in his mind into the rain, as if the whole township was looking at him. Mpiyakhe? He did not even deserve a glance.

When the cold water of the rain hit him, Thoba had the impulse to run back on to the veranda. But when he got into the street, he felt nothing but exhilaration. There was something freeing in the tickling pressure of the soft needles of rain on his skin. And then he ran in spurts: running fast and slowing down, playing with the pressure of the rain on him. It was a pleasant sensation; a soft, pattering sensation. And the rain purred so delicately against his ears. And when he waded in and out of puddles, savouring the recklessness, it was so enchanting to split the water, creating his own little thunder from the numerous splashes. He was alone in the street with the rain. He was shirtless in the rain. How many people were watching him from the protective safety of their houses? How many? They were sitting round their kitchen stoves, taking no challenges. Mpiyakhe? Was he watching him? Of course. Mpiyakhe, the vanquished. Everybody would know. Vusi and Simangele would know that he, Thoba, had bravely followed them into the cold rain.

He passed the A.M.E. church and crossed Thipe Street. Where were the boys of that street? They would not come out to fight on such a day. Weaklings, the lot of them. Up he went, crossing Ndimande Street. Where were the boys of that street? Weaklings too. They were not in the rain.

He ran up towards the crèche now. He had been there as a child, when he was younger than he was now. Would he be recognized from the windows as the man who had been there as a child? Would the matron see him? Would she say, "There is my little man?" Should he slow down and be seen? No. The man broke into a sprint. Wouldn't it be better for them to say, "Doesn't that look like Thoba?" They wouldn't be sure. That way they would think about him a little longer, trying to be sure. He wished he were a blur. The wind and the water! He could not feel them any more, for they had dissipated into the sustained alacrity of speed.

Beyond the crèche was the Dutch Reformed Church, and beyond that, far out of the township, were the rugged, rocky hills where men and women always went in pairs, on Sunday afternoons. Thoba slowed down somewhat. If he ran further up the street, he would get nearer those hills, and one could never be sure about those hills. It was said there was a beast there which swallowed up little children, especially in bad weather. He wondered if Vusi and Simangele had gone further up. No, he would not go towards the hills. Thoba passed the church, but instead of going up, he turned left into Twala Street. Even though he could outrun the beast, it would be foolish to go nearer it first.

As he turned into Twala Street, he tried to increase his speed once more, but noted with faint anxiety that he was unable to. He was slowing down now, and that was not good. He was very far from home now. Did he reach the limits of his endurance so soon? And yet the surge of exhilaration was definitely beginning to fade away. But he would have to keep up the pace at least until the crèche was well out of sight. Why did people tire? Did Vusi tire, or did he run all the way? There was no sign of him. Maybe it was the Dutch Reformed Church; he shouldn't have looked at it. He should have closed his eyes when he passed it, for that was the church of ill luck. Everybody said so. But he would have to run, all the same. At least until the crèche was well out of sight. And as soon as he made that commitment, Thoba suddenly felt as he had the day his mother had beaten him with a wet dishcloth for cracking open an egg that had a half-formed chick in it.

Thoba had vowed that he would cry until his father came back home to deal with his mother. His father did not come. So long after the tears and the anger had gone, Thoba had continued to cry with his voice only. It had been painful in his throat and somewhere in his chest. And now, as he continued to run, Thoba realised that the fire was going out of him. There was left only the pain of tiring legs. Yet, he was too far from home to tire. He looked back briefly. The crèche was out of sight; and just then, the tiredness assailed him. He could feel the ache in his calves. He slowed down to an easy trot. If only he could reach Nala Street; that would take him back home.

Then he became conscious of the sound of water rushing down in two streams on the sides of the street, towards the Dutch Reformed Church. His eyes followed the direction of the water until he saw the church in the distance back there. He turned away quickly. What would happen if the water went into the church and flooded it? Would it float like Noah's ark?

When he turned left at Mosotwana Street, he saw Nala Street some five houses away. And only then did he realise why he had heard the sound of the rushing streams so clearly. It had stopped raining. There was a heavy stillness

around him, for the roofs of houses had gone silent. And
the sound of rushing water made the streams sound bigger
than they actually were. He began to feel exposed. He
broke his trot and walked, arms akimbo. He was tired, and
the rain was as embarrassingly tired, for it was now falling
in tiny droplets as weak as the sprays at the edge of a water-
fall. There was no one else in the street, not even a stray
dog. And then he began to feel cold.

He was about three houses from Nala Street when a
familiar taxi turned into Mosotwana Street, forcing him to
run towards the nearest fence away from danger. He wondered if Mpiyakhe's father had seen him. Thoba stopped,
rested his arms on the fence, so that those in the taxi could
see only his back. He enjoyed the wonderful sensation of
stillness. But that was not to last very long. The taxi
stopped only about ten yards away from Thoba. A man got
off and ran into the next house as if he thought it was still
raining. Thoba heard Mpiyakhe's father shout after the
man: "Love your wife!" In a few seconds, the taxi started
up, but it did not go forward; instead it reversed and
stopped about two yards from Thoba. Thoba froze. So the
man had recognised him.

"Hey, boy!" shouted Mpiyakhe's father. "Are you not
teacher Mbele's son?"

Thoba turned his head and nodded. The passengers in
the taxi were all looking at him. Why did Mpiyakhe's father
not leave him alone?

"Yes, I thought so," said Mpiyakhe's father. "Do your
parents know you are here?"

Thoba looked away and did not answer.

"Boy, I'm talking to you."

Thoba looked at the man again. His head was sticking
out of the driver's open window. What would happen if
another car came and the head was still sticking out?
Surely that head would be sliced off.

"Boy, I'm talking to you."

First it was Mpiyakhe; now it was his father.

"Now get into this car, and let me take you home."

It could not be. To be taken home like a drenched chicken! To be taken home in his enemy's car! It could not be. His own feet would carry him home.

"Come on. Get into the car."

Thoba began to walk away.

"Boy, I will not let your parents accuse me of killing you!"

Thoba continued to trudge away.

"Boy, get into this car!"

Nothing would stop him.

"You all saw him defy me, didn't you!"

When Thoba heard the engine of the car revving up, he tried to run. But he needn't have: the car went on its way in the opposite direction. Thoba ran for only a few yards before he reached Nala Street.

When he looked down Nala Street in the far distance, Thoba saw something which discouraged him further. Two buses were lugging up slowly towards the township. They were the first afternoon buses bringing workers who knocked off early. If only he could reach the bus stop and pass it before the buses got there. If not it would be embarrassing. All those people! What would they say? What was a shirtless boy doing in the cold rain? But the pain in the calves. The pain in the thighs. He just wanted to stand still. Then he began to shiver violently. It always got colder after the rain. He must move on. But try as he might, he could not run. He knew then that he would never beat the buses to the bus stop. And by the time they got there, and the passengers were streaming out of them like ants, Thoba was still very far from the bus stop, and would surely meet the workers coming up.

And he saw them: the bulk of them. Women. They knocked off early. That was their problem. They were coming up: a disordered column of women with shopping

bags balanced on their heads. He would meet them somewhere in the middle of the street. If only he could run so
fast that when he passed them, they would be a blur to
him; and he would be a blur to them. He knew he
wouldn't make it. He felt so exposed: shirtless; shoeless; a
wet body in a dripping pair of pants that clung tightly and
coldly to him. They would surely see the outline of his
buttocks. And his penis? Would they see it too? That
would be worse.

Indeed, there was mother Mofokeng, one of Thoba's
mother's many friends. Everybody knew his mother.
Mother Mofokeng would certainly recognise him. Then he
stepped on to a pointed stone. At first the pain was dull,
but once it cut through his almost iced foot, it tore up to
his chest. He jerked to a stop, grimacing with pain, as he
raised the hurt foot ever so slightly as if he wanted to keep
it on the ground at all costs. He felt like a sleeping horse
when it lifts one hoof a fraction from the ground. He was
far from home. And he felt tears forming in his eyes. But
he fought them back by blinking repeatedly.

"Wonder of wonders!" exclaimed mother Mofokeng.
"What am I seeing? God in heaven what am I seeing?
Curse me if this isn't the nurse's child!"

"Which nurse?" asked another mother.

"Staff nurse Mbele's son," said mother Mofokeng.

"Is this the nurse's child? He looks so much like her!"

"Son," inquired mother Mofokeng, "what are you doing
here in the cold?"

Thoba looked at her, and then looked at the battered
leather shopping bag balanced on her head. It was bulging
with vegetables. Some spinach and carrots were peeping
from a hole on the side.

"Here's a child who will die of cold," said a mother who
had just joined the crowd.

"And you think his mother would know better," said
another.

"Where's your shirt, son?" asked mother Mofokeng.

"This is what I've always maintained about school holidays," said another. "You are busy working your heart out at the white man's, and your children are busy running wild. I don't know why they have these holidays."

"And in this weather of all weathers in the world," said another.

"Woman!" exclaimed another. "I'm telling you, what else can you do with children?"

How could Thoba explain? Should he walk away or continue to listen? The questions were piling up; being as many as there were women returning from work. He would wait. Surely it would be disrespectful to walk away from elders. Yet the questions came; and the piercing cold; and the stinging pain of muscles. His teeth began to chatter.

"Whose child is this?"

"Shame! What happened to him?"

"Where's his shirt? Did anybody take your shirt, son?"

"Who has done this sin?"

"Leave the child alone! Run home, son!"

"It's so easy to die!"

"Exposure!"

"Sponge wet. Look how the trousers cling to him."

"Women of the township! Why don't you leave this child alone?"

Thoba had crossed his arms across his chest as if that way he could create some heat. Better the rain than the cold which follows it. He was far from home, and the women had created a cordon of humiliation around him. Then he felt two thin lines of heat flowing down his cheeks. His tears had betrayed him. And the eyes grew painful. Instead of the speed he had desired, it was now tears that had turned the women into a blur. He could not see them now. That was the time to leave.

"Here's my jersey, son," said mother Mofokeng. "Bring it back tomorrow."

Thoba felt the warm wool settle on his shoulders. But he had begun to move. And he saw the forms before him part; and then came a grey emptiness. He limped away, wounded with sympathy. A few feet away from the women, he impulsively began to run. He did not see where he was going; as he picked up speed, the jersey slipped from his shoulders. And he heard the countless voices of women shouting: "It has slipped! It has fallen! Pick it up! The jersey has fallen! Pick it up, son! Stop him! Stop him!" Thoba broke into a sprint. It was the most satisfying sprint, for it was so difficult, so painful. It had led him out of humiliation.

When he finally cleared his eyes with the back of his hand, Thoba realised that he was at the junction where Nala, Moshoeshoe, and Ndimande Streets met. Just across the street was the Police station. More buses were coming up. More women were coming. Thoba definitely felt no pain now. He flew past the Police station, the bus stop, Thipe Street . . . Mayaba Street was the next. Where were the boys of Mayaba Street? Would they be waiting for his return? As he took the corner into Mayaba Street, Thoba increased his speed; and, spreading his arms out like the wings of an aeroplane, he banked into Mayaba Street.

The street was as empty as he had left it at the other end. No Vusi, no Simangele, no Mpiyakhe, no Nana. No boys had come out yet to race little twigs on the streamlets in the street. Was anybody looking through the window? Was Mpiyakhe, the vanquished, still on the veranda? Or had his father rescued him? Thoba wondered if he should run on to the veranda to collect his shirt. No. Let it lie there on the floor of the veranda of Simangele's home. It would be tomorrow's testimony.

There was no one at home yet when Thoba arrived. He would have to make the fire before his mother came. But the stillness inside his home suddenly made him feel lonely, and all the pain came back again. No, he would not make the fire. Let his mother do whatever she liked with him. He would not make the fire. He passed on from the kitchen into his bedroom. There, he took off his trousers, and left them in a wet little heap on the floor close to his bed. He felt dry, but cold, as he slipped into the blankets. He felt warm, deep inside him. And as he turned over in bed, looking for the most comfortable position, he felt all the pain. But, strangely enough, he wished he could turn around as many times as possible. There was suddenly something deeply satisfying and pleasurable about the pain. And as he slid into a deep sleep, he smiled, feeling so much alive.

HOW, WHY TO GET RICH—
LESSON #1

༄

(United States)

by J. California Cooper

Whoever works without knowledge works uselessly.
  — African Proverb

I don't like money actually, but it quiets my nerves.
  — Joe Louis (boxer, 1914–81)

You know, I'm just a kid, but I got nerves, and sometimes grown-up people just really get on em! Like always talkin about how kids don't have no sense "in these days." Like they got all the last sense there was to get. Everybody with some sense knows that if grown-up people had so much sense the whole world wouldn't be in the shape it's in today!

Cause don't nobody in the world seem to get along together, nowhere. Not even here, where they sposed to have most of the sense!

I came up, long with some war. It's so many wars you can't always remember which one. My mama and daddy moved to the big city to get rich workin at one of them shipyards. Gramma too. It was real exciting coming, drivin all cross the country of the United States. Coming to where the streets was paved with gold and all everybody was makin money. We was gonna save up a lot of it and go home. Change our lives, Daddy said. Get rich.

Well, we didn't get rich or nothing like it. We got changed, tho. We got a lot of other things, too. Like separated and divorced. Daddy met one of them ladies out from under one of them weldin hats was workin at the shipyard. And Mama was sweet-talked, or somethin, by somebody else was workin in the same shipyard! They sposed to be makin boats and ships and things down there and it look like they mostly made love and troubles, breakin up families!

Daddy's lady like to party and stuff, so lotta our saving money went out that way. And him and Mama began to fuss and fight a lot, with Gramma runnin round sayin, "Now you all, now you all. . . ." But it didn't help nothin.

Then, Mama put him out and locked the door one night after he got off the "night shift." See, he really worked days. We had to move then, cause our money was cut in half or just even way down.

After while we moved into some cockroach's house. I don't know was it because of bein poor or nothin, maybe just cause it so crowded round here. Ain't hardly no place to rent near bout nice as our house what we was buyin back home what we left from to come out here and get rich.

Mama kept workin, naturally, and Gramma took to workin part-time domestic. It was just the three of us then, but things were high-priced and soon Gramma had to work full-time cause Daddy didn't bring no money much.

You could see everybody if you stayed out in the streets long enough, so I used to hang around places where he might be going to. Bars, gamblin shacks, Bar-B-Q shops. When I see him on the street he would always go in his pocket and give me some money, a big kiss and a hug. But not Mama. He wouldn't give her nothin, he said, cause she had a man-friend now. I didn't see no sense in that cause I was his child and he was the only man-friend in my life. Help me! But he didn't, if I didn't catch him.

Gramma didn't like Mama's man-friend so, soon, Mama was stayin away over to his room and it was just Gramma and me. Gramma tryin to work and make me a home so I'd be a good girl and grow up to be a good woman, and me tryin to catch my daddy on the streets with his bad woman for that extra five or ten dollars he would give me. This new place didn't have no streets paved with gold for us, but it sure did change our life. If I was a cussin person I could tell you what my Gramma says the streets are paved with!

Then, Gramma's other children who had come out here started havin problems too. Either the mama or the daddy left and each one sent their children to live with us. With us! There was two, both boys.

Our life changed some more. Scuffelin round with Gramma on what chores everybody else ought to do, who ate the most, got the dirtiest jobs and things like that. We all went to school. And we were poorer than ever. People sure can forget their kids! Just love em and leave em. They knew we had to eat and Gramma was workin hard as she could. We was poor. Government said we wasn't, but it sure felt like poor to us!

About this gettin rich, it's very easy to understand why anyone wants to be rich. One big reason, for us, was we was poor, black, and living in a ghetto. All three of us, my two fourteen-year-old boy cousins and thirteen-year-old me, were single children. That is we had one parent each . . . Gramma.

I will call one "John" (the slick one) and the other one "Doe" (the kinda dumb one), and you can call me "Einstein" cause I was the smart one. Now Doe had come from the country, but John and me were from the city; leastways, a little city close to a big City. We always had the ideas, Doe was a hard worker, but very lazy at it.

Anyway, going on a paper route in the mornings (I went along to manage things because my grandmother had to have absolute peace and quiet to sleep as late as she could before we helped her cook breakfast and she went to work), we always saw this gang of people on the street corner. Befuddled, dirty, poor-lookin, some winos, stuff like that, waiting for the bus to haul them to the country to pick fruit or something like that all day. Then they would be brought back to the same corner where they all began to stuff their hands in their pockets, hunch their shoulders and walk hurriedly away, kinda a tired hurry.

Now, we knew they must have made some money and were rushing off to buy things with it! So, one morning I asked the bus driver how the job went, you know, how much and all? Well, he said fifteen cents a sack or a box depending on what was picked. That sounded pretty good to me when I thought of my two big strong cousins, so I asked what we had to do to get the job. The answer was to get a social security card and be on the corner at 5:00 A.M.

I thought about that for a week or so, then held a meeting and we all went down and lied and got our social security cards. I said I was twenty-six years old, so you know that was some government worker who wasn't thinking bout nothin cause she gave me my card and after my two cousins lied, gave them theirs, too!

We rushed home and explained everything to our grandmother, who listened and laughed a little when she told us that was hard work. Wellll, we know ALL work was hard to her so that didn't stop us!

She gave us some money to buy bologny and some other stuff after we arranged to pay her back. We fixed our lunches in the best happy mood we had been in, in a long time! We made a beautiful fat bologny sandwitch each and a piece of fruit; set them neatly in the refrigerator with our names printed neatly on each bag. We then went to bed to sleep, dreamin of all the money we were going to have!

I even counted up to maybe a year between the three of

us and we could let me keep the money, some of it, save it and then maybe find a little business we could go into to get away from cockroach alley, the dirty looking characters and the winos round here. Set Gramma down. Not have to wait around waitin to catch my daddy. I had all our lives planned. I slept good that night!

Anyway, we woke up early, ate a little cold cereal, grabbed our lunches and rushed to the corner. Wellll, the bus was halfway down the block, leaving us! We screamed and hollored, but to no avail, cause he kept right on truckin. Oh! We were mad! And disgusted! After we got through blaming each other, we went home and got ready to eat our lunches when Gramma told us we better save em for the next day if we was gonna try again cause she wasn't buying no more! See? I knew I had to get rich! We sat the lunches in the refrigerator and went on out to get the papers we had stashed and deliver them to the people who almost didn't get them!

The next morning we skipped the cereal and rushed to the corner, but they were gone again! My Lord!! We were mad! We went home and put our lunches back in the frig. You know them sandwitches were beginning to turn up at the edges! Much less the fruit! We ate that soggy fruit stuff on the way home in the dark morning. We hardly spoke for half a day or so . . . we all blamed each other.

The next morning, the THIRD one, we didn't even go to the bathroom or nothin. Went to bed dressed and ready and got up, grabbed them beat-out tired lunch bags and made it to the bus . . . on time.

Now, there was a very disgusting group we were goin with and we felt so superior to them mentally and physically. We knew we would be the champs that whole year and we laughed at them and everything! Especially one old lady who looked like she was 109 years old.

We just laughed at everything! We almost rolled in the

aisle of the bus, but we kept it down except for that piece of laugh that sometimes busts out in spite of all you can do to hold it in!

One old wino-lookin man was telling everybody bout his experience as a picker and everything he said he would add, "Don't you know? Don't you know?" That cracked us up! We didn't listen to what he said, just how he said it. We found out later we shoulda just listened to what he was sayin.

Well, daylight was coming fast now, and the farther we drove, the hotter it was gettin to be. It didn't look hot, but when that big, ole red sun shone down on you through that ole dusty window, it was hot! The scenery was nice tho. You know, space and trees and a big sky and all. To a city kid, it was different. It was good. Like back home. I had forgot I missed it, with all the other stuff I had to have on my mind. We finally just relaxed and enjoyed it. I know it's some birds in the city, but we could SEE these, justa flying way out all over in the sky. The tall trees wavin and stretchin, like us, in the morning sun. And the sky . . . the sky was so clear . . . and blue. I got so relaxed and dreamy, I even dozed off a few times. Doe slept. John was still sniggling at the old wino til I told him to quit it cause he was nudging me with his elbow, lettin me know to listen to somethin and all I wanted, at that time, was to look out the dirty window and dream about stuff.

Anyway after bout two hours or so, the bus arrived at a field and we stretched quickly and flexed our muscles and jumped off. We were ready! Ready to get started on our big money! Everybody else just walked off, natural like. We grabbed two or three sacks each and told the man to point to our part. He said, "You all kin take any part but just stay in this section." Okey!!

It was an onion field. We started right in diggin and pullin them onions to load our sacks just like we was throwin money in them sacks. We threw the extra sacks around our necks, but in two minutes that sun was so hot on our backs we threw them sacks off, watching where, so we would know how far we had to come back for them. We were organized!

Well, fifteen minutes later the bus driver came out and, waving his hands over his head, he hollered, "Wrong field, wrong field!" and pointed toward the bus to let us know to head back. Oh shit! we said to the sun (and we didn't even curse much usually). He continued, "Throw em down, leave em here!" We said to each other, "Not us! Hell, this is hard work!" Everybody else must have said the same thing cause everybody took a few onions out and threw them on the ground, then took their sacks on the bus with them. My cousin John, the city boy, grabbed all ours back when nobody was looking and some of the other ones too! He got on the bus with onions falling every-whichaway, saying they were all his.

Now, that onion smell . . . in that hot bus . . . was over-powering, so we were really glad to get to the right field. That took about ten minutes or so, then we were hopping out to get going again!

The sun wasn't even up very high, maybe it was about 9:30, but it was like it had been up there shining all week! I wanted to take some of my clothes off! But I'm a girl, and a lady, as my grandmama taught me, so I kept em on, even that thick cotton undershirt she had made me put on. Chile, I was hot!

We got started. The field was still onions. I stayed close to my cousins because the 109-year-old lady and I were the only two women and she didn't get no eye action, but the men seemed to look at me a lot from under their hats. See, I kinda had a little bust line, you know. So I was careful to stay close to protection should anybody lose their mind out there lookin at my new shape I was gettin! Anyway, now we could go to work for real.

Don't you ever let anyone tell you that an onion is smooth! You had to pull so hard to get them things out of the ground! My smooth, young skin started comin off on them onions. I went over to the bus man and asked for a knife to dig them with and he asked me, "How old are you?"

I lied, "Sixteen."

He said, "That ain't old enough, you have to be eighteen." He smiled with some yellow teeth between his cracked lips.

Darn! I hadn't lied enough! So I gave him a mean look and went on back to my row and my sack. I had about half a sack only. John and Doe were not too much further ahead of me, but everybody else was on their second row and their third or fourth bag! The 109-year-old lady even was workin on her third sack! Maybe she was only a hundred years old!

Well, anyway, at lunch time, two and a half hours later, I had a bag and a half. John had two bags and Doe had about two and a half! I know John had stole some of them onions from the other sacks when he went to start a new row. At fifteen cents a sack, we had made ninety cents! Altogether.

Ach! (This picking was teaching me how to speak German.) We only had three hours more to go and it was goin to cost us $1.25 each to pay for the bus trip! Ach! We hadn't asked Gramma for no money because that didn't make sense! WE were going to make plenty money! Besides, she would have screamed anyway. One, for waking her up, and two, for the money. The hundred-year-old lady had fifteen sacks. Fifteen! All by herself!

Lunch time. We got our lunch bags from the bus and looked for some shade. Quick as we wipe the sweat away it would come right back. It was hot, hot, HOT! I have to say it three times! We were hot, sweaty and dirty and tired. Oh Lord, we was tired. My hands were raw. The sack was heavy and only half-filled. I had to lug mine with me everywhere just to keep my own cousins from takin any.

We looked at each other and we almost cried! But . . . we were too strong for that. Besides, nobody wanted to be first to cry. We all knew one thing tho . . . we HAD to get enough onions to get home. That $1.25 each!

We opened our lunch bags (under no shade) and those bologny sandwitches were almost rolls, they had turned up so far! The lettuce, an ugly shade of greenish-brown, we threw away. The tomato, we just sqwished and threw in the dirt (even the birds flew away from em). We ate the rest.

Then a bean lunch truck drove up. Those beans were smelling GOOD! All over that field! And we didn't have any money! Now . . . I knew enough to know that some of those men had been eyeing me all day and so I just walked over to the bean truck and stood there lookin like a hungry fool. My cousins just stood back and watched me. Somebody beckoned me to the bean window, but I shook my head with the saddest face I could make, I wasn't playin either, and said I didn't have any money. After a little while, the wino-lookin older man bought me a bowl of beans. A whole bowl of beans! Oh! they smelled so good! I smiled down at them and almost screamed with delight as I walked away from the man, thanking him. I even forgot how hot and tired I was. Only for a minute tho.

I had swallowed two mouthfulls when I felt the heat from the peppers. The stuff was loaded with peppers! Flames seemed to, and did, come out on my breath! I wished I was still starvin again. I gave the bowl to my cousins who began to fight over it as I rushed to the water can! I was still drinking water when they got there in a little while and pushed me away from the water. Them beans was hot! Now we were burning up on the outside from the sun and on the inside from the beans. We were broke and had about six sacks between us! I went to sit on the bus, mad, to try to think this out, since I am the one with the brains. I snatched that paper contract we had signed, that the busman gave me a copy of, from my pocket and started to read the fine print. Could they leave us out here, God only knows where? If we didn't have the dollar twenty-five each? You had to pay them when they paid you, just before you left for home. Home. Oh, home, home, home. Oh, Gramma, Gramma, sweet Mama, sweet Daddy. I woulda cried cept I had to save my strength. But my heart felt like it was too big for my chest, and it hurt to swallow.

My associates came on the bus to get the lowdown and I gave it to them! We had to have the money. As we sat there, I looked out the window and saw the old lady; she had bout eighteen sacks or more now. That beat-up old lady! She had gone back to work early! She was taking care of her business. You know? I looked at that old lady and I respected her! I respected her because she was doing what she had to do and she was doing it good!

I turned back to my problems cause I meant to solve em and respect myself too.

I looked at my cousins . . . two of my problems! I told em where we all stood. Doe, the country cousin, went back out there and really started packing those onions. John, the city cousin, went out there to see whose onions he could steal; his eyes darting back and forth over the people in the field. My grandmama say you can just about tell who is gonna go to jail in life, just by watchin what people do in their daily livin. I began to understand her more. Then, I went to talk to the busman and show him my sore, raw hands, so I could get some sympathy and maybe a free ride home, but he was busy, he said, so I got my sack and started digging onions again, with tears in my eyes and evil in my heart!

I don't know where they got that song from, "Shine On, Harvest MOON," cause I will never forget that sun shining on me in that harvest. We really worked, tho. Doe was tryin to tear up those rows, and John was stealin so fast that a man stopped him and musta told him a few hard things that made him see the benefit of diggin his own onions cause he did work a few rows of his own for awhile. For awhile. No-body wanted to walk home after this hot, bone-tired day. We didn't talk, laugh or even smile any-more. Cause wasn't nothin funny no more.

Well . . . we got on the bus when it was time to go home. Somehow we had made it! We had thirteen cents over the fare. Don't ask me how. Just thirteen cents, thats all. We sat with our mouths poked out all the way home. Thinking hard.

We had never really thought about labor and unions and all that stuff. Or given too much attention to the civil rights movements, cause it didn't seem to touch us too much where we lived. But, now, we noticed there were not but two white people on the bus. All the rest of us were black, with a few mexicans, I guess, all colored in some way. But all poor, even the white ones.

I looked at that hundred-year-old lady who had worked so hard. She might have been twenty years old for all I knew. Just tired and wore out, thats all! A hundred years worth of tired! My respect grew and something else I didn't know what to call it.

I tried to give the man who had bought the beans for me the thirteen cents, but he just shook his head, "No." Said, "Help somebody else on down the road someday." Then cracked his face into a kinda smile and waved me on away.

We were even too tired to doze off after we were crumbled in our seats. We didn't see the trees and the sky on our way home. But I'm glad the space was out there . . . we needed it in that old, creaking, rattling, heaving bus that was hot and funky with the sweat of a hard day's "honest" work.

But there was something more . . . the smell of poor . . . the smell of somebody's home being worse than those fields. Some had packed a few onions in their pockets or lunch bags. What, I wondered, would they buy with that body-breaking little money to go with those onions? I felt something . . . something but I don't know what it was. It was just there in my mind.

My grandmama, even my mama, my daddy had done this kinda work a little. I didn't want to talk about it. I just wanted to be quiet and feel it til I knew what it was. It felt a little like resignation . . . I seemed to catch it from the people in the bus. Something in me refused it. I changed it to indignation. For myself.

When we got off the bus at home, I knew why the people walked hurriedly away. To rest . . . and forget, until tomorrow or . . . death, I guess. I don't know. I only know that day has made me think so hard. So hard.

We started home with the thirteen cents. Somehow, I started crying and they almost did, until we started laughing. Then we each took a penny and threw it in the street. Then we almost cried again from our aching bones, til we laughed again. We finally got home and told Gramma about it. She laughed so hard at us, we got mad at her and cried til we couldn't help laughing at each other.

She made us bathe. We didn't want to, we just wanted to fall out in the bed. After, we were glad we had washed all the onion, dirt and sweat off. Gramma gave us a good hot meal, store bought, then we hit that bed and I believe I was sleep midair on my way to the pillow. Gramma said we all snored like old men.

We always have to go to church every Sunday, whether we feel like it or not because Gramma says we have to learn what road to take in life. Nowwww, I understand what that means a little better, cause I'm not takin that road out to them fields again! Not if I can help it! We like God too, I guess, because when we really couldn't think of what to spend that dime on and how hard we had worked for it, we decided to give it to Him. I don't know what the preacher did with it, but we gave it to God.

I don't know what John and Doe thought, but I said a prayer for that hundred-year-old lady, then for the man who bought the beans, then broke down and included them all. But the last thing I said to God was, "Please, please, don't let me make my life like that. Please."

Lately, I pay more attention to the labor and black movements. Or just poor people movements. Maybe I would be a labor official or something where you have some say bout what you do. I don't know. All I do know is I don't ever want to go pick nothing in no field no more unless it is my field, my own. Or I was the boss.

You know, you don't have to be white to be president of anything. Even of the United States. I could be president! Black as I am! And if you white and poor, you don't have to be rich to get to be president either.

I could be president! Even being a girl, a lady. Cause some of these laws and rules got to be changed!

I think about life too . . . my mama . . . my daddy. Maybe there is a reason or something for why they act like they do when they be working and tryin to make a livin. Separating and divorcin and all. They got to go out there and do it everyday! Work! I only did it for one day . . . and I was so tired and evil. I even cried, only for a minute tho.

Oh, I don't know. But I understand more what my grandmama is tryin to teach me. I remember that hundred-year-old lady!

Yea. I think about all those things now.

I think I'm gonna hate onions for a long, long time, too.

And dumb boys.

Yes . . . I'm doing a lot of thinking. On how to get rich. Even just how to make a real good livin for my life! Cause I already know why.

JOHNNY BLUE

꧁

(Australia)

by Archie Weller

*Greater love has no one than this, than to lay down one's
life for one's friends.*
                    — John 15:13

No one liked Johnny Blue much. They reckoned he was
a larrikin, a rebel and a lout.

But I liked Johnny all the time he was here, because he
was the Nyoongah's[1] mate, and mine especially. The only
person who ever understood me and the only white bloke
to notice me as a human instead of just a hunk of meat
who could run fast.

You see, when me old man went to jail, Mum and me
moved down the country because now me old man was a
crim like, us Maguires had got a bad name. So we moved
to Quarranocking.

There wasn't much at Quarra: only a school, a pub, a
store, and a few houses settled in the yellow dust like a
flock of tired cockatoos. We went and lived down the
camp, near the river with the other Nyoongahs, and Mum
sent me to school.

All of the other kids there, most of them off farms, was
older than me, and brainier and bigger too, so, being
coloured as well, I got smacked up first day out. That's
what the kids down these little towns is like.

---

[1] Once the name of the Bibbulmum people of Southwest Australia, Nyoongah
has come to mean any Aborigine—as black Australians are called as a whole—
who is part white. Aborigine, or aboriginal, literally means "from the beginning" and is used to refer to the people who were the original inhabitants of a
land. The Australian Aborigines are not a monolithic group but represent many
different peoples with related, but distinct, cultures.

There was these two big blokes pushing me around when, out of the shadows where I hadn't seen him stepped this cruel big bloke and says, quiet like,

"Youse buggers let the kid alone and fight me."

Well, I see the big bloke's got a name about, because the two bullies let go of me like I was a tiger snake, and scooted off. Then the big bloke said, "What's ya name, skinny ribs?"

So I says back me name, which is Jesse Maguire, then he said, "Well my name's Johnny Blue, but I got others what people call me, whenever they find sumpin's missin'." Then he laughed. An' I reckon he sounded like a kookaburra.[2]

Then he tells me to come and sit in the shade and have a fag,[3] so I do. He was me mate from that very day and us two stuck together like feathers on a bird.

He was the only white bloke ever to show any real kindness to me, except perhaps me dad. Most white blokes have always pushed me round until sports days or footie[4] seasons come around, then they lay off and even suck up because I'm a good runner.

But in Quarranocking no one touched me while I was Johnny's mate. Once Eddie Callanan tried to fight me when he reckoned Johnny wasn't around. But he was, and he came in like a cornered boomer.[5] He gave a right that lifted Callanan off his feet, then a haymaker to the Irish kid's belly that laid him stiff as a board.

That was one of the things I admired about me cobber.[6] He could fight like a bunch of wildcats and he was as game as a dozen Ned Kellys.[7]

Like the time he jumped off Dogger's Ledge, sixty feet

[2] A kingfisher.
[3] A cigarette.
[4] A sport with similarities to soccer and rugby.
[5] Something exceptionally large, like a huge animal.
[6] Buddy, pal.
[7] Ned Kelly was a 19th-century bandit who became a folk hero. The saying "To be as game as Ned Kelly" means to be very brave.

into the waterhole, just for something to do, or when he fought five chicken kids who reckoned they would have a chance of beating him in a mob. But he laid them flat, every one of them, on his own. Or when he kicked the priest's gate down because the father had abused his mum.

No one else would have touched the priest because most of them was Catholics anyhow. Besides, the priest would go straight to the town cop, who was another mick, if anyone even gave him so much as a dirty look. But this didn't stop Johnny after he come home and found his mum howling.

Johnny really loved his old mum, but he never liked his dad, who was always drunk, fat, dirty and vicious. He was bigger and stronger than Johnny, too, so the kid got hell. Once when he come to school with a real beaut black eye he swore to me he'd get his old man one day.

Johnny was kind to all us Nyoongahs. He was a real good carpenter and made ripper toys for us, like the hill trolley he made for the Innitts, which lasted until Riley Johns smashed it into a rock and nearly brained himself. He was a good carver too and made tons of bonzer carved things for the kids down the river. He made me a horse out of red gum on a wandoo stand. Struth,[8] it looked good—real muritch, you know—all red and shiny and all.

He loved making us kids laugh, though he never laughed much himself. He'd get us up by the dump and dress up as Miss Raymond, our teacher for maths. He'd stick an old pillow in his shorts, put a wig of mattress stuffing on his head and, speaking in a high voice, "teach" us maths. By Jeeze he was funny, and he had us rolling around in stitches. Sometimes he'd stick a tin on his head and put on a pair of broken glasses and, with an old piece of piping, creep stealthily among the rubbish acting like the town cop.

He was funny allright, a real good actor, and I felt pretty proud that such a clever bloke was my mate.

And I admired him because he never treated us any different. When we was all laughing and fooling around together at

---

[8] An oath; short for "God's truth," as in "Swear to God."

the dump, we was all equal and all mates. And at school or at town, in front of the other white folk, he was just the same. And that's really something. A lot of white folk are friendly if no one's looking, but when there's a crowd around, they don't want to know you if your skin's black.

Johnny Blue never had a girlfriend, but he wasn't queer.

He was handsome enough in a rugged sort of way. His eyes were black like the backs of beetles and were often hidden behind a fringe of his curly black hair that grew thick and long enough to hang over his broad brown shoulders. Sometimes his eyes squinted up with laughter but mostly they were as cold as the middle of a dam in winter, them eyes of Johnny's. His nose was flat and broken like Billy Keith the boxer's, who smacked up the shearers every year in the local show. Except when he was fooling around with us kids, his mouth was always drawn back in a half-snarl, like one of them dingoes in the South Perth zoo. But his teeth was big and white and he had a ripper whistle—better than anyone else.

Another thing about Johnny Blue, he could fight, chuck boondis,[9] spears or boomerangs, spit and run better than anyone, but he never bragged or boasted. He let other kids think they could beat him in everything, except fighting.

Winter came and the dust turned to mud around the town. The kids had mud fights instead of using boondi or conky nuts, and the old man was due out of jail soon.

Johnny and me was sharing a fag under the tank stand[10] when Mickey Rooselett came and told me Acky wanted to see me. Acky was our nickname for Mr Ackland, the headmaster. I gave a grin to Johnny and says, "Silly bugger'll probably cane me for not doing me maths."

Johnny gave a snarl. There was no love lost between him and old Acky, they were always getting into yikes together like a pair of male dingoes fighting over a bitch. Acky

---

[9] Boondis: rocks or stones.
[10] The structure that supports a water tank.

didn't like us Nyoongahs either so, since I was the only one in his class, I got the lot, too.

I got into his room and it was dark with only a bit of light shining through the cobwebby, dusty, flyspotted window panes. Acky was in a shirty mood that day, and he grabs me shoulder and yanks it around so me neck fair gets twisted. I could smell the beer on him, so I reckons, "Look out, Jesse, this bloke's as drunk as Johnny's old man." I was buggered if I was going to get caned by him in such a temper, 'cos I reckoned he'd half-kill me. I was scared—so I done a silly thing.

I sticks me hand in me pockets and says, "If you hit me, I'm gonna get my old man onto you when he comes 'ome next week."

Well, that gets him as wild as a dog in a cat's home. He pulls me about and drags me hands out and tries to lay six across them. The thing is, only one of them hit me hand and, since me fist was clenched, it only hit me knuckles but it still felt like me fingers was cut off.

Another hit me face and fair near took me eye out, and the rest got me around the shoulders, and when he'd finished he chucked me out the door.

Me arm was numb right up to me elbow and the mark on me face starts to hurt like the time Mickey Redgum, a stockman on a station where the old man was working one time, sent his stock-whip across me face accidentally. I had to bite back the tears: it would never do for a Nyoongah to cry in front of our number one enemies, by whom I mean our loving white brothers. But when I got to Johnny I couldn't keep the tears back. He wouldn't tell, and besides he was me mate.

When he saw me hand and face, he up and goes for the head's office before I can say "struth" and, by the time I can get after him, it's too late. I hear a cry, then Acky yelling out something about ringing up Johnny's dad and Johnny shouting out that he can do what he likes but no one is going to push his little cobber around. Then Acky tells him not to come back to school, and Johnny says he won't come back for a million quid.

So Johnny was expelled. But he didn't care.

That night me life was changed. I aren't no scholar and I don't know any big words, but I guess after that night I was never really a kid any more.

I was lying in me bag and newspaper bed, watching the lightning flash like spears across the black sky. I loved the rain pelting onto the tin roof of our home-made house, though when it came through the cracks in the rusty walls and all the old nailholes in the roof, it wasn't so good.

Suddenly, I hears a thudding on me window that's not hail, so I up and opens it and in hops Johnny, looking like the bunyip[11] coming up out of a muddy creek. I says, surprised like, "What's up, Johnny mate?"

And he says, in a dull voice, "I killed me dad and you've gotta help me."

Now Johnny never lied, and anyhow, what sort of a galah[12] would swim through all that mud to bull to a kid? Not Johnny Blue, I can tell you. So I asks him what he wants me to do and he tells me.

What happened was, after he got home from school after the stoush with Acky, the silly old coot *had* rung up like he said he would. Johnny's dad was angrier than a wounded grizzly and told the boy all sorts of things, like he had to quit fighting, to stop going around with the Nyoongahs, and that he was going to belt Johnny good for being such a fool. Then he pulls off his belt and starts to lay into him, but Johnny's mum steps in. Now old man Blue was in a cruel, wild mood, so he pushes Missus Blue out of the way and lashes her across the face with his belt.

Then Johnny went mad, because, you see, he loved his mum. He grabbed the bread knife and stuck it into his

[11] A legendary creature akin to Bigfoot.
[12] A stupid person, a fool; also, a pink-and-gray bird.

Dad's fat belly. Johnny stuck old man Blue so full of holes he was looking like a sieve, then he took off, because he didn't want to go to jail. So he came to our place, to his only mate—to me.

And he worked out a bit of a plan, and it was a pretty smart idea.

He reckoned they'd be looking for him pretty soon, and they'd know, with the river in flood, he couldn't swim over, and the bridge was fifteen miles down. But us Nyoongahs had made a raft out of old four-gallon kerosene drums and bits of wood, and his plan was that we both cross over then I would bring the raft back and tie it up again and hop into bed, and don't know about anything. See, if he just took the raft they'd know straight away that he'd got over. But this way, they'd spend all day tomorrow looking on this side and by then he'd be up in East Perth with his Mum's family, and they'd hide him until maybe he could go over east or something.

Well I got out of bed and into me trousers and we went off down to where the raft was. The river was all white foam, and brown, and green; and rushing and twisting like a giant koodgeeda,[13] dashing itself against rocks and snags. It was the only way Johnny could hide from the fuzz, else I wouldn't have even gone near it, let alone try and cross it. But Johnny was the only bloke I'd have done it for, no sweat.

So we got on and pushed off from the bank with the two poles, then we're off like a flaming rodeo steer, bucking and tossing, pigrooting and rearing. But we was getting across.

We was in the middle when it happened.

I was using the pole to keep the raft off a dirty big boulder, sticking its head above the water like a water spirit. Suddenly the pole broke and the raft rammed full pelt into the rock, smashing into a thousand pieces.

Well, I wouldn't know how many pieces, really. All I

[13] A snake.

know is that there was water instead of wood under me feet, and I was being dragged along like a bleeding racing car driver. I never been so fast in me life.

I couldn't swim, and I reckoned I was done. Not a nice way to croak, thinks I, so I yell for nothing in particular. Then I feel a strong arm under me and Johnny soothing me down. He used his body to protect mine, so it was him that bumped into most of the rocks and snags, but I didn't realise that at the time. Only a horrid roaring in me ears and brain, and being tossed along by the Quarra's green-brown hands.

Then we hit the bank. I felt Johnny give me an almighty push, and that's all I remember, until morning came and there I was lying flat as a tack among the reeds, like a drowned possum.

Johnny was gone and at first I thought he'd got away, but not for long. Actually, they found him before they found me. When morning came and they found me and the raft missing too, they drove down the river and over the bridge and started to come up the other side, and they found his body wrapped around a tree about half a mile down river.

Well that was the end of Johnny Blue, the Abos' mate.

He was kind to us, he fought our battles, he made us laugh and stopped our crying, he made toys for us and shared what little he had in life with us. And for all those things I admired him.

But most of all I admired him because he really *did* treat us as equals, not just people to be kind to.

You see he was a strong swimmer, he could have made it to the opposite bank alone.

I was only a skinny little Nyoongah, a quarter-caste, a nothing. But to him I was a person and an equal and his mate, and he gave his life for me.

MARIGOLDS

❧

(United States)

by Eugenia Collier

*It may be easier to be mad than to be sad, but it's not very
productive.*

When I think of the home town of my youth, all that I
seem to remember is dust—the brown, crumbly dust of late
summer—arid, sterile dust that gets into the eyes and
makes them water, gets into the throat and between the
toes of bare brown feet. I don't know why I should remember only the dust. Surely there must have been lush green
lawns and paved streets under leafy shade trees somewhere
in town; but memory is an abstract painting—it does not
present things as they are, but rather as they *feel*. And so,
when I think of that time and that place, I remember only
the dry September of the dirt roads and grassless yards of
the shantytown where I lived. And one other thing I
remember, another incongruency of memory—a brilliant
splash of sunny yellow against the dust—Miss Lottie's
marigolds.

Whenever the memory of those marigolds flashes across
my mind, a strange nostalgia comes with it and remains
long after the picture has faded. I feel again the chaotic
emotions of adolescence, illusive as smoke, yet as real as
the potted geranium before me now. Joy and rage and wild
animal gladness and shame tangled together in the multi-
colored skein of fourteen-going-on-fifteen as I recall that
devastating moment when I was suddenly more woman

than child, years ago in Miss Lottie's yard. I think of those marigolds at the strangest times; I remember them vividly now as I desperately pass away the time waiting for you, who will not come.

I suppose that futile waiting was the sorrowful background music of our impoverished little community when I was young. The Depression that gripped the nation was no new thing to us, for the black workers of rural Maryland had always been depressed. I don't know what it was that we were waiting for; certainly not for the prosperity that was "just around the corner," for those were white folks' words, which we never believed. Nor did we wait for hard work and thrift to pay off in shining success as the American Dream promised, for we knew better than that, too. Perhaps we waited for a miracle, amorphous in concept but necessary if one were to have the grit to rise before dawn each day and labor in the white man's vineyard until after dark, or to wander about in the September dust offering one's sweat in return for some meager share of bread. But God was chary with miracles in those days, and so we waited—and waited.

We children, of course, were only vaguely aware of the extent of our poverty. Having no radios, few newspapers, and no magazines, we were somewhat unaware of the world outside our community. Nowadays we would be called "culturally deprived" and people would write books and hold conferences about us. In those days everybody we knew was just as hungry and ill-clad as we were. Poverty was the cage in which we all were trapped, and our hatred of it was still the vague, undirected restlessness of the zoo-bred flamingo who knows that nature created him to fly free.

As I think of those days I feel most poignantly the tag-end of summer, the bright dry times when we began to have a sense of shortening days and the imminence of the cold.

By the time I was fourteen my brother Joey and I were the only children left at our house, the older ones having left home for early marriage or the lure of the city, and the two babies having been sent to relatives who might care for them better than we. Joey was three years younger than I, and a boy, and therefore vastly inferior. Each morning our mother and father trudged wearily down the dirt road and around the bend, she to her domestic job, he to his daily unsuccessful quest for work. After our chores around the tumbledown shanty, Joey and I were free to run wild in the sun with other children similarly situated.

For the most part, those days are ill-defined in my memory, running together and combining like a fresh watercolor painting left out in the rain. I remember squatting in the road drawing a picture in the dust, a picture which Joey gleefully erased with one sweep of his dirty foot. I remember fishing for minnows in a muddy creek and watching sadly as they eluded my cupped hands, while Joey laughed uproariously. And I remember, that year, a strange restlessness of body and spirit, a feeling that something old and familiar was ending, and something unknown and therefore terrifying was beginning.

One day returns to me with special clarity for some reason, perhaps because it was the beginning of the experience that in some inexplicable way marked the end of innocence. I was loafing under the great oak tree in our yard, deep in some reverie which I have now forgotten except that it involved some secret, secret thoughts of one of the Harris boys across the yard. Joey and a bunch of kids were bored now with the old tire suspended from an oak limb which had kept them entertained for awhile.

"Hey, Lizabeth," Joey yelled. He never talked when he could yell. "Hey, Lizabeth, let's go somewhere."

I came reluctantly from my private world. "Where you want to go? What you want to do?"

The truth was that we were becoming tired of the form-lessness of our summer days. The idleness whose prospect had seemed so beautiful during the busy days of spring now had degenerated to an almost desperate effort to fill up the empty midday hours.

"Let's go see can we find some locusts on the hill," someone suggested.

Joey was scornful. "Ain't no more locusts there. Y'all got 'em all while they was still green."

The argument that followed was brief and not really worth the effort. Hunting locust trees wasn't fun anymore by now.

"Tell you what," said Joey finally, his eyes sparkling. "Let's go over to Miss Lottie's."

The idea caught on at once, for annoying Miss Lottie was always fun. I was still child enough to scamper along with the group over rickety fences and through bushes that tore our already raggedy clothes, back to where Miss Lottie lived. I think now that we must have made a tragicomic spectacle, five or six kids of different ages, each of us clad in only one garment—the girls in faded dresses that were too long or too short, the boys in patchy pants, their sweaty brown chests gleaming in the hot sun. A little cloud of dust followed our thin legs and bare feet as we tramped over the barren land.

When Miss Lottie's house came into view we stopped, ostensibly to plan our strategy, but actually to reinforce our courage. Miss Lottie's house was the most ramshackle of all our ramshackle homes. The sun and rain had long since faded its rickety frame siding from white to a sullen gray. The boards themselves seemed to remain upright not from being nailed together but rather from leaning together like a house that children might have constructed from cards. A brisk wind might have blown it down, and the fact that it was still standing implied a kind of enchantment that was stronger than the elements. There it stood, and as far as I know is standing yet—a gray rotting thing with no porch, no shutters, no steps, set on a cramped lot with no grass, not even weeds—a monument to decay.

In front of the house in a squeaky rocking chair sat Miss Lottie's son, John Burke, completing the impression of decay. John Burke was what was known as "queer-headed." Black and ageless, he sat, rocking day in and day out in a mindless stupor, lulled by the monotonous squeak-squawk of the chair. A battered hat atop his shaggy head shaded him from the sun. Usually John Burke was totally unaware of everything outside his quiet dream world. But if you disturbed him, if you intruded upon his fantasies, he would become enraged, strike out at you, and curse at you in some strange enchanted language which only he could understand. We children made a game of thinking of ways to disturb John Burke and then to elude his violent retribution.

But our real fun and our real fear lay in Miss Lottie herself. Miss Lottie seemed to be at least a hundred years old. Her big frame still held traces of the tall, powerful woman she must have been in youth, although it was now bent and drawn. Her smooth skin was a dark reddish-brown, and her face had Indian-like features and the stern stoicism that one associates with Indian faces. Miss Lottie didn't like intruders either, especially children. She never left her yard, and nobody ever visited her. We never knew how she managed those necessities which depend on human interaction— how she ate, for example, or even whether she ate. When we were tiny children, we thought Miss Lottie was a witch and we made up tales, that we half believed ourselves, about her exploits. We were far too sophisticated now, of course, to believe the witch-nonsense. But old fears have a way of clinging like cobwebs, and so when we sighted the tumbledown shack, we had to stop to reinforce our nerves.

"Look, there she is," I whispered, forgetting that Miss

Lottie could not possibly have heard me from that distance.
"She's fooling with them crazy flowers."

"Yeh, look at 'er."

Miss Lottie's marigolds were perhaps the strangest part of
the picture. Certainly they did not fit in with the crumbling decay of the rest of her yard. Beyond the dusty brown
yard, in front of the sorry gray house, rose suddenly and
shockingly a dazzling strip of bright blossoms, clumped
together in enormous mounds, warm and passionate and
sun-golden. The old black witch-woman worked on them
all summer, every summer, down on her creaky knees,
weeding and cultivating and arranging, while the house
crumbled and John Burke rocked. For some perverse reason, we children hated those marigolds. They interfered
with the perfect ugliness of the place; they were too beautiful; they said too much that we could not understand; they
did not make sense. There was something in the vigor with
which the old woman destroyed the weeds that intimidated
us. It should have been a comical sight—the old woman
with the man's hat on her cropped white head, leaning over
the bright mounds, her big backside in the air—but it was-
n't comical, it was something we could not name. We had
to annoy her by whizzing a pebble into her flowers or by
yelling a dirty word, then dancing away from her rage, rev-
eling in our youth and mocking her age. Actually, I think it
was the flowers we wanted to destroy, but nobody had the
nerve to try it, not even Joey, who was usually fool enough
to try anything.

"Y'all git some stones," commanded Joey now, and was
met with instant giggling obedience as everyone except me
began to gather pebbles from the dusty ground. "Come on,
Lizabeth."

I just stood there peering through the bushes, torn
between wanting to join the fun and feeling that it was all
a bit silly.

"You scared, Lizabeth?"

I cursed and spat on the ground—my favorite gesture of phony bravado. "Y'all children get the stones, I'll show you how to use 'em."

I said before that we children were not consciously aware of how thick were the bars of our cage. I wonder now, though, whether we were not more aware of it than I thought. Perhaps we had some dim notion of what we were, and how little chance we had of being anything else. Otherwise, why would we have been so preoccupied with destruction? Anyway, the pebbles were collected quickly, and everybody looked at me to begin the fun.

"Come on, y'all."

We crept to the edge of the bushes that bordered the narrow road in front of Miss Lottie's place. She was working placidly, kneeling over the flowers, her dark hand plunged into the golden mound. Suddenly "zing"—an expertly aimed stone cut the head off one of the blossoms.

"Who out there? Miss Lottie's backside came down and her head came up as her sharp eyes searched the bushes. "You better git!"

We had crouched down out of sight in the bushes, where we stifled the giggles that insisted on coming. Miss Lottie gazed warily across the road for a moment, then cautiously returned to her weeding. "Zing"—Joey sent a pebble into the blooms, and another marigold was beheaded.

Miss Lottie was enraged now. She began struggling to her feet, leaning on a rickety cane and shouting, "Y'all git! Go on home!" Then the rest of the kids let loose with their pebbles, storming the flowers and laughing wildly and senselessly at Miss Lottie's impotent rage. She shook her stick at us and started shakily toward the road crying, "Black bastards, git 'long! John Burke! John Burke, come help!"

Then I lost my head entirely, mad with the power of inciting such rage, and ran out of the bushes in the storm of pebbles, straight toward Miss Lottie chanting madly, "Old witch, fell in a ditch, picked up a penny and thought she was rich!" The children screamed with delight, dropped their pebbles and joined the crazy dance, swarming around Miss Lottie like bees and chanting, "Old lady witch!" while she screamed curses at us. The madness lasted only a moment, for John Burke, startled at last, lurched out of his chair, and we dashed for the bushes just as Miss Lottie's cane went whizzing at my head.

I did not join the merriment when the kids gathered again under the oak in our bare yard. Suddenly I was ashamed, and I did not like being ashamed. The child in me sulked and said it was all in fun, but the woman in me flinched at the thought of the malicious attack that I had led. The mood lasted all afternoon. When we ate the beans and rice that was supper that night, I did not notice my father's silence, for he was always silent these days, nor did I notice my mother's absence, for she always worked until well into evening. Joey and I had a particularly bitter argument after supper; his exuberance got on my nerves. Finally I stretched out upon the pallete in the room we shared and fell into a fitful doze.

When I awoke, somewhere in the middle of the night, my mother had returned, and I vaguely listened to the conversation that was audible through the thin walls that separated our rooms. At first I heard no words, only voices. My mother's voice was like a cool, dark room in summer—peaceful, soothing, quiet. I loved to listen to it; it made things seem all right somehow. But my father's voice cut through hers, shattering the peace.

"Twenty-two years, Maybelle, twenty-two years," he was saying, "and I got nothing for you, nothing, nothing."

"It's all right, honey, you'll get something. Everybody's out of work now, you know that."

"It ain't right. Ain't no man ought to eat his woman's food year in and year out, and see his children running wild. Ain't nothing right about that."

"Honey, you took good care of us when you had it. Ain't nobody got nothing nowadays."

"I ain't talking about nobody else, I'm talking about *me*. God knows I try." My mother said something I could not hear, and my father cried out louder, "What must a man do, tell me that?"

"Look, we ain't starving. I git paid every week, and Mrs. Ellis is real nice about giving me things. She's gonna let me have Mr. Ellis' old coat for you this winter—"

"God damn Mr. Ellis' coat! And God damn his money! You think I want white folks' leavings? God damn, Maybelle"—and suddenly he sobbed, loudly and painfully, and cried helplessly and hopelessly in the dark night. I had never heard a man cry before. I did not know men ever cried. I covered my ears with my hands but could not cut off the sound of my father's harsh, painful, despairing sobs. My father was a strong man who would whisk a child upon his shoulders and go singing through the house. My father whittled toys for us and laughed so loud that the great oak seemed to laugh with him, and taught us how to fish and hunt rabbits. How could it be that my father was crying? But the sobs went on, unstifled, finally quieting until I could hear my mother's voice, deep and rich, humming softly as she used to hum to a frightened child.

The world had lost its boundary lines. My mother, who was small and soft, was now the strength of the family; my father, who was the rock on which the family had been built, was sobbing like the tiniest child. Everything was suddenly out of tune, like a broken accordion. Where did I fit into this crazy picture? I do not now remember my thoughts, only a feeling of great bewilderment and fear.

Long after the sobbing and the humming had stopped, I lay on the pallete, still as stone with my hands over my ears, wishing that I too could cry and be comforted. The night was silent now except for the sound of the crickets and of Joey's soft breathing. But the room was too crowded with fear to allow me to sleep, and finally, feeling the terrible aloneness of 4:00 A.M., I decided to awaken Joey.

"Ouch! What's the matter with you? What you want?" he demanded disagreeably when I had pinched and slapped him awake.

"Come on, wake up."

"What for? Go 'way."

I was lost for a reasonable reply. I could not say, "I'm scared and I don't want to be alone," so I merely said, "I'm going out. If you want to come, come on."

The promise of adventure awoke him. "Going out now? Where to, Lizabeth? What you going to do?"

I was pulling my dress over my head. Until now I had not thought of going out. "Just come on," I replied tersely.

I was out the window and halfway down the road before Joey caught up with me.

"Wait, Lizabeth, where you going?"

I was running as if the furies were after me, as perhaps they were—running silently and furiously until I came to where I had half-known I was headed: to Miss Lottie's yard.

The half-dawn light was more eerie than complete darkness, and in it the old house was like the ruin that my world had become—foul and crumbling, a grotesque caricature. It looked haunted, but I was not afraid because I was haunted too.

"Lizabeth, you lost your mind?" panted Joey.

I had indeed lost my mind, for all the smoldering emotions of that summer swelled in me and burst—the great need for my mother who was never there, the hopelessness of our poverty and degradation, the bewilderment of being neither child nor woman and yet both at once, the fear unleashed by my father's tears. And these feelings combined in one great impulse toward destruction.

"Lizabeth!"

I leaped furiously into the mounds of marigolds and pulled madly, trampling and pulling and destroying the perfect yellow blooms. The fresh smell of early morning and of dew-soaked marigolds spurred me on as I went tearing and mangling and sobbing while Joey tugged my dress or my waist crying, "Lizabeth stop, please stop!"

And then I was sitting in the ruined little garden among the uprooted and ruined flowers, crying and crying, and it was too late to undo what I had done. Joey was sitting beside me, silent and frightened, not knowing what to say. Then, "Lizabeth, look."

I opened my swollen eyes and saw in front of me a pair of large calloused feet; my gaze lifted to the swollen legs, the age-distorted body clad in a tight cotton night dress, and then the shadowed Indian face surrounded by stubby white hair. And there was no rage in the face now, now that the garden was destroyed and there was nothing any longer to be protected.

"M-miss Lottie!" I scrambled to my feet and just stood there and stared at her, and that was the moment when childhood faded and womanhood began. That violent, crazy act was the last act of childhood. For as I gazed at the immobile face with the sad, weary eyes, I gazed upon a kind of reality which is hidden to childhood. The witch was no longer a witch but only a broken old woman who had dared to create beauty in the midst of ugliness and sterility. She had been born in squalor and lived in it all her life. Now at the end of that life she had nothing except a falling-down hut, a wrecked body, and John Burke, the mindless son of her passion. Whatever verve there was left in her, whatever was of love and beauty and joy that had not been squeezed out by life, had been there in the marigolds she had so tenderly cared for.

Of course I could not express the things that I knew

about Miss Lottie as I stood there awkward and ashamed. The years have put words to the things I knew in that moment, and as I look back upon it, I know that that moment marked the end of innocence. People think of the loss of innocence as meaning the loss of virginity, but this is far from true. Innocence involves an unseeing acceptance of things at face value, an ignorance of the area below the surface. In that humiliating moment I looked beyond myself and into the depths of another person. This was the beginning of compassion, and one cannot have both compassion and innocence.

The years have taken me worlds away from that time and that place, from the dust and the squalor of our lives and from the bright thing that I destroyed in a blind childish striking out at God-knows-what. Miss Lottie died long ago and many years have passed since I last saw her hut, completely barren at last, for despite my wild contrition she never planted marigolds again. Yet, there are times when the image of those passionate yellow mounds returns with a painful poignancy. For one does not have to be ignorant and poor to find that his life is barren as the dusty yards of our town. And I too have planted marigolds.

MY LUCY

(United States)

by Howard Gordon

First love! Oh, the thrill of it! And . . . uh-oh, the madness!

I had never meant to force her into doing anything she had not wanted to do when I clumsily threw her down in her own hallway that day. Even now I remain convinced that while my passion may have been induced by that sudden and uncontrollable metamorphosis that accompanies puberty, my actions were influenced by literature.

That was so long ago, and it is never easy returning to a place you have been away from for nearly twenty years. Yet it is not at all difficult to recall those minute details of one's life, or relive even entire experiences as precisely as if they occurred seconds ago, as if they could be capsulized and put away in a shirt pocket to be examined at leisure under the lens of a microscope. When I walked along Adams Street I was not the least bit surprised that I encountered such pleasure. It was there that I saw a young girl who looked exactly like my Lucy.

She was about the same age—fourteen robust years of modest height and weight wrapped in a slender body of slouching shoulders and knocking knees. Her hair was neatly braided in cornrows, and her dark chestnut skin glowed a little from too much Vaseline generously applied by an overly ash-conscious mother. The girl had my Lucy's wide brown eyes, the same tiny, almost nonexistent nose, and the same dimpled smile, all surrounded by the slightest bit of baby fat.

I tried not to hesitate in front of her, uncomfortably aware that stares or my very presence might startle her. But she was too deeply involved in reading a book to notice me, as she sat unperturbed on the steps of an apartment duplex. In fact, a smile was drawn across her face, as if no one else in the world but she and the characters in her book were alive. I had not seen that smile on a living person in years, even though I would see it materialize like a naked apparition every day of my life after my Lucy ran screaming from my arms. I tried to move on, but the girl's thin, tea-colored legs with heavy white socks up to her calves were crossed under her body in one of those difficult positions that young girls easily assume, and, from my vantage point in front of her, I noticed the tiniest piece of blue silk peeking out from beneath her dress.

Now, I am no Humbert Humbert,[1] and I have never entertained even the remotest fantasies involving the flesh of little children. Yet, it struck me that my actions, or lack of them, might have been mistaken for some clandestine perversion by an angry mother storming out of the front door, armed with a broom or baseball bat. Quickly, I walked by the girl, past the next duplex, and over to the adjacent lot of grass. The grass was uncut and ankle-high. Tangled brown weeds grew among it, and in several spots patches of dirt-covered gravel embowered flecks of glass, splintered bits of dried wood, and yellowing scraps of paper.

My house had stood there once. Three stories of gray lumber with a large picture window, a crumbling porch with its loosened handrail. It was about that time of day when my mother would push her head through the hole in the front-door screen and shout, "Dinner, Kevin!" and I would come running from a game of matching pennies or a conversation with friends near the corner. "What, Ma?" I

[1] The main character in the novel *Lolita* by the Russian American writer Vladimir Nabokov.

would whine, even though I had clearly heard her first command.

Inside, the apartment was small, yet there was room enough for me, my parents, my three brothers, and my sister. It was a walk-through flat, as we called them, and you could walk through the living room, which was furnished with only a couch, an old floor-model television, and two antique-looking chairs; straight through to the dining room, which served as a modest sleeping space for young Evelyn; through my parents' bedroom, with a plaque nailed over their bed asking, "Keep This House, Lord"; and into my bedroom, where Steve and Butchy, my older brothers, slept in one twin-size bed, and Earl and I slept in the other. After my bedroom, there was a kitchen, bathroom, and the backdoor, and you could walk right out of the house as if you passed through a tunnel.

Three other families lived in this house. Through the wall on my side of the room, I heard the Gilsons as they walked noisily up the staircase and into their rooms. And, if I placed my ear against the wall just right and listened carefully, I could hear nearly everything they said. Usually, there was no need to do more than just sit back in bed and listen. Mr. Gilson and his wife argued just about every evening. He would threaten to break her back, or cave her chest in, and she would swear she would leave him "cold and dry if you *ever* put your crusty, black hands on me!" The two of them would carry on for hours into the night, yelling insults and bumping furniture against the walls but never actually striking one another. My mother and father were used to it. They would fall asleep quickly, as if nothing more than a television had been blaring. Evelyn would start and occasionally whimper from under the blanket if the noise scared her, but soon she would place her thumb in her mouth and rock herself to sleep. My brothers would listen for a while, laughing and clowning over the obsceni-

ties the Gilsons hurled at each other, until finally they too
would fall asleep, creating a chorus of snores.

But I would prop my pillow against the wall and push
Earl's cumbersome feet off my stomach, and begin reading
Sister Carrie or *Ivanhoe*, or one of the many other fascinat-
ing books I had discovered at the school library. The din of
the Gilsons fighting faded away as soon as I opened a book.
Before long, a paragraph would take me into a city far away
from Rochester, sometimes even into another world. I
would read for two or three hours after everyone had fallen
asleep, or until Evelyn would get up in the middle of the
night to use the bathroom. On her way back to bed, she
would habitually yell, "Daddy! Kevin's got that light on
again."

It was there, in my books, that I discovered Lucy. In
what particular novel or by what author I cannot remember. It may have been Lucy Scanlan in *Studs Lonigan* or
the Lucy in *Lucy Temple*, or perhaps it was Melville's Lucy
in *Pierre*. But she was everywhere, my Lucy, sometimes
using the name of another character, sometimes nameless.
She could be found in Hawthorne, in Wright, in Lawrence,
or in Porter—in all of literature there was a Lucy, a young
girl who gradually evolved into a saintly, potentially passionate and beautiful woman whose love was meant to be
won by only one man. She fascinated me in *Camille*, she
dumbfounded me in *The Rainbow*, and she escaped me in
Madame Bovary. The more I read, the more I realized
I had to find her outside of my literature, away from the
eighteenth-century settings of Farquhar's *The Recruiting
Officer* or Thackeray's *Henry Esmond*. I needed to possess
her outside the limited sphere of my books and plays, outside of Wordsworth's haunting "Lucy" poems or those
seventeenth-century dramas by Wycherley, Congreve, and
Sheridan, whose Lucys always seemed to turn up in the
unattractive role of maid.

Each time I finished reading a story, I would lay the book across my chest and dream of discovering my own mature, stupid, virtuous, tainted, good, evil, feminine, tomboyish heroine. I would dream of finding that one girl who on every occasion, unless the story ended in tragedy, had been won over by the hero. At the age of fourteen, though other boys went to the movies and dreamed of emulating their celluloid heroes, we all had the same dream: to walk away holding the horse by the reins and the girl by the hand. I knew you could never get a horse into the ghetto, but I was absolutely confident I would one day walk away with my Lucy.

It had been raining the day I first saw my Lucy. I had entered my final year of junior high school, had sadly predicted that the occasion would be no more than the beginning of another frustrating year in pursuit of my dream. But she sat right across from the desk that the teacher pointed out as mine. As I passed by that girl my legs buckled, and I nearly knocked the desk over. I tried to sit down immediately, but my feet no longer felt the floor. She sat still, barely acknowledging the noise I made, but almost sneering at the other children's laughter.

She wore her hair in two braided ponytails joined at the back of her head by a single bobby pin. Her skin was pepper brown and her arms and neck so perfectly thin that it appeared her clothes had been ironed on to her body. Finally, I managed to push myself into my chair as class began.

I knew that she was the most beautiful girl in the room, because every other girl was suddenly without a face. She stared straight ahead while listening attentively to the teacher call roll. Her head was perched high and proud on her neck like a new hat. She pursed her lips in a tight pout.

"Miss Gray?" She stood up, replied "Present," and sat

down again, looking annoyed at two boys who had giggled when her name was called. *My* Lucy. So proud, so mature, so beautiful. From the corner of one eye she glanced over at me and assured herself that I had been staring. She lifted her chin even higher and did not look at me again, and for the rest of the day I thought of nothing but her.

When the bell rang at the end of the school day I waited at my desk for my Lucy to get her coat from the closet before I approached her. But she threw the coat over her shoulder and quickly left the room. By the time I reached the bottom of the stairs, she was walking out of the building.

"Hey, wait!" She glanced back, then pretended she had not heard me call her. I managed to catch up to her skipping-walk pace and slightly tapped her on the shoulder.

"I'm Kevin." She did not answer, but the look in her eyes said, "So?" I walked at her side.

"What's wrong? I just wanted to talk to you."

"'Bout what?" she finally asked, but still did not look at me. Her nut-brown eyes looked straight ahead, as if I were simply a distraction—not completely ignoring me, but waiting for me to speak and then go away. We walked, and I suddenly realized I had nothing to say. After boys outgrow that sexless period of their lives where everyone is merely a playmate, they have the tendency to store a lot of excitement in their heads before approaching a girl; but, as soon as there is a need for the expression of mature emotion, nothing results except silly remarks or silence.

"Well?" she said emphatically. "What you want?"

I was speechless. There she was, walking at my side, this girl whom I had waited a lifetime to encounter, who had swept me through ages of love in my books—my treasure, my sweetness, my prize. There at only arm's length she waited for me to make the first move. And, like a confused child whose toy had been taken away from him, I fumbled for words and felt my legs buckle again.

"Why you walking like that?" she asked, finally looking at me. "You retarded or somethin'?"

"Lucy, I just—"

"My name ain't no Lu-cy, boy. It's Debra."

I had walked with her more than two blocks along Adams and onto Clarissa Street without realizing it, until she stopped and turned into the front yard of a tall, wood-frame house. I could feel myself begin to panic, as if I might not ever see her again.

"Hey . . . Okay . . . Look, I just want to talk to you." She emitted a strange laugh, not a giggling sort of laugh, but the mocking snicker used by older children when they attempt to ridicule their younger brothers and sisters. I followed her into the yard and reached a hand out to her.

"I think you *are* retarded," she said. She moved backward, though she remained facing me, and raised her thick, black eyebrows, slightly wrinkling her forehead. Somehow, she was on the porch walking up the stairs, then almost running as she pushed the door behind her open. And somehow, I had my hand on the coat she had been carrying, and was pulling her toward me. We were in a hallway not unlike the one in my own house. A long flight of freshly varnished stairs led up to a single door. She tried to pull her coat free while running up the stairs, but she slipped backward during our tug-of-war, and I fell on top of her. I was surprised that she did not scream. Instead, she made sort of a half-moaning noise and tried to push me off of her.

"Please," I said, "I didn't mean to make you fall."

"Hush," she whispered, "and get offa me." Again I was surprised. She was talking to me—pushing me away, yes, but talking to me. I felt encouraged, and lost all sense of embarrassment. She smelled of lotion and new clothes, and one of her braids had come undone. I could feel her flat, mannequin stomach pressed against my own, and the chill of her cold but soft skin rubbing against my arms.

Awkwardly, I tried to kiss her, but she pushed her head away from my face. She moved under me again, tightening the muscles in her neck.

"Yuuck!" she said as my lips found and wet her ear. "Get off."

"C'mon," I pleaded. I was sweating, and a pleasure swelled within me that I had previously experienced only while reading books.

"What you tryin' to do?" She was still whispering.

"I wan—" I coughed as the unpinned braid fell into my mouth. "I wanna kiss you."

"Hmph." She moaned again. "Get offa me before my mama comes." She twisted her body to one side, moving me over. Again, I tried to kiss her lips, but we straightened up and stood against the wall. In one motion she tugged at her coat, which was still tangled around my hand, and pressed her mouth against my own so hard that the back of my head bumped the wall.

"Now, go'an, boy," she commanded. And for the first time ever, I saw her smile. Unable to move, I stood against the wall and watched her as she ascended several steps.

"Go'an!" she repeated almost desperately. Then she stopped walking and turned suddenly. "I hate all you boys, and you can take this." With the last word she patted her hand against the seat of her dress.

"Debra Ann!" came a throaty shout from the top of the stairs. She ran up, and I nearly fell running down. As I stumbled through the front door I could hear my Lucy shout, "Home, Ma!"

The next day at school, she ignored me once again. Yet at least twice I caught her looking over at me from the corner of her eye. I had not slept more than a few hours the night before. I tried to read *Daisy Miller*, but could get no further than a page or two before losing my concentration. James was too difficult for me, I admitted. I tried "Rappaccini's Daughter," but read only the first five paragraphs. Earl's feet on my stomach nauseated me. They were nothing compared to what I pictured as the Cinderella delicacy of Lucy's elfin feet. I watched Earl's toes stretch and then curl from beneath the covers and thought of how I would adorn Lucy with priceless gifts once I had won my fortune, or at least had gotten a job. Soft fur slippers, velvet nightrobes, and silk dresses—all for her. I would playfully hide a tiny box behind my back until she pleaded to know what it contained, and then I would slip a gold ring on her finger while she worshipped me with her eyes. Finally, the words would come easily; they would flow from my mouth with the confidence of a hero. I repeated the words over and over as I fell asleep. "I love you, Lucy. I love you."

I sat alone in the playground eating my lunch and practicing my I-love-yous. She was in gym class as I ate, and I fantasized about carrying her books home for her if she were too tired. We would walk arm in arm.

I was getting ready to go to the bathroom and comb my hair for the third or fourth time that day when a group of my friends wandered over to my bench. I sniffed the air and hoped that my father's cologne was not too obvious because I knew they would tease me about it, but when I smelled the pleasing fragrance, only my Lucy really mattered. She was a special girl, a girl different from anyone else in the world. For her, I had taken two baths that morning, and I had changed my clothes at least four times before leaving the house. Even my socks and belt matched my clothes. For her, I had dabbed small amounts of after-shave over the three hairs just beginning to grow on my chin, and I had rubbed it into all of the other places I was confident she would kiss.

"Hey, Kevin." Robert McCullough stood in front of me with a wide grin splashed across his face. "Heard it didn't turn out all right."

"Huh?"

"Aw, c'mon, man. It ain't nothin' to be 'shamed about." The boy everyone called White Henry (because his skin was so light that the veins in his arms stood out like dark blue tracks) joined me. They looked at each other and laughed, and two others, Sonny Curtis and Wilbur Trenton, walked over.

"What ya'll talkin' about?" I asked. Sonny turned to Wilbur and lowered his voice for an attempted bass effect.

"C'mon, baby. C'mon, please." Wilbur extended his arms, pretending to push away from Sonny who moved toward him clumsily. Then Wilbur closed his eyes. From his mouth came a squeaking falsetto voice.

"No! No! I ain't givin' you nothin'!"

"Aw, c'mon, baby. I just wanna kiss you," boomed Wilbur.

I stood up. Robert clutched his stomach and laughed. White Henry jumped in front of me and closed his eyes so tightly that the eyelids shook, then, he protruded his lips in front of my face and made a loud, whistle-like kissing noise. They all laughed, and I confronted White Henry.

"How did . . . What you tryin' to say, man?" Still laughing, Wilbur stepped between us.

"Man, you don't have to try to hide nothin' from us. Everybody knows Debbie."

"That's right," said Sonny. "You just gotta approach it a little different. You know, make her feel good first." I started to feel queasy.

"You're a liar!" I shouted. They looked at me as if I were stupid. Sonny elbowed Wilbur.

"Now ain't he somethin'? Tryin' to play true blue. We know what you tried to do."

"Eah-haah," said Robert, "you tried to get some coody."

"No, I didn't!" They laughed, and Robert pointed a finger in my face and taunted me in a singsong chant.

"Kevin-tried-to-get-him-some-coody—"

"I did not!"

"But-all-she-gave-him-was-a-little-boody!"

"Shut up! Leave me alone!" I broke away from them and ran into the building. For the five minutes until the bell rang, ending recess, I stayed in the bathroom. I was having trouble thinking and I prayed I would not get sick. Those boys knew nothing, I convinced myself as I half stood, half leaned over one of the toilets. They hadn't made fun of any ordinary girl. It was not Fielding's Lucy, or Spenser's. It was *my* Lucy, unshared, unknown, untouched. And they had made ugly insinuations about her. I stood there staring into the water, then, defiantly, I spat into the bowl.

"Not my Lucy!" I shouted. "Not her."

My house had stood there. I had kissed the wall in my bedroom good-bye on the day we moved to another street. How a neighborhood could change so drastically in the space of only twenty years was beyond me. How an entire age could evaporate into memory defied my sense of history. A mile or so away I could see the only places trees had grown. They were gone now, replaced by solid concrete. The buildings, the sidewalks, even a new public library, were all made of concrete. Like huge pieces of an industrial erector set, slabs of gravel, water, and cement towered over the city, shading it from the sun. I walked slowly around the grass lot. It was like walking through a graveyard after the death of a best friend.

❧

At the end of the day, my Lucy waited for me at the door while I gathered up my books. She wore a lime-colored skirt and a matching blouse, and stood smiling at me as I approached her. We walked out of the building, saying nothing, but we looked at each other, smiling with embarrassment. I took her books from her and she seemed pleased. It was working perfectly. We walked. I wished that there were objects in our path—obstacles, so that I might lift her over them and reveal how strong I was and how much a gentleman. She took my hand in hers.

"You almost got me in trouble," she said, finally breaking the silence that had grown between us. "My mama gets home from her cleanin' early in the afternoon, and—*pee-you!* You smell like perfume."

"Didn't mean to. I mean, I didn't know your mother was home." We were silent again. I had desperately wanted to say something else. I had wanted to charm her with adult words, but they would not come. If only I had Dumas in my mind to quote from; if only Tolstoy were alive to guide me.

"Well—" She stopped and looked at me, then turned away shyly. "We could go over to the tracks, off Plymouth. Nobody can see you when you go over there."

"The tracks?"

"Uh-huh. And there's lots of grass and stuff so you don't—" She stopped again, but this time she lowered her face and looked up at me from the top of her shy eyes. "So you don't get your clothes all dirty," she said.

"Oh, I don't want to go all the way over there. I figured we would maybe walk over to Ford Street and maybe sit in the park. There's a lot of things we could talk about."

"Talk?"

"Yeah. I think you and me could talk about—"

"You mean you don't wanna do nothin'?"

"What you mean?"

"You know what I mean. Hey, you tryin' to play me for a fool or somethin'?"

"I just wanted to tell you . . ." I struggled with the words. But I knew I had to force myself to tell her.

"Tell me what?" I would shake the words out of my mouth or choke on them.

"Lucy, I—"

"I done told you, my name ain't no damn Lucy!"

"Okay, okay. Don't be mad at me. Lu—Debbie, I love you."

She stood back and looked at me as though I slapped her. Then, almost violently, she shook her hand free of mine.

"Somethin's wrong with you, boy. I thought you was cute—kinda. But you crazy."

"I thought *you* would understand. I thought you would have what they call *propriety* in literature."

"Pra . . ."

"Propriety."

Her face formed a strange look. It was the kind of queer look that parents have when a young child suddenly knows something he is not supposed to know. I was overwhelmed again with the urgent need to kiss her, with the need to press her against me until she understood. I tried to take her hand back, but when I grabbed her wrist, she screamed—the exact scream I had expected, but not heard the day before in her hallway. Now, I could hear the scream clearly. It echoed in my ears, then was muted by a loud rip. So startled had I been by her scream, and so tightly had I held her wrist, that the sleeve of her blouse had been torn.

"Leave me alone," she grunted, and pulled with both arms to free her wrist, half-dragging me a yard or so along the sidewalk. Somehow, I managed to say the only thing I thought might comfort her.

"I love you."

She shot a hard look at me. And, just as quickly, she stuck out her tongue.

"Ma!" she yelled in the direction of her house. She pulled her arm from me and started to pat herself on her backside. But, instead, she raced away. I stumbled to the edge of the sidewalk.

"Lucy!" I shouted after her. But she was gone. I sat on the curb and cried.

"Hey mister? Hey, you all right?"

I felt something shake inside my chest, the way a heart rattles when one is startled by an unexpected hand on the back of the shoulder, or by a voice that interrupts the solitude of an empty room. I was back in the grassy lot. The girl with the braided hair had not actually touched me, but she stood so close, so unafraid, looking down at me with an intense concern in her eyes. I turned my head for a moment, not wanting her to see my tears. But she did see. She smiled at me as I stood and moved away from the curb.

The girl said nothing more, but shook her head and smiled again as I wiped my eyes with my shirt sleeve and walked away from her.

DREAMING THE SKY DOWN

❧

(Britain)

by Barbara Burford

To rise (perchance to soar!) above people's put-downs is a major mark of maturity.

She woke bumping gently against the ceiling, like a fairground-bought helium filled balloon. Even while she knew it was another waking dream, Donna gloried in the feeling, the light as airiness of her twelve stones[1] drifting way above her bed.

Donna remembered to look especially at her bed this time. No, she was not there. She drifted down closer in the darkness. No, definitely not. She'd have to remember to tell shit-face Dawn Sullivan, that *she* was not having some kind of "primitive spiritualist experience," she *was* dreaming.

She arched her back and did a slow elegant backward roll, skimming the carpet, avoiding the knob on the wardrobe with a skilled half-twist of her swiftly ascending torso.

"Yah!" she whispered triumphantly to her gym teacher, wherever the hell she was. "Eat your heart out, Miss Howe!" Always going on about how elegant Black athletes were, and how much stamina and natural rhythm they had.

"You must be the exception that proves the rule, Donna!" Hah! Bloody hah! And everybody else falling about laughing at her.

Yeah, but they should see me now, she thought, as she skimmed the long diagonal of the ceiling, leaving the blue

---

[1] A British unit of weight equivalent to 14 pounds.

fringes on the lampshade adrift on the wind of her speed. She pushed off from the topmost corner of the room the way the swimmers did it on TV and coasted past her enemy, the mirror, rolling slowly over in order to catch a glimpse of herself as she slipped by.

In the dim glow that was all that the curtains let in from the street lamp in the road outside, she saw herself slide by, as elegant as a dolphin. "A dolphin that wears pyjamas!" she giggled, and drifted back to hang upside down and grin at herself.

I can see my reflection, so at least I'm not a vampire.

She made fangs at herself in the mirror, but had to get up close before she could catch the gleam of her teeth in the glass. She arced over to the light switch, but putting pressure on the toggle ricocheted her backwards towards the ceiling; and only an adroit twist saved her from cannoning off that, flat splat into the wardrobe. She grabbed at her duvet, and when that started to lift, managed to snatch hold of the rail at the bottom of her bed.

She hung there, like a balloon tied to a kid's pushchair,[2] while the racing of her heart steadied. Gradually she remembered how it worked, had always worked in these dreams, and slowly her feet drifted down till she was no longer upended, but resting lightly at the very top of the pile on the carpet. Very carefully, holding on to the fitted bottom sheet, she got into bed, and pulled the duvet over her. There was still a tendency for her body to bounce gently if she made any sudden movements, so she lay carefully still, eyes wide open, waiting to wake up.

Donna was walking Ben to school before she remembered her dream. She looked down at her younger brother, watching the blue bobble on his knitted hat bounce, as he trotted along beside her. She wondered if Ben dreamed of flying. She couldn't remember dreaming that way until she

---

[2] A stroller.

was nearly thirteen, just after her periods started, in fact. But maybe she had just forgotten, the way she had forgotten the house they lived in when she was younger.

Ben spotted one of his friends, and after checking for traffic, Donna let him tow her across the road, and then charge off along the pavement. But he waited for her at his school gate, and gave her a hug, before he ran to join the playground melée.

Donna liked Ben. The others all complained about their brothers, but despite the fact that she couldn't hang around to chat after school because she had to pick him up, and couldn't have a peaceful laze in the bath without him climbing in *and* bringing his flotilla of empty shampoo bottles, Donna enjoyed having him around.

Gurpreet, Zoe, and Tina were going round to Dawn's house after school to listen to her new *Articulated Donut* LP. Donna pretended nonchalance, insulted their new sex object, the lead singer, by saying he sounded like a frog with one testicle; and set off to collect Ben.

"Frogs don't *have* testicles, Big Bum!" Zoe shouted after her.

"That explains the way he walks then!" Donna got in the last word, before she turned the corner.

At home, she gave Ben his tea, put the TV on for him, and settled down to do her homework before the table was needed for dinner. If she didn't get it done before, she couldn't watch any TV after dinner till it *was* done. And it wasn't any good lying, her mother always checked.

God, what a life! she thought, trying to dredge up what she knew about the Equatorial Forests of Brazil. Everyone else had parents who let them watch TV till all hours, even videos, yet she had to go to bed at nine. According to the others, the discos didn't even start till then. And as for letting her go out with boys, no chance! Not, she reminded

herself grumpily, that any had ever expressed an interest in
taking her out. And they certainly wouldn't, now that the
story of her flooring Zoe's brother at Tina's birthday party
was all round the school.

Yeuk! She'd do it again, Donna thought. *"Act like a
girl!"* he'd kept saying, pinning her against the wall in the
passage, squeezing her breasts till they hurt, all the time
trying to shove his horrible wet tongue into her mouth.

Her mother came home just before six, and brought her a
cup of tea while she was finishing off her english. Donna
wished that she looked like her mother, well not exactly
like her, she was old after all: Nearly forty! But Donna
wished that she too was slim, and could walk without her
breasts bouncing. Even in her highest heels, nothing
bounced on her mother when she walked. Yet, she
wouldn't let Donna diet, talking about puppy fat.

If I had a puppy this fat, Donna thought sourly, and fourteen years old, I'd shoot it.

Then her dad came in from work and started to chase
Ben round the place, so that he could tickle him. Donna,
knowing that her dad had only to wriggle his fingers at her,
to have her giggling helplessly, removed herself.

Oh, my God! Donna thought, taking refuge in the down-
stairs toilet. Don't parents ever grow up? And, I wish he'd
get another job, so he wouldn't come home on the bus in
his railway uniform. It's so *embarrassing* meeting him at
the top of the road when he was on early shift.

After she had turned out the light that night, Donna got
out of bed and opened the curtains. She did not know if the
light streaming in from the sodium street lamp would last
into a dream, but it was worth a try. After all, in all her flying dreams, her room was always exactly as it was when
she went to sleep.

Donna woke, but knew she was dreaming. She was still

under the duvet, and the room was the colour of her mother's amber earrings. Wanting did it, she knew, and gradually she drifted up out of bed, the duvet sliding down her tilting body. She arched her toes, bent backwards from the waist, and turned gently over and over, lifting slowly till her hand brushed the ceiling. She hung suspended turning slowly to look down at her room. It was the same as when she had gone to sleep: her clothes ready for tomorrow over the chair, the book she had been reading in bed, on the bedside table. And the curtains were open!

Donna pushed off from the ceiling, and hung, legs drifting up behind her, one hand clinging to the rim of the sash window. Outside the street was deserted, the leaves on the plane tree across the way rustling secrets at her.

What would it be like, she wondered, to be out there? To drift hand over light hand up the branches of the tree, till she sat in the swaying tufts at the very top? But perhaps it would be scary. Perhaps only the ceiling of her bedroom kept her from floating off the world, and out in the open she would begin to fall up off the earth. Even in a dream, that would be scary, Donna decided, and slid away from the window.

For a long time, Donna disported herself in the air of her bedroom, the light from the window gilding her mirrored reflection. She spent ten laughing tumbling minutes trying to get out of her pyjamas in mid-air, before she tethered herself with a foot under her bed rail, and watched her clothes flop to the carpet. They did not float, even in a dream. The phenomenon interested her, and she went down after them, and taking them up to ceiling height, released them. They dropped just as they would have done if she'd tossed them out the window. She tried several other things. Her pillow was easier to lift than her dictionary; and what's more the book made a sharp noise as it hit the floor.

Donna froze, but there was no response from her parents'

room, and soon she was doing lazy naked pinwheels in front of her mirror, trying to see if she could keep the reflected shadow of her navel always in the middle of the glass, while the rest of her moved around her centre.

In the weeks following, despite the occasional snide joking inquiry from the others, Donna no longer wanted to talk about her flying dreams, and the subject was dropped. At home she went to bed promptly, without any of her vast repertoire of procrastinating tactics. Yet, nowadays she seemed extra tired in the mornings, reluctant to get out of bed.

Her mother said it was because she had put on another growing spurt. And indeed she seemed to be growing: upward this time—and despite her increased appetite—not outward; muscles fining out, gaining definition, where once there were just rounded limbs.

Despite this, Miss Howe, once having cast Donna in the role of gymnastic buffoon, still singled her out for ridicule.

"Donna Hamilton!" as Donna clung with a sudden attack of vertigo, unable to tell up from down, to the top of the gym bars. "You're an absolute disgrace! Have you no pride, girl?"

"Donna Hamilton!" she said today when on dinner duty in the refectory.[3] "If you put as much energy into moving the rest of you, as you put into moving your mouth to eat, you wouldn't have all that blubber."

That night, for the first time, Donna's room could not contain her—her angry energy batting her backwards and forwards between the furniture, the floor, and the ceiling. Finally she gripped the sash of her window to steady her body, through which storm winds blared, and gazed hungrily out at the space outside.

She tried to turn the knurled knob of the window lock,

---

[3] In Britain and many other countries (and once upon a time in America), "dinner" is our "lunch," and "supper" is our "dinner." A refectory is a dining hall or lunchroom.

and turned herself instead. Gradually she added weight to her body, letting her feet sink to the floor, till she could gain purchase on the knob without her body shifting. Quietly, cautiously, she lifted the sash, then lightened until she could swing her body through.

She hung there, at first floor level, one hand clinging to the window frame, then she let go. She bobbed gently, controlling her weight, then with a now skilled flick of her body, she pushed off from the sill in a long shallow dive, lifting as she went. Her reaching hands grasped a handful of summer-dusty plane leaves, and she propelled herself gently, hand over careful hand, along the branch towards the centre of the tree. She added enough weight to let her rest on the branch, and one hand grasping a knobbly outgrowth of the tree trunk, looked down.

Beneath her bare feet, the leaves shifted, green as angelica; restored to springtime translucency by the lamp directly below her. She lightened and drifted carefully up the inner space of the tree, halting once to whisper, in response to startled bird cheeps: "It's okay! I'm dreaming."

There was more wind at the top of the tree, and Donna clung to the dipping swaying crown branch, her body curving gently this way and that like a lazy banner. She let go, drifted up, then added weight in a panic, and found herself chin deep in scratchy twigs and leaves, her feet floundering for a hold. Just then, Miss Howe's face, with that sarcastic twist to the lips, flashed across her mind, and Donna let go.

One fisted hand crooked above her head, she exploded up into the night, her breath escaping in a soundless scream of helpless rage. Then, up where the night wind snapped and pulled at her pyjamas, she slowed, limbs pulling inwards as if on strings, curling in on herself, as she began to tumble slowly, then faster, back towards the skein of orange diamonds that marked the road.

Gradually she regained control, shedding weight, till she

stopped with a bob, and began to drift. She was in the open space directly above the road, with nothing to push off from, and her open window away from the direction of the light wind. She lifted, then sent herself in a long sliding slanted glide, her body rolling, turning gently as she added weight to first one side and then the other, beginning to smile, then laugh, the wind of her going cold against her teeth and lips.

With a flick of her wrist, she pulled herself neatly under the sash into her room, remembering to add weight before she slid down the window and thumbed the screw lock fast.

"How on earth did you manage to get those scratches under your chin?" Her mother's question at breakfast sent Donna hurtling to the mirror in the kitchen.

"I'm sure they weren't there last night," her mother came after her. "You must have done it in your sleep." She took one of Donna's hands in hers, inspecting her nails. "You used to do that when you were a baby; scratch yourself. I'll have to make you sleep in mittens again." But she smiled and gave her a hug.

Donna desperately wanted to go up to her room before she left the house, but her mother was buttoning Ben into his coat, and they always left with her. At the corner, her mother straightened from hugging Ben, and caught Donna gently exploring the scratches with unbelieving fingers.

"Better leave them alone, Donna, or you'll get them infected." She tilted Donna's chin and looked at the scratches, shaking her head. "I can't imagine how you got them. We'd better remake your bed tonight, just in case there's a pin or hairclip in it."

At school there was assembly, then double maths, before Donna could shut herself in a cubicle in the toilets. She touched the scratches with wondering fingers, then looked carefully at her short cut nails, her smile growing. She closed her eyes, shedding weight gently, lifting until her head was level with the partition. Grinning, she patted herself about the tiny space, promising herself the whole of the night sky.

"For chrissake, Donna!" Tina shouted, banging the outer door open. Donna added weight and sunk to the floor so rapidly that she turned her ankle. "We'll be late, and you know how Miss Howe loves you."

Miss Howe looked as if she had had iron filings for breakfast, and her response to Donna's request that she be excused gym because of a turned ankle, was to turn her around brusquely by the shoulders, and inspect the ankle like a farrier with a horse, before shoving her towards the changing room. All without a word in response.

Donna changed and went in with her commiserating friends. Her heart sank as she saw the range of equipment laid out like an assault course; it was going to be one of *those* sessions.

The first part of the gym session, consisting of gentle stretching exercises, was not too bad, but at the end Donna's ankle was puffing out over her plimsoll rim.[4] She watched the others line up and begin their first run at the vaulting horse, with a sinking heart.

She'd hurt herself, she knew she would, she thought, listening to the thumps of their landings.

"Come along, Donna!" Miss Howe was waiting impatiently by the horse.

"I can't!" Donna said. "My ankle's really hurting now, *and* it's swollen."

"Nonsense! Come along!"

"No!" Donna took a step backwards, her hands fisting by her sides.

Miss Howe marched over. "I can't see any swelling or

---

[4] The top of her sneaker.

inflammation," she barely flicked a glance at Donna's ankle. "You'll use any excuse, won't you?" she sneered.

Donna looked steadily back at her. Just because I'm not pink and white, and bruise like a rainbow; you won't see, will you? But she said nothing.

"Very well. I'm giving you an hour's detention this evening, now go and—"

"But, you can't!" Donna gasped. "I have to collect my brother from school!"

"You should have thought of that before you were so insolent, shouldn't you? Report to me outside the staffroom at three-thirty." She turned away.

Donna left school premises during the lunch break, praying that no one would catch her, and tried to get through to Ben's school, but the phone was busy, no matter how many times she dialled. Directory inquiries did not have another number listed for the school, and after several fruitless tries, Donna gave up and snuck dispiritedly back into school. She spent the rest of the day worrying about Ben, and what her parents would say when they found out.

The afternoon lessons dragged, and it was a miracle that she did not collect any more detention orders because of her lack of attention. Her mum would kill her. And Ben . . . Just the thought of how worried and frightened he would be when she did not turn up to collect him on time made Donna want to burst into tears.

At the end of the afternoon, she waited outside the staffroom, and eventually Miss Howe came along. Donna had considered pleading with her, but one look at that cold antagonistic face stilled the words.

"What is your home room?" Miss Howe contrived to speak at her without looking at her.

"Room Three Twelve, Miss Howe," Donna filtered any emotion out of her voice.

"Very well. Go to your home room and draw me up a day by day list of everything that you've eaten for the last week. I'll be along presently." She vanished into the staffroom.

Misery overcoming her rage, Donna climbed slowly back to the third floor, and her empty home room. She had just put her name and the date on a sheet of paper, when a prefect stuck her head round the door.

"Donna Hamilton? Miss Howe says you can go."

Donna hurtled along the corridor to the staircase at the end, pushing open the swing doors with such force that they swung back and caught her bad ankle. She limped down the first flight of stairs, weak tears welling. Instinctively favouring her bad leg she must have shed weight for she found herself bouncing slightly.

She looked quickly over the banisters; the stairwell was empty. She lifted and slid over the rail and let the weight of her school bag take her purposefully down the well between the flights of stairs. She found she had to hug the bag to her bosom in order not to be dragged head first, and her uniform skirt soon ballooned out, further obstructing her view downwards.

Mary Poppins never has this trouble, she thought aggrievedly, trying to count the flights of stairs as they slid swiftly by.

Miss Howe was standing open-mouthed at the top of the first flight of stairs, hands gripping the banisters, the knuckles gleaming bone white. She made a sudden ineffectual grab at Donna as she slid past, then covered her eyes with both hands, her shoulders cowering up round her ears.

Donna touched down gently, and brushed her skirt down and headed for the outer doors.

"Oh, my God!" Miss Howe's hoarse shout echoed in the stairwell. "Help! Somebody help! She fell . . ." Her feet pounded down the stairs and she halted suddenly, horror-struck eyes raking the concrete floor, then lifting, widening, as Donna walked back towards her.

Miss Howe backed, hands going out in a warding gesture. "I came to tell her that her brother's school phoned . . . and she fell!" And all the time her eyes turned from Donna to the empty concrete floor.

"Who fell, Miss Howe?"

"Donna Hamilton . . . *You* fell! I saw you!"

"But you couldn't have," Donna said reasonably, and left to collect Ben.

Ben was waiting forlornly by the locked school gates, when Donna ran breathlessly up. She had shed weight in empty streets, moving in long leaping bounds when there was no one in sight. The schoolkeeper arrived, keys jangling, to let Ben out, and to read Donna a lecture on the "irresponsible kids nowadays." Donna didn't listen, stooping to hug Ben tightly.

When her mother came home that night, Donna immediately told her about being late for Ben.

"Well," her mother said, fixing her with a stern look. "It's a good thing you've owned up. One of your teachers phoned me at work, a Miss Howe, she sounded very worried about you. Something about hurting your ankle and getting detention and falling down the stairs, . . . I couldn't quite understand her. Then the headmistress took over the phone and said that you were going to be a bit late collecting Ben, through your own fault. And that Miss Howe was just upset because she hadn't realized when she gave you detention, quite justifiably that you had to pick up your younger brother."

Donna felt her heels begin to lift slightly off the floor, and grounded herself so hard that she winced.

"I'll put a compress on your ankle," her mother guided her into a chair. "But, first thing tomorrow, you are going to go to the staff room, and apologize to that teacher." Her hand lifted Donna's chin, and the stern look was bent on her. "Do you hear me?"

"Yes, Mum."

Next morning, Donna waited outside the staffroom while the teachers were arriving. They all ignored her, intent it seemed on gaining the sanctuary of the staffroom. Mrs. Pullen, her form mistress, came along eventually. "Donna?" she paused, looking down at one of her better pupils. "Is there something wrong?"

"I'm waiting for Miss Howe, Mrs. Pullen."

Mrs. Pullen looked at the clock above Donna's head. "She's usually in by now. Did you knock?"

"No, Mrs. Pullen." Donna shifted her satchel, wishing she was anywhere else in the world.

Mrs. Pullen went in, and a minute later Miss Howe came out, carefully closing the door behind her. Donna felt her cold stare like a battering ram, and with an effort met her eyes.

"My mother says I'm to apologize for being rude to you," she said through stiff lips, and waited to be dismissed.

"Well?"

Donna shouldered her satchel, and at her movement Miss Howe took a step back.

"Well, I'm waiting."

"Can I go now, Miss?"

Miss Howe's face whitened with anger. "Do you consider that an apology, girl?"

"I apologize, Miss Howe," Donna said at the point of her shoulder.

"And I do not accept your apology. Now get out of my sight."

Donna turned abruptly away, feeling eyes like sharp splinters of ice drilling through her back. Her heels lifted slightly, as if to get her out of range as fast as possible. Donna grounded herself, pouring weight on, so that she felt as if she was trying to walk through the polished concrete of the floor.

"Donna!" The voice was cold but insistent. "What country do you come from?"

Donna turned, meeting those glacial eyes, limpidly, with all the strength of her waking reality.

"Battersea,[5] Miss Howe," she replied, and walked away.

High in the night sky, with the multicoloured fairy lights of Battersea Bridge directly below her, the cobweb fantasy of Chelsea Bridge beyond that, and the dark squatting bulk of the power station brooding over the oily glisten of the Thames; Donna spoke into the wind:

"Not from outer space, Miss Howe! Not from some strange foreign place, Miss Howe! Battersea, Miss Howe!"

---

[5] A former borough of London, now part of Wandsworth, on the Thames.

MY MOTHER AND MITCH

꼭꼭

(United States)

by Clarence Major

Adults are only human beings— no more and no less.

*H*e was just somebody who had dialed the wrong number. This is how it started and I wasn't concerned about it. Not at first. I don't even remember if I was there when he first called but I do, all these many years later, remember my mother on the phone speaking to him in her best quiet voice, trying to sound as ladylike as she knew how.

She had these different voices for talking to different people on different occasions. I could tell by my mother's proper voice that this man was somebody she wanted to make a good impression on, a man she thought she might like to know. This was back when my mother was still a young woman, divorced but still young enough to believe that she was not completely finished with men. She was a skeptic from the beginning, I knew that even then. But some part of her thought the right man might come along some day.

I don't know exactly what it was about him that attracted her though. People are too mysterious to know that well. I know that now and I must have been smart enough not to wonder too hard about it back then.

Since I remember hearing her tell him her name she must not have given it out right off the bat when he first called. She was a city woman with a child and had developed a certain alertness to danger. One thing you didn't do was give your name to a stranger on the phone. You never knew who to trust in a city like Chicago. The place was full of crazy people and criminals.

She said, "My name is *Mrs.* Jayne Anderson." I can still hear her laying the emphasis on the Mrs. although she had been separated from my father twelve years by 1951 when this man dialed her number by accident.

Mitch Kibbs was the name he gave her. I guess he must have told her who he was the very first time, just after he apologized for calling her by mistake. I can't remember who he was trying to call. He must have told her and she must have told me but it's gone now. I think they must have talked a pretty good while that first time. The first thing that I remember about him was that he lived with his sister who was older than he. The next thing was that he was very old. He must have been fifty and to me at fifteen that was deep into age. If my mother was old at thirty, fifty was ancient. Then the other thing about him was that he was white.

They'd talked five or six times I think before he came out and said he was white but she knew it before he told her. I think he made this claim only after he started suspecting he might not be talking to another white person. But the thing was he didn't know for sure she was black. I was at home lying on the couch pretending to read a magazine when I heard her say, "I am a colored lady." Those were her words exactly. She placed her emphasis on the word *lady*.

I had never known my mother to date any white men. She would hang up from talking with him and she and I would sit at the kitchen table and she'd tell me what he'd said. They were telling each other the bits and pieces of their lives, listening to each other, feeling their way as they talked. She spoke slowly, remembering all the details. I watched her scowl and the way her eyes narrowed as she puzzled over his confessions as she told me in her own words about them. She was especially puzzled about his reaction to her confession about being colored.

That night she looked across at me with that fearful look that was hers alone and said, "Tommy, I doubt if he will ever call back. Not after tonight. He didn't know. You know that."

Feeling grown-up because she was treating me that way, I said, "I wouldn't be so sure."

But he called back soon after that.

I was curious about her interest in this particular white man so I always listened carefully. I was a little bit scared too because I suspected he might be some kind of maniac or pervert. I had no good reason to fear such a thing except that I thought it strange that anybody could spend as much time as he and my mother did talking on the phone without any desire for human contact. She had never had a telephone relationship before and at that time all I knew about telephone relationships was that they were insane and conducted by people who probably needed to be put away. This meant that I also had the sad feeling that my mother was a bit crazy too. But more important than these fearful fantasies, I thought I was witnessing a change in my mother. It seemed important and I didn't want to misunderstand it or miss the point of it. I tried to look on the bright side which was what my mother always said I should try to do.

He certainly didn't sound dangerous. Two or three times I myself answered the phone when he called and he always said, "Hello, Tommy, this is Mitch, may I speak to your mother," and I always said, "Sure, just a minute." He never asked me how I was doing or anything like that and I never had anything special to say to him.

After he'd been calling for over a month I sort of lost interest in hearing about their talk. But she went right on telling me what he said. I was a polite boy so I listened despite the fact that I had decided that Mitch Kibbs and his ancient sister Temple Erikson were crazy but harmless. My poor mother was lonely. That was all. I had it all figured out. He wasn't an ax murderer who was going to sneak up on her one evening when she was coming home from her job at the factory and split her open from the top down. We were always hearing about things like this so I knew it wasn't impossible.

My interest would pick up occasionally. I was especially interested in what happened the first time my mother herself made the call to his house. She told me that Temple Erikson answered the phone. Mother and I were eating dinner when she started talking about Temple Erikson.

"She's a little off in the head."

I didn't say anything but it confirmed my suspicion. What surprised me was my mother's ability to recognize it. "What'd she say?"

"She rattled on about the Wild West and the Indians and having to hide in a barrel or something like that. Said the Indians were shooting arrows at them and she was just a little girl who hid in a barrel."

I thought about this. "Maybe she lived out west when she was young. You know? She must be a hundred by now. That would make her the right age."

"Oh, come on, now. What she said was she married when she was fourteen, married this Erikson fellow. As near as I could figure out he must have been a leather tanner but seems he also hunted fur and sold it to make a living. She never had a child."

"None of that sounds crazy." I was disappointed.

"She was talking crazy, though."

"How so?"

"She thinks the Indians are coming back to attack the house any day now. She says things like Erikson was still living, like he was just off there in the next room, taking a nap. One of the first things Mitch told me was his sister and he had moved in together after her husband died and that was twenty years ago."

"How did the husband die?"

She finished chewing her peas first. "Kicked in the head by a horse. Bled to death."

I burst out laughing because the image was so bright in my mind and I couldn't help myself. My pretty mother had a sense of humor even when she didn't mean to show it.

She chewed her peas in a ladylike manner. This was long before she lost her teeth. Sitting there across the table from her I knew I loved her and needed her and I knew she loved and needed me. I was not yet fearing that she needed me too much. She had a lot of anger in her too. Men had hurt her bad. And one day I was going to be a man.

When I laughed my mother said, "You shouldn't laugh at misfortune, Tommy." But she had this silly grin on her face and it caused me to crack up again. I just couldn't stop. I think now I must have been a bit hysterical from the anxiety I had been living with all those weeks while she was telling me about the telephone conversations that I wanted to hear about only part of the time.

It was dark outside and I got up when I finished my dinner and went to the window and looked down on the streetlights glowing in the wet pavement. I said, "I bet he's out there right now, hiding in the shadows, watching our window."

"Who?" Her eyes grew large. She was easily frightened. I knew this and I was being devilish and deliberately trying to scare her.

"You know, Mister Kibbs."

She looked relieved. "No he's not. He's not like that. He's a little strange but not a pervert."

"How'd you know?"

By the look she gave me I knew now that I had thrown doubt into her and she wasn't handling it well. She didn't try to answer me. She finished her small, dry pork chop and the last of her bright green peas and reached over and took up my plate and sat it inside of her own.

She took the dishes to the sink, turned on the hot and cold water so that warm water gushed out of the single faucet, causing the pipe to clang, and started washing the dishes. "You have a vivid imagination," was all she said.

I grabbed the dishcloth and started drying the first plate she placed in the rack. "Even so, you don't know this man.

You never even seen him. Aren't you curious about what he looks like?"

"I know what he looks like."

"How?"

"He sent me a picture of himself and one of Temple."

I gave her a look. She had been holding out on me. I knew he was crazy now. Was he so ugly she hadn't wanted me to see the picture? I asked if I could see it.

She dried her hands on the cloth I was holding then took her cigarettes out of her dress pocket and knocked one from the pack and stuck it between her thin pale lips. I watched her light it and fan smoke and squint her eyes. She said, "You have to promise not to laugh."

That did it. I started laughing again and couldn't stop. Then she started laughing too because I was bent double, standing there at the sink, with this image of some old guy who looked like the Creeper in my mind. But I knew she couldn't read my mind so she had to be laughing at me laughing. She was still young enough to be silly with me like a kid.

Then she brought out two pictures, one of him and the other one of his sister. She put them down side by side on the table. "Make sure your hands are dry."

I took off my glasses and bent down to the one of the man first so I could see up close as I stood there wiping my hands on the dishcloth. It was one of those studio pictures where somebody had posed him in a three-quarter view. He had his unruly hair and eyebrows pasted down and you could tell he was fresh out of the bath and his white shirt was starched hard. He was holding his scrubbed face with effort toward where the photographer told him to look which was too much in the direction of the best light. He was frowning with discomfort beneath the forced smile. There was something else. It was something like defeat or simple tiredness in his pose and you could see it best in the heavy lids of his large blank eyes. He looked out of that face at the world with what remained of his self-confidence and trust in the world. His shaggy presence said that it was all worthwhile and maybe even in some ways he would not ever understand also important. I understood all of that even then but would never have been able to put my reading of him into words like these.

Then I looked at the woman. She was an old hawk. Her skin was badly wrinkled like the skin of ancient Indians I'd seen in photographs and the westerns. There was something like a smile coming out of her face but it had come out sort of sideways and made her look silly. But the main thing about her was that she looked very mean. But on second thought, to give her the benefit of the doubt, I can say that it might have been just plain hardness from having had a hard life. She was wearing a black iron-stiff dress buttoned up to her dickey which was ironically dainty and tight around her goose neck.

All I said was, "They're *so* old." I don't know what else I thought as I looked up at my mother who was leaning over my shoulder at the pictures too, as though she'd never seen them before, as though she was trying to see them through my eyes.

"You're just young, Tommy. Everybody's old to you. They're not so old. He looks lonely, to me."

I looked at him again and thought I saw what she meant.

I put the dishes away and she took the photographs back and we didn't talk any more that night about Mitch and Temple. We watched our black-and-white television screen which showed us Red Skelton acting like a fool.

Before it was over, I fell asleep on the couch and my mother woke me up when she turned off the television. "You should go to bed."

I stood up and stretched. "I have a science paper to write."

"Get up early and write it," she said, putting out her cigarette.

"He wants me to meet him someplace," my mother said.

She had just finished talking with him and was standing by the telephone. It was close to dinner time. I'd been home from school since three-thirty and she'd been in from work by then for a good hour. She'd just hung up from the shortest conversation she'd ever had with him.

I'd wondered why they never wanted to meet then I stopped wondering and felt glad they hadn't. Now I was afraid, afraid for her, for myself, for the poor old man in the picture. Why did we have to go through with this crazy thing?

"I told him I needed to talk with you about it first," she said. "I told him I'd call him back."

I was standing there in front of her looking at her. She was a scared little girl with wild eyes dancing in her head, unable to make up her own mind. I sensed her fear. I resented her for the mess she had gotten herself in. I also resented her for needing my consent. I knew she wanted me to say go, go to him, meet him somewhere. I could tell. She was too curious not to want to go. I suddenly thought that he might be a millionaire and that she would marry the old coot and he'd die and leave her his fortune. But there was the sister. She was in the way. And from the looks of her she would pass herself off as one of the living for at least another hundred years or so. So I gave up that fantasy.

"Well, why don't you tell him you'll meet him at the hamburger cafe on Wentworth? We can eat dinner there."

"We?"

"Sure. I'll just sit at the counter like I don't know you. But I gotta be there to protect you."

"I see."

"Then you can walk in alone. I'll already be there eating a cheeseburger and fries. He'll come in and see you waiting for him alone at a table."

"No, I'll sit at the counter too," she said.

"Okay. You sit at the counter too."

"What time should I tell him?"

I looked at my Timex. It was six. I knew they lived on the West Side and that meant it would take him at least an hour by bus and a half hour by car. He probably didn't have a car. I was hungry though and had already set my mind on eating a cheeseburger rather than macaroni and cheese out of the box.

"Tell him seven-thirty."

"Okay."

I went to my room. I didn't want to hear her talking to him in her soft whispering voice. I'd stopped listening some time before. I looked at the notes for homework and felt sick in the stomach at the thought of having to write that science paper.

A few minutes later my mother came in and said, "Okay. It's all set." She sat down on the side of my bed and folded her bony pale hands in her lap. "What should I wear?"

"Wear your green dress and the brown shoes."

"You like that dress don't you."

"I like that one and the black one with the yellow at the top. It's classical."

"You mean classy."

"Whatever I mean." I felt really grown that night.

"Here, Tommy, take this." She handed me five dollars which she'd been hiding in the palm of her right hand. "Don't spend it all. Buy the burger out of it and the rest is just to have. If you spend it all in the hamburger place I'm going to deduct it from your allowance next week."

When I got there I changed my mind about the counter. I took a table by myself.

I was eating my cheeseburger and watching the revolving door. The cafe was noisy with shouts, cackling, giggles, and verbal warfare. The waitress, Miss Azibo, was in

a bad mood. She'd set my hamburger plate down like it was
burning her hand.

I kept my eye on the door. Every time somebody came
in I looked up, every time somebody left I looked up. I finished my cheeseburger even before my mother got there,
and, ignoring her warning, I ordered another and another
Coca-Cola to go with it. I figured I could eat two or three
burgers and still have most of the five left.

Then my mother came in like a bright light into a dingy
room. I think she must have been the most beautiful
woman who ever entered that place and it was her first
time coming in there. She had always been something of a
snob and did not believe in places like this. I knew she'd
agreed to meet Mister Kibbs here just because she believed
in my right to the cheeseburger and this place had the best
in the neighborhood.

I watched her walk ladylike to the counter and ease herself up on the stool and sit there with her back arched.
People in that place didn't walk and sit like that. She was
acting classy and everybody turned to look at her. I looked
around at the faces and a lot of the women had these real
mean sneering looks like somebody had broke wind.

She didn't know any of these people and they didn't
know her. Some of them may have known her by sight,
and me too, but that was about all the contact we had with
this part of the neighborhood. Besides, we hardly ever ate
out. When we did we usually ate Chinese or at the rib
place.

I sipped my Coke and watched Miss Azibo place a cup of
coffee before my mother on the counter. She was a coffee
freak. Always was. All day long. Long into the night.
Cigarettes and coffee in a continuous cycle. I grew up with
her that way. The harsh smells are still in my memory.
When she picked up the cup with a dainty finger sticking
out just so, I heard a big fat woman at a table in front of

mine say to the fat woman with her that my mother was a snooty bitch. The other woman said, "Yeah. She must thank she's white. What she doing in here anyway?"

Mitch Kibbs came in about twenty minutes after my mother and I watched him stop and stand just inside the revolving doors. He stood to the side. He looked a lot younger than in the picture. He was stooped a bit though and he wasn't dressed like a millionaire which disappointed me. But he was clean. He was wearing a necktie and a clean white shirt and a suit that looked like it was two hundred years old but one no doubt made of the best wool. Although it was fall he looked overdressed for the season. He looked like a man who hadn't been out in daylight in a long while. He was nervous, I could tell. Everybody was looking at him. Rarely did white people come in here.

Then he went to my mother like he knew she had to be the person he'd come to see. He sat himself up on the stool beside her and leaned forward with his elbows on the counter and looked in her face.

She looked back in that timid way of hers. But she wasn't timid. It was an act and part of her ladylike posture. She used it when she needed it.

They talked and talked. I sat there eating cheeseburgers and protecting her till I spent the whole five dollars. Even as I ran out of money I knew she would forgive me. She had always forgiven me on special occasions. This was one for sure.

She never told me what they talked about in the cafe and I never asked but everything that happened after that meeting went toward the finishing off of the affair my mother was having with Mitch Kibbs. He called her later that night. I was in my room reading when the phone rang and I could hear her speaking to him in that ladylike way—not the way she talked to me. I was different. She didn't need to impress me. I was her son. But I couldn't hear what she was saying and didn't want to.

Mister Kibbs called the next evening too. But eventually the calls were fewer and fewer till he no longer called.

My mother and I went on living the way we always had, she working long hours at the factory and me going to school. She was not a happy woman but I thought she was pretty brave. Every once in a while she got invited somewhere, to some wedding or out on a date with a man. She always tried on two or three different dresses, turning herself around and around before the mirror, asking me how she looked, making me select the dress she would wear. Most often though she went nowhere. After dinner we sat together at the kitchen table, she drinking coffee and smoking her eternal cigarettes. She gave me my first can of beer one night when she herself felt like having one. It tasted awful and I didn't touch the stuff for years after that.

About a day or two after the meeting in the hamburger cafe I remember coming to a conclusion about my mother. I learned for the first time that she did not always know what she was doing. It struck me that she was as helpless as I sometimes felt when confronted with a math or science problem or a problem about sex and girls and growing up and life in general. She didn't know everything. And that made me feel closer to her despite the fear it caused. She was there to protect me, I thought. But there she was, just finding her way, step by step, like me. It was something wonderful anyway.

ABOUT THE CONTRIBUTORS

AMA ATA AIDOO (b. 1942) was born in Abeadzi Kyiakor, Ghana, and is one of her country's most highly acclaimed writers. Her writings include several plays, the books of poetry *Someone Talking to Sometime* (1985) and *A Very Angry Letter in January* (1992), and the novels *Our Sister Killjoy; or, Reflections from a Black-Eyed Squint* (1976) and *Changes: A Love Story* (1991). "The Late Bud" is taken from her collection of stories *No Sweetness Here* (1970).

TONI CADE BAMBARA (b. 1939) spent her growing-up years in Harlem, Brooklyn, and Queens, New York, and in Jersey City, New Jersey. "Raymond's Run," which she adapted into a screenplay (PBS, 1985), is taken from her first collection of short stories, *Gorilla, My Love* (1972). Her second collection is entitled *The Seabirds Are Still Alive* (1977). Bambara's other works include several screenplays, the editing of the anthologies *The Black Woman* (1970) and *Tales and Stories for Black Folks* (1971), and the novel *The Salt Eaters* (which won the 1981 American Book Award).

BARBARA BURFORD (b. 1945) was born and raised in England. Her poetry and short stories have appeared in various magazines and other publications, including *A Dangerous Knowing: Four Black Women Poets* (1984) and *Everyday Matters: 2* (1984). "Dreaming the Sky Down" is taken from her first collection of stories, *The Threshing Floor* (1987).

JOHN HENRIK CLARKE (b. 1915) was born in Union Springs, Alabama, and grew up in Columbus, Georgia. In addition to being a fine short story writer and poet (*Rebellion in Rhyme*, 1948), he is a renowned scholar of

African and African American history. He has edited
numerous works of fiction and nonfiction, including
American Negro Short Stories (1966; revised and expanded
edition, *Black American Short Stories: A Century of the
Best*, 1993), *Malcolm X: The Man and His Times* (1969),
and *Marcus Garvey and the Vision of Africa* (with Amy
Jacques Garvey, 1974). Among his more recent books are
Notes for an African World Revolution (1991) and *African
People in World History* (1993).

EUGENIA COLLIER (b. 1928) was born and raised in
Baltimore, Maryland. Her literary essays and reviews have
appeared in *First World Journal, Phylon,* and the book
Black Women Writers (1950–1980): A Critical Guide,
among other publications. Her short stories have been pub-
lished in numerous periodicals and anthologies, including
*Negro Digest/Black World, Indigene, Literati Inter-
nationale, Black American Short Stories: A Century of the
Best,* and *The New Cavalcade.* Collier's *Breeder and Other
Stories* and novel, *Spread My Wings,* are scheduled for publication in 1994. Her story "Marigolds" received *Negro
Digest's* Gwendolyn Brooks Literary Award in 1970.

J. CALIFORNIA COOPER was born in Berkeley,
California. She is the author of seventeen plays, the novel
Family (1991), and four short story collections: *A Piece of
Mine* (1984), *Homemade Love* (1986), *Some Soul to Keep*
(1987), and *The Matter Is Life* (1991), from which "How,
Why to Get Rich" was taken.

PEARL CRAYTON (ca. 1930) was born in Natchitoches
Parish, Louisiana, and grew up in nearby Alexandria. Her
short stories and poems have been published in *USL
Chapbook, Suisun Valley Review, Pudding Magazine,
Reed,* and the anthologies *The Best Short Stories by Black*

Writers, Out of Our Lives: A Selection of Contemporary Fiction, and *Trials, Tribulations and Celebrations*, among other publications. Crayton's literary awards include the California Arts Council Poet in the Schools Fellowship (1987–90) and the Frances Shaw Creative Writing Fellowship from Ragdale Foundation at Lake Forest, Illinois (1990).

QUINCE DUNCAN (b. 1940) was born in San José and raised in Limón, Costa Rica. He is the author of five novels and several short story collections, including *Una canción en la madrugada* (1970; from which "Swan Song" is taken), *Los cuentos del Hermano Araña* (1975), and *La rebelión Pocomía y otros relatos* (1976). A bilingual edition of his stories, *Los mejores cuentos de Quince Duncan/The Best Short Stories of Quince Duncan*, is scheduled for publication by Editorial Costa Rica in 1994. His translator, **DELLITA L. MARTIN-OGUNSOLA** (b. 1946), was born and raised in New Orleans, Louisiana. She is chairperson of the Department of Foreign Languages and Literatures at the University of Alabama at Birmingham. Her literary reviews and essays have appeared in *Afro-Hispanic Review, College Language Association Journal, Journal of Caribbean Studies, South Atlantic Review*, and other scholarly periodicals. She has translated all of the stories from *Una canción en la madrugada* and *La rebelión Pocomía y otros relatos* for the bilingual collection cited above.

CECIL FOSTER (b. 1954) was born and raised in the parish of Christ Church, Barbados, and emigrated to Canada at the age of twenty-five. His essays and short stories have appeared in numerous magazines in Canada and the United States. His first novel, *No Man in the House* (1992), is about a boy—not unlike our hero here—coming of age in

Barbados in the 1960s, amid the turmoil of the island's "soon coming" independence from Britain. His second novel, *Dance Suzanne, Dance!*, is scheduled for publication in 1994.

HOWARD GORDON (b. 1952) was born and raised in Rochester, New York. His poetry and short stories have appeared in various publications, among them *Essence, Obsidian*, and the anthology *Imagining America: Stories from the Promised Land*. "My Lucy" is one of the nine stories in *The African in Me* (1993), his first collection of short stories. Gordon is presently at work on two novels: *Pretending to Be Negro* and *Neutered by the Colored Wash*.

MARTIN J. HAMER (b. 1931) was born and raised in Harlem, New York. His short stories have appeared in *Negro Digest, The Atlantic Monthly* (which awarded his story "One, Two, Three O'Leary" an *Atlantic Monthly* "First" Award), and various anthologies, including *The Best Short Stories of 1965, Brothers and Sisters*, and *Black American Short Stories: A Century of the Best*, among other publications. His story "Sarah" was the basis for a student film by Spike Lee.

CHARLES JOHNSON (b. 1948) was born and raised in Evanston, Illinois. He is the author of two collections of drawings, *Black Humor* (1970) and *Half-Past Nation-Time* (1972), and has contributed about a thousand drawings and cartoons to an array of magazines and newspapers. His teleplays include "Charlie's Pad" (PBS series, 1970) and "Booker" (which received the Writers Guild Award for the Best Children's Show of 1986). Johnson is also the author of *The Sorcerer's Apprentice: Tales and Conjurations* (1986), which was nominated for the 1987 PEN/Faulkner

Award; *Being and Race: Black Writing Since 1970* (1988); and three novels: *Faith and the Good Thing* (1974); *Oxherding Tale* (1982); and *Middle Passage* (1990), winner of the 1991 National Book Award for Fiction.

CLARENCE MAJOR (b. 1936) was born in Atlanta, Georgia, and grew up in Chicago, Illinois. He is the author of ten books of poetry and the editor of several anthologies. He has also written seven novels. Among his most recent ones are *My Amputations*, which won the 1986 Western State Book Award; *Such Was the Season*, a 1987 Literary Guild Selection; and *Painted Turtle: Woman with Guitar*, a *New York Times Book Review* Notable Book of the Year for 1988. "My Mother and Mitch" is taken from his collection of short stories *Fun and Games* (1988). In 1991, Major served as fiction judge for the National Book Awards.

NJABULO NDEBELE (b. 1948) was born in Johannesburg and grew up in Nigel, South Africa. His poetry has appeared in *Black Poets in South Africa* (edited by Robert Royston, 1973), among other anthologies and periodicals. His short stories have also been published in many anthologies, including *Hungry Flames and Other Stories* (edited by Mbulelo Mzamane, 1986) and *Contemporary African Short Stories* (edited by Chinua Achebe and C. L. Innes, 1992). "The Test" is taken from his collection *Fools and Other Stories*, which won the 1983 Noma Award for Publishing in Africa.

OLIVE SENIOR (b. 1941) grew up in the parishes of Trelawny and Westmoreland in Jamaica, West Indies. "Bright Thursdays" is one of the ten stories in her first collection, *Summer Lightning and Other Stories* (1986), which won the 1987 Commonwealth Writers' Prize. Senior's other works include several plays; the reference book *A–Z of Jamaican Heritage* (1983); a volume of poetry, *Talking of Trees* (1985); *Working Miracles: The Lives of Caribbean Women* (1991); and the short story collection *Arrival of the Snake Woman and Other Stories* (1989).

CHARLOTTE WATSON SHERMAN (b. 1958) is a native of Seattle, Washington. Her poetry and short stories have been published in numerous publications, among them *The Black Scholar, CALYX Journal, Ikon, Painted Bride Quarterly*, and the anthologies *When I Am an Old Woman, Memories and Visions*, and *Gathering Ground*. "BigWater" is taken from her first collection of stories, *Killing Color*, winner of the King County Arts Commission Fiction Award and the 1992 GLCA New Writer's Fiction Award. Her first novel, *One Dark Body*, was published in 1993.

ARCHIE WELLER (b. 1957) was born in Subiaco, Western Australia. He is one of the most well known and highly regarded black Australian writers. His works include plays, screenplays, poetry, the novel *The Day of the Dog* (1981), and an anthology of Aboriginal writings, *Us Fellas* (1988), coedited with Colleen Francis-Glass. "Johnny Blue" is taken from his first collection of short stories, *Going Home* (1986).

PAULETTE CHILDRESS WHITE (b. 1948) was born and raised in Ecorse, Michigan. Her poetry has appeared in *Callaloo, Essence*, and *The Watermelon Dress* and her short stories in *Redbook, Essence, Harbor Review, Michigan Quarterly Review*, and the anthology *Memory of Kin: Stories About Family by Black Writers* (edited by Mary Helen Washington, 1991), among other periodicals and books.

ABOUT THE EDITOR

TONYA BOLDEN is a Harlem-born, New York–based free-lance writer. Her articles and book reviews have appeared in *Essence, Black Enterprise, Small Press,* the *New York Times Book Review,* and the 1989 and 1990 *Black Arts Annual,* among other periodicals. She is presently the book columnist for *YSB* ("Young Sisters & Brothers") magazine. With Vy Higginsen she coauthored the novel *Mama, I Want to Sing* (1992), based on the musical of the same name. Her works in progress include a children's book, a young adult novel, and a book on African American women, also for young adults.

We gratefully acknowledge the following for granting us permission to include their stories:

"Raymond's Run" from *Gorilla, My Love* by Toni Cade Bambara. Copyright © 1971 by Toni Cade Bambara. Reprinted by permission of Random House, Inc. and The Women's Press, Ltd, London.

"The Scar" by Cecil Foster. Copyright © 1994 by Cecil Foster. Printed by permission of the author.

"The Day the World Almost Came to an End" by Pearl Crayton. Copyright © 1965 by Pearl Crayton. First published in *Negro Digest*, August 1965. Reprinted by permission of the author.

"The Late Bud" from *No Sweetness Here* by Ama Ata Aidoo (Longman Group UK Ltd, 1970). Copyright © 1970 by Ama Ata Aidoo. Reprinted by permission of the author.

"The Mountain" by Martin J. Hamer. Copyright © 1962 by Martin J. Hamer. Copyright © renewed 1990 by Martin J. Hamer. First published in *Negro Digest*, June 1962. Reprinted by permission of the author.

"Bright Thursdays" from *Summer Lightning and Other Stories* by Olive Senior (Longman Caribbean Writers Series). Copyright © 1986 by Longman Group UK Ltd. Reprinted by permission of Longman Group UK Ltd.

"The Boy Who Painted Christ Black" by John Henrik Clarke. Copyright © 1940 by John Henrik Clarke. Copyright © renewed 1968 by John Henrik Clarke. First published in *Opportunity* magazine, 1940. Reprinted by permission of the author.

"BigWater" from *Killing Color* by Charlotte Watson Sherman. Copyright © 1992 by Charlotte Watson Sherman. Reprinted by permission of Calyx Books, Corvallis, Oregon.

"Swang Song" from *Una canción en la madrugada* by Quince Duncan Moodie. Copyright © 1970 by Editorial Costa Rica. This translation is from the forthcoming *Los mejores cuentos de Quince Duncan/The Best Short Stories of Quince Duncan* copyright © 1993 by Editorial Costa Rica. Translated by Dellita L. Martin-Ogunsola. Reprinted by permission of Editorial Costa Rica.

"Getting the Facts of Life" by Paulette Childress White. Copyright © 1989 by Paulette Childress White. First published in *Memory of Kin: Stories About Family by Black Writers*, edited by Mary Helen Washington (Anchor/Doubleday, 1991). Reprinted by permission of the author.

"The Test" from *Fools and Other Stories* by Njabulo Ndebele. Copyright © 1983 by Njabulo S. Ndebele. Reprinted by permission of the author and the Shelley Power Literary Agency.

"How, Why to Get Rich" from *The Matter Is Life* by J. California Cooper. Copyright © 1991 by J. California Cooper. Used by permission of Doubleday, a division of Bantam Doubleday Dell Publishing Group, Inc.

"Johnny Blue" from *Going Home* by Archie Weller. Copyright © 1986 by Archie Weller. Reprinted by permission of Allen & Unwin Pty. Ltd.

"Marigolds" by Eugenia Collier. Copyright © 1969 by Eugenia Collier. First published in *Negro Digest*, November 1969. Reprinted by permission of the author.

"My Lucy" from *The African in Me* by Howard Gordon. Copyright © 1992 by Howard Gordon. Reprinted by permission of George Braziller, Inc.

"Dreaming the Sky Down" from *The Threshing Floor* by Barbara Burford. Copyright © 1989 by Barbara Burford. Reprinted by permission of Firebrand Books, Ithaca, New York.

"My Mother and Mitch" from *Fun & Games* by Clarence Major. Copyright © 1990 by Clarence Major. (Holy Cow! Press, Duluth, Minnesota). First published in *Boulevard* magazine, September 1989. Reprinted by permission of Holy Cow! Press and Susan Bergholz Literary Services, New York City.